BOOKS BY N...

CW00858700

TRAINWRECK 1
TRAINWRECK 2

A Standalone Romantic Comedy
Baby Daddy

An OTT Insta-love Standalone
The Big O

THAT MAN Series
THAT MAN 1
THAT MAN 2
THAT MAN 3
THAT MAN 4
THAT MAN 5

Gloria
Gloria's Secret
Gloria's Revenge
Gloria's Forever

An Erotic Love Story
Undying Love
Endless Love

Writing as E.L. Sarnoff
DEWITCHED: The Untold Story of the Evil Queen
UNHITCHED: The Untold Story of the Evil Queen 2

Boxed Sets
THAT MAN TRILOGY
THAT MAN: THE WEDDING STORY
Unforgettable: The Complete Series
Gloria's Secret: The Trilogy
Seduced by the Park Avenue Billionaire
Naughty Nelle

Endless Love

The Sequel
to Undying Love

Endless LOVE

NELLE L'AMOUR

NICHOLS CANYON PRESS
Los Angeles, CA USA

Endless Love
By Nelle L'Amour

Cover by Arijana Karcic/Cover It! Designs
Formatting by BB eBooks
Proofreading by Mary Jo Toth and Virginia Tesi Carey

For all my readers who urged me to write this book and never lost faith in me.

A true love story never ends.

—Richard Bach

PROLOGUE
Allee

Four Years Earlier

Madewell~

By the time you read this letter, I will be gone. I have no clue where I'm going or why this is happening to me. I only know I will miss you.

Your name, Ryan, comes from the French word "roi" which means "king." My name Allee is almost identical to the French word "allée" which means "gone." LOL. When I am gone, Madewell, I want you to rule with your heart and live your life. You have so much potential, so much to live for. You have a great future ahead of you, with me or without me.

I know one day you will fall in love again. You will because I'm telling you to. I don't want you to mope around mourning me. Why mourn what you can't have? I'm sure whomever you meet will be someone I would like.

There's one other thing I want you to do. Make up with your father. He is the only one you will ever have.

We have all erred in our lives, but we all deserve the chance to be forgiven. I hope you will forgive me for leaving you too soon. It's not your fault, my Superman, I could not be saved.

Go on living, my sweet superhero. Although our time together was so short, it was the best time I ever had. You gave me everything—love, laughter, Paris, and all of you. Just because I've stopped living my life, don't stop living yours.

One last thing...Write, Madewell, write. Write for me. I'll be reading every word from wherever I am. Always remember...

I love you more~
Allee

ONE

Willow

I'd started crying from the minute Allee found out she had incurable cancer. I felt her pain and Ryan's in every bone of my body. The words on the page became blurs as my teary eyes brushed over their first and last dance...their fateful trip to Allee's beloved Paris...Allee's final words as Ryan lay beside her in her death bed. Their song, "I Won't Give Up," played in my head as I flipped the pages. Then, I totally lost it when I came to Allee's love letter to her Superman. Big fat ugly tears pouring down my face, my sobs clogging my ears, I bawled until there were no more tears to shed. The last page of the book was soaked. Ready to fall apart like me. Emotionally drained, I closed the book and gazed at the cover. A beautiful young couple in love. They had everything to live for; unexpectedly, death took all that away. But their love, immortalized in this memoir, would never die.

The title of the book stared me in the face. I had experienced my own *Undying Love*. I'll never forget the day I came home from high school, and my father sat me down at one of the tables in his deli. In fact, it was the very one I was sitting at today.

"Pumpkin, I have to tell you something you're not going to want to hear."

My eyes searched his misty, bloodshot ones. It looked as if he'd been crying.

"Mom is no longer with us."

A chill traveled down my spine. "What do you mean, Pop?"

And then he told me. My mother, Belinda, had been hit by a cab. Instant death. She was only thirty-five. The tears just poured and poured. Enough to make brine in a barrel of pickles. The sadness was unbearable, the guilt unshakable. I never told her how much I loved her during my rebellious teenage years nor did I get a chance to say goodbye.

Pop and I went on with life without mom. His deli, Mel's Famous, was a landmark institution on New York's Lower East Side, and regular customers kept him busy. As for me, I threw myself into my dancing at Julliard. An aspiring ballerina, my dancing kept the pain away. My father was concerned about my obsessive-compulsive behavior and made me see a shrink. I'd become dangerously anorexic. All skin and bones. Dr. Jules Goodman saved my life.

Dr. Goodman was now saving my life again. I was on a sabbatical from the Royal Latvia Ballet. On my way to becoming a world-class ballerina, I had collapsed on stage while performing in Vienna. The in-house doctor said I was exhausted and malnourished. That's what my dad was told. Only Dr. Goodman knew what really brought me almost to complete destruction. Physical and emotional. The real extent of the damage. For now, as I healed, that secret needed to stay between us. Gustave Fontaine, the company's infamously handsome and brilliant artistic director, had gone on to another dancer. And not just any ballerina. Mira Abramovitch. My archrival since we'd been in tutus together in pre-school. I had given him everything—my heart, my soul, my body. My passion. But I was just another conquest. Stupid, stupid me should have known better. The other girls in the troupe had warned me, but foolishly I thought I was different. Special.

Being back home in New York, living with my dad, was good for me. Afraid of losing the other great love of his life, he took care of me, feeding me lots of homemade chicken soup—the soup that made Mel's Famous legendary. Slowly, I put back on the weight I'd lost though I was still very thin by most standards. But the obsessive desire that had almost consumed me was gnawing at me. Now six months away from the stage, I was aching to put on a leotard and my pointe shoes. To dance for *him.*

Gustave had been my master. He possessed me, both figuratively and literally. Hungering to please him, I surrendered to the power he had over me as if he were a drug. He would be showing me how he wanted my leg to extend and before I knew it, my legs were extended around him, and he was fucking me without mercy until orgasms pirouetted through my body. One after another.

No place was sacred. He fucked me anywhere, anytime he could. Or should I say wanted. I was at his command. Between acts. During intermissions. In my dressing room. Behind the curtain. On the stage floor after the lights dimmed.

I don't know if I loved him. But for sure, I was obsessed. Maybe more. I worshipped him like a god. His beauty and sexuality were irresistible, and the control he exerted over me trumped the gut-wrenching pain of being pushed to the limit. I even withstood the harsh punishments for not being good enough. For not being perfect. How many tears had I shed? Yet, more than anything, no matter what it took, I wanted to be his. So when I found him humping Mira in my dressing room, I was crushed to the bone. I was nothing to him. Just another beautiful body to fuck and control. My downward spiral began and accelerated at the speed of a bullet train until I was a shell of the person I was. Thinking back to the devastating events of the past year, self-loathing seeped into my bloodstream.

Don't go there.

"What's the matter, pumpkin?

The husky voice stopped me before I could descend into darkness. I looked up. My father. In his perpetually stained, floor-length deli apron over his ill-fitting baggy pants and a Mel's Famous T-shirt. There was alarm in both his voice and warm chocolate brown eyes. His bushy brows furrowed.

"Oh, Pop! I just read the saddest book ever." I showed him the cover.

My burly father smiled with relief as he wiped away my tears with the edge of his apron. "The author's a regular. He comes in here from time to time."

"Ryan Madewell? Really?" My tears subsided. "Do you think he'd be willing to sign my book the next time he comes in?"

My father's smile broadened. "It doesn't hurt to ask."

"And, Pop, it doesn't hurt to lose weight."

Ryan Madewell showed up at my father's deli exactly one week later. I recognized him instantly because I'd spent the whole week Googling him.

With a laid back but confidant gait, he strode up to the well-stocked deli case and surveyed the contents. An Indian summer kind of day, he was wearing black jeans and a simple white T-shirt. God, he was gorgeous. Tousled sandy hair, gemstone blue eyes, a movie star-handsome face, and a six foot-plus lean, buff body that shouted, "I work out." In his Google images, he was gorgeous too. Just not this insanely gorgeous. His hair was now longer, the scruff on his face thicker, and his muscles more pronounced, making him even more impossibly sexy.

I was minding the store while my father was at the bank making a deposit. Almost three in the afternoon, it wasn't very busy. In fact, he was the sole customer.

My gaze stayed fixed on him while he lingered in front of the meat counter. Finally, he said, "I'll have my regular—a pastrami sandwich to go with a side of slaw."

"Would you like it hot?" I asked, my eyes meeting his.

There was a short stretch of silence before he replied. "Yeah, I like it hot."

His soft, raspy voice was so damn sexy. I swear my temperature rose ten degrees.

"What kind of bread?"

"Rye, please."

Rye bread for Ry-man. I wondered what it would feel like to be sandwiched between him and a mattress. Oh God. This guy was making my mind travel to places it hadn't been for a long time.

I prepared the sandwich for him. I was good at this, having made deli sandwiches ever since I could remember. Putting the slab of pastrami onto the meat slicer, I held out my plastic-gloved hand as one lean piece of meat after another fell onto my palm. After heating it, I set the three-inch high pile on the counter.

"Would you like mustard?"

"Just mayo, please."

Without overthinking it, I squeezed some mayonnaise from a nearby plastic bottle onto the two slices of bread. Something about the way the creamy white condiment squirted out from the pointed cap sent a rush of tingles to my core. It was totally erotic. *Jesus! What was I thinking?*

I felt his eyes on me as I spread the mayo with a knife and then transferred the pastrami onto one of the slices of bread.

"That looks delicious," he said as I completed the mouthwatering sandwich.

So do you.

I wrapped up the sandwich and threw it with the pre-packed slaw into a paper bag.

"Would you like anything else?" I managed.

"A cream soda would be great. In fact, I'll have that now."

Retrieving a bottle from the cooler, I handed him the soda, my fingers brushing against his. They were long, strong, and purposeful. The fingers of a writer.

He held the bottle in his right hand, and for the first time, I noticed the gold band around his ring finger as he popped off the cap with his other hand. His wedding band. I was surprised he still wore it. Obviously, he was still clinging to Allee. Maybe he wasn't ready to let go. My stomach tightened. I tried not to linger on it or on what it symbolized and instead focused on his lush lips as they wrapped around the bottle. Tilting his head back, his eyes closed as he savored the cold, carbonated beverage, and as he swallowed, a satisfied moan escaped his throat. A pulse beat between my legs, and I wondered if this is what he looked like after having an orgasm. In my head, I began to undress him, imagining how beautiful he must look in the raw. Then, I remembered his beloved late wife's last words to him—telling him how beautiful he was. Indeed, he was.

"How much do I owe?" he asked, bringing me out of my reverie.

"It's on the house if you sign my book."

His beautiful squiggle of a brow arched before he quirked a wry smile, made sexy by the way the left corner curled upward. "So, you know who I am?"

I quirked a shy smile. "Yeah. I loved your book. Will you sign it?"

"Sure."

I was taken aback. I suddenly realized that the book was upstairs in our apartment above the deli. "I have to get it. Would you mind watching the store for just a few minutes?"

"Not a problem."

I hurried to the back of the restaurant and raced up the flight of stairs to the apartment my dad and I shared. The book was on a nightstand in my bedroom. I reread passages of the book every night before I went to sleep. I think it helped me from having the nightmares that haunted me.

When I jogged downstairs, book in hand, Ryan was behind the counter, attempting to cater to a twitchy elderly man. I had to bite down on my bottom lip to stifle my laughter. The customer, one of our pickiest, was asking for an extra lean roast beef sandwich, ketchup on the side, and French fries well done. Poor Ryan. No matter how many pieces of meat he sliced, it was never lean enough for Mr. Picky Wicky.

Scurrying behind the counter, I said, "I'll handle this while you sign my book." He let out a loud sigh of relief.

"What's your name?" he asked, taking my book from me.

"Willow. Willow Rosenthal."

"Willow." My skin prickled as he repeated my name. He made it sound like pure poetry.

"That's a beautiful name." He smiled a dimpled smile that rendered me breathless. It stretched across his magnificent face as he pulled out a pen from his back pocket. Being a writer, I guess he always carried one with him. You could never tell when or where inspiration would hit.

I took care of the curmudgeon while watching Ryan sign my book from the corner of my eye. I had mechanically signed dozens of ballet programs for fervent fans, but I hadn't been on the other side of the table for a long time. It was simultaneously nerve wracking and exhilarating. After I got rid of Mr. Picky, I handed Ryan the bag with his sandwich. He, in turn, handed me back the book.

"Thanks," we said in unison, our eyes never straying from one another.

A saucy grin spread across his lips as he headed to the front door with his sandwich bag in hand.

When he was gone, I eagerly opened my book. On the inscription page were these words:

Willow~

I look forward to seeing you again.

~Ryan

What did that mean? Did he want to go out with me? Or was he talking about coming back for another sandwich? My heart pounded with anticipation and anxiety. The truth was I couldn't wait to see him again.

TWO
Ryan

*W*illow. I said her name aloud. I liked saying it. It was breathy and beautiful. And so fitting for this willowy, wisp of a girl. There was something about her I thought as I walked to the pub where I was meeting my best bud, Duffy McDermitt. We had a standing boys' night out every Wednesday night. It was a way of staying in touch and keeping up with what was going on with *Arts & Smarts* of which he was now editor in chief. He had replaced me after I quit following a major and painful blow up with the publisher—my father—one I tried not to think about since my father and I were making amends. Slowly but surely with the help of a top Manhattan shrink. Duffy was doing a great job just as I predicted. The online magazine was flourishing and advertising sales were at an all-time high, the latter being the only thing that mattered to my powerful, cutthroat father. Mr. Bottom Line.

It had been a long time since a girl had an effect on me. Almost five years. With the success of my memoir, *Undying Love*, and my family name, I was, like it or not, one of New York's most eligible bachelors. A minor celebrity. I had no need—or desire—to put my profile up on one of those online dating sites like Tinder or Match.com Everyone, from my editor to my drycleaner, was trying to fix me up. Without meaning to sound boastful, I could have my pick of any girl in the city. Even top supermodels. The truth: I wasn't ready. I still couldn't get the love of my life, Allee Adair, out of my head. Or out of my heart.

But there was something about this girl Willow that got under my skin. That shock of wild, fiery red hair. Her delicate, pale Boticellian features. The soulfulness in her wide-set olive green eyes. And that lithe, legging-clad body that peeked through her apron. I couldn't take my eyes off her tight heart-shaped ass or her long, toned legs as she flew up the stairs with the lightness and grace of a butterfly to retrieve my book. The fact that she really loved my book and wanted me to sign it was a turn-on too. And, man, she really knew how to make a man a sandwich. Why the hell didn't I ask her out?

The pub was dark and crowded, especially at the bar, which was known for being a hot pick up spot. Eschewing the bar, I spotted my ginger-haired buddy at our usual booth toward the back. He already had a beer.

"Hey, dude," said Duffy as I took a seat opposite

him. An attractive blond waitress came by and I ordered what Duffy was drinking. A Guinness on tap. She eyed me flirtatiously before disappearing into the crowd.

Duffy grinned. "That babe has the hots for you."

Ignoring his comment, I responded, "The last issue of *Arts & Smarts* was the bomb." I still regularly read the magazine even though I was no longer editor or had any desire to be associated with it again.

"Thanks, bro." Beaming, Duffy gave me an affectionate fist bump and took a gulp of his beer.

"How's my old man treating you?"

"He leaves me alone. I think he's gotten used to the idea that *A&S* is his rebellious child."

My father, Ryan Madewell III, was the founder and CEO of Madewell Media, a Fortune 500 company that controlled broadcast outlets and publishing entities around the world. He was worth 1.8 billion dollars the last time I checked. *A&S* was just a small cog in his vast media empire.

"How are things with you and Sam?" I asked as the flirty waitress returned and lowered my mug of beer onto the distressed wood table. Sam, short for Samantha, was his beautiful fiancée. Like Duffy, she came from Southern California and loved to surf. He had met her at my wedding to Allee. She was Allee's friend and colleague at The Met. It was love at first sight for Duffy, who had never managed to score in the girlfriend department. Ironically, had I chosen Sam to show me a hidden treasure at the museum, I may have never married Allee. Sometimes, I wished I had so that I wouldn't have had to endure the tragedy of Allee dying so young. Life could be just so fucking unfair.

Duffy took another took chug of his beer. "She's great, dude. She's starting to show. She's nervous she'll be as fat as a cow at the wedding."

Duffy had been living with Sam almost from the beginning. Before Sam, he hadn't gotten laid in years. When she discovered she was pregnant a couple of months ago, they finally decided to tie the knot. They were getting married in a few weeks in Malibu at a hotel close to her parents' house. Aptly, on the beach since they both loved the ocean. Duffy had asked me to propose a toast and I'd agreed.

"Cheers." After clinking my mug against Duffy's, I took a swig of my beer. "Sam's going to a beautiful bride. How's the wedding stuff going?"

"Bitchin'. Sam's got it under control." He stroked his scruffy beard. "But the daddy thing is already freaking me out."

"Relax, man, you're going to do great." A pang of envy shot through me. A baby with Allee had not been in our cards. At least while she was alive. The frozen embryos that were being stored at a renowned Manhattan fertility clinic flashed into my mind. Having made a last minute decision not to include that part of our story in my memoir, no one knew about their existence—except my shrink and my sister Mimi, who had offered to be a surrogate. I'd declined her kind offer because following Allee's death I was in no shape or form to be a single parent. And after the release of the book, I traveled too much doing talk shows and book signings.

"So, dude, what's up with you?" my buddy asked, catapulting me back into the moment.

I told him how the movie version of *Undying Love* was moving along. While I was in California for his wedding, I had meetings set up with the Hollywood producer who was bringing my story to the big screen. The studio had already approved the screenplay and selected a director. Both Ryan Gosling and Ryan Reynolds were being considered to play me. Emma Stone had already committed to the role of Allee. As much as I was pleased with this casting decision, no one could be my Allee.

"Man, that movie is going to be a blockbuster. Every girl in America's going to be in love with Ryan Madewell."

I rolled my eyes at him. "Nah, they're going to be in love with Ryan Gosling or whoever plays the part."

Duffy snorted. "So, dude, what's going on with the rest of your life? You get laid yet?" Duffster was constantly telling me that I needed to start dating again. It had been almost five years since Allee had passed away, and I wasn't getting younger. He was convinced my dick was going to wither away and fall off.

I took a big gulp of my beer and then I said it. "I met someone." A sharp pause followed before I took several more gulps of the frothy beverage.

"Hey, man, don't go AWOL on me. Talk to me."

I reluctantly told my pal all about Willow and our encounter. In the end, it actually felt good to confide in him.

"Seriously, dude, I can't believe you wrote in her book that you wanted to see her again and you didn't ask her out. Or jot down your phone number or email address. What a doof!"

Maybe I blew it. Maybe I just wasn't ready. Maybe I really didn't want to. Maybe, maybe, maybe, maybe. I drained my beer.

"Madewell, get your big dick back to that deli before it disappears and ask that chick out."

"Okay, okay."

"And buy yourself a pack of condoms."

Duffy ordered another round of beers. I guzzled mine. The cold beverage seeped through my veins while a beautiful girl named Willow danced in my head.

My downtown loft was not far from the pub. I walked home. The buzz I got from the beer mixed nicely with the crisp autumn air. I wrapped my cashmere scarf, a gift from Allee, around my neck to shield myself from the wind.

When I got home, it was always the same. I came home to the ghost of Allee. As soon as I stepped out from the elevator that took me to my loft, a former millinery factory, I saw her curled up on the leather couch she favored, reading one of her art books. Her dark hair gathered up in a high ponytail, her espresso bean eyes meeting mine, already undressing me in my mind's eye. I always imagined her beautiful and radiant, not the faded beauty she had become when she got sick. There were photographs of her everywhere.

"Hi, baby."

"Hi, Madewell. Where've you been?"

"Just down the street at a pub. Hanging with Duff."

"That's good. You need to get out more, Golden Boy."

"It's hard."

"I betch'ya it can't be that hard." So Allee-like. *"Did'ya meet someone?*

I cringed as if she had caught me cheating.

"You look different."

My perceptive Allee. Always the voice of reason. Never one to hold back.

My cock stiffened. My balls ached. Fuck. When was it going to stop? I could taste her, smell her, feel her. My shrink told me I needed to move. Get a new place. A new bed. A new life. I just couldn't bring myself to do it. I wanted to stay connected to her anyway I could.

I blinked my eyes, and when I opened them, like magic, she was gone. Once again I felt so alone in my vast loft. Trudging to the kitchen, I checked my phone messages before winding up the spiral stairs to *our* bedroom. I shucked my clothes, putting on some pajama bottoms and a T-shirt. I did my normal bathroom routine and then hopped into bed. The beautiful antique four-poster bed that I shared with the love of my life. Usually, I did a little reading before I went to sleep, but tonight I wasn't in the mood. Besides, I needed a good night's rest. Tomorrow morning I had an interview on *Good Morning America,* so I had to be up bright and early.

No matter how hard I tried, I couldn't fall asleep. My cock was throbbing. I needed relief. My eyes shut, I slipped my hand under the duvet and began jerking myself off. Harder. Faster. I imagined her long, limber fingers around my shaft, her warm breath heating my cheeks. The ends of her long hair dancing on my flesh. My breathing grew ragged. I was heading fast and furiously toward an orgasm. With a shudder, I exploded, spurting hot cum all over my hand. Still breathing heavily, I opened my eyes halfway. In the shadows of the night was the image of a beautiful girl. She had flaming red hair and glittering green eyes. Willow!

THREE

Ryan

My segment on *Good Morning America* went well. Now that *Undying Love* was finally being made into a movie, the producers of the early morning talk show wanted to give viewers an inside scoop on my involvement in the production process. Truthfully, after consulting on the script, it was rather minimal although I did have casting approval. They were all over *Lalaland* Oscar-winner Ryan Gosling to play the lead. One of the hosts asked me if I ever considered playing the part myself. With a nervous laugh, I told her I was no actor, silently adding that I could never relive my life with Allee. That led to the final question: "Was I going to see the movie?" My answer: a straight forward: "NO." I was glad it was time for a commercial break so that I wouldn't have to elaborate.

After the interview, I stopped at a Starbucks for a latte and then walked uptown to the office of my shrink. I had a standing appointment with him on Thursdays at ten a.m. His office was located in a stately pre-war building on Central Park West and Seventy-Fifth Street, not too far from ABC studios where I'd taped the *GMA* segment.

I always felt at ease in his office. It was filled with unpretentious antiques, Hollywood memorabilia (his passion), and impressive awards and degrees. Like Father and me, he was Harvard all the way. The two of them, in fact, had been classmates. Class of '74. Dr. Goodman had treated me as a child when I was going through a bout of depression, thanks to my dysfunctional family. He was like a surrogate father to me. The warm, loving, caring man my father never was. I felt comfortable telling him everything… and he was the sole person other than my sister who knew about the frozen embryos.

Seeing the state of despair I was in following Allee's death, my sister Mimi, who had also seen Dr. Goodman during her conflicted teenage years, had urged me to seek his help. God bless, Mimi. Dr. Goodman, who was a saint, had been instrumental in helping me overcome my grief. When I got back from Paris, after scattering Allee's ashes in the Tuileries Gardens, my pain morphed into anger. Or should I say rage. I was so fucking mad that Allee had been taken from me at such a young age. Mad enough to want to take someone down. My temper was never one of my strong points to begin with.

"Ryan, your rage is normal," Dr. Goodman explained. "Especially when people you love die so young."

She wasn't even twenty-five when I lost her. It was unfair. So goddamn unfair that someone as young, beautiful, and talented as my beloved Allee could be denied the potential of her life. Dr. Goodman worked with me patiently, letting me express my feelings of pain, guilt, remorse, denial, and fear. There were times when I thought she might come back, and others when I hated myself for not being able to save her.

He was now working on getting me to accept Allee's death and to move forward. To rebuild my life and feel again. Trust me, feeling nothing was worse than depression. Way fucking worse.

"Will I ever be able to love again?" I had asked him recently.

"Yes, Ryan, you will. Broken hearts mend."

"But I don't think I can ever get over Allee."

Dr. Goodman quirked a smile. "That's because love never dies. But you are capable of loving another. The mighty heart has a lot of room."

Today, as I reclined on the couch that by now probably had a permanent imprint of my body, I thought about those words; I was feeling very conflicted. I began by telling him about my interview on *Good Morning America*.

He listened intently behind his large mahogany desk without interrupting. "It's very understandable, Ryan, why you would not want to see the movie version of *Undying Love*. It will certainly dredge up sad memories and evoke great pain, and there's also the possibility that it will not live up to your emotional or artistic expectations."

I had to say, Dr. Goodman was brilliant. Without thinking twice, I told him about my previous night's masturbation experience. That I had imagined another woman jerking me off.

With a smile, Dr. Goodman nodded. "Ryan, that's good. Progress. Tell me more about her."

Without mentioning her name, I simply told him that it was some girl who worked at a restaurant. "She made me a killer sandwich."

Dr. Goodman chuckled. "Any woman who knows how to make a good sandwich scores points in my book. Ryan Madewell, I want you to ask her out."

It was an order. A firm order. That made two…Duffy and the Doc. Okay, I was going to ask Willow out. I just didn't know when and how I was going to do it.

On the way home, I made a quick stop at a drug store and picked up a box of condoms.

FOUR

Willow

Confession. When Ryan Madewell had agreed to sign my book, I clambered upstairs to my room and had a mini-panic attack. My heart was beating a mile a minute, and butterflies swarmed my stomach. I could barely breathe. Sliding down against my bedroom door into a crouching position, I gulped in a big breath of air, ready to swoon. No one had ever had this effect on me...not even Gustave.

Over a week went by without hearing from him. Or seeing him. With each passing day, my heart sank deeper with disappointment. Maybe he had second thoughts. He probably was still suffering from the loss of Allee. The love of his life. I understood that.

Fortunately, my father's restaurant was crazy busy, which helped keep me distracted. The Jewish holidays had snuck up, and the eve of Yom Kippur, the holiest of days, was approaching, this year falling on a Friday. All day long, people had been flocking here from all over the city to order platters from Mel's Famous for their break-fasts tomorrow night. Mel's had the reputation of preparing the finest deli and dairy platters in the city. There was no one—except my mother—who could make a more beautiful platter of lox than me. She had taught me how to do it. Around a mound of cream cheese, layer the tender, shimmering pieces of smoked salmon like delicate petals, and then surround the salmon with slices of cucumber, onion, and tomato plus some lemon. Then decorate the platter with parsley and capers. And voilà!

I was exhausted but not alone. My father had a lot of loyal help—including the sandwich guys, servers, hosts, busboys, cashiers, and short order cooks—and everyone pitched in. My extended family. This was hard work, but it kept my mind off the dark places it could travel. And assembling the platters along with slicing bagels also kept my mind off Ryan.

As I sliced an onion bagel, a familiar raspy voice captured my attention with one breathy little word— "Hi." My breath hitching, I almost cut myself as I looked up. Oh my God! It was him. Ryan Madewell. As beautiful as the day I met him in a ridiculously sexy leather bomber jacket and a pair of faded jeans. My gaze met his. A smile twitched on his gorgeous face. If I didn't know better, I'd say he looked a little nervous. But there was no way he could be as nervous as me. Every nerve in my body was buzzing. The heart palps and butterflies were back with a vengeance.

"You should be careful with that knife," he commented as I fumbled with it.

"I'm an expert," I muttered, floundering for words. "Can I get you something?"

"No thanks; I'm good." He paused, the sparks between us palpable. "Hey, I know this is spur of the moment, but I was wondering—do you want to catch a movie with me tonight?"

My heart was practically beating out of my chest. His gorgeousness had no idea of the effect he was having on me. I should have been smiling brightly— even done a happy dance—I mean, he just asked me out, but instead I inwardly sighed with regret.

"I'm sorry; I can't. It's Yom Kippur. My dad and I are closing up early and going to temple for Kol Nidre."

His face flashed a blank look. Then, I remembered he was the penultimate WASP. From a Mayflower descended family.

"My mom...she passed away." My already heavy heart grew heavier. "We always go to temple on Yom Kippur to remember her."

He surprised me.

"I'd like to come with you."

Shocked, I uttered two letters: "O. K."

The synagogue was packed. Every seat taken. Luckily, Pop and I arrived early and found three together. On the walk over, I told him that Ryan Madewell was joining us. "I didn't know he was Jewish," my father commented. I told him he wasn't...that he was just interested in seeing what the service was like...maybe doing research for a new book. In my peripheral vision, I saw my father raise a skeptical brow. "Maybe he's checking something else out." Not responding, I left it at that.

Once we sat down, I kept looking out for Ryan and staving off congregants who were not too pleased that I was saving the seat next to mine. Just as the service was about to begin, Ryan came dashing through the entrance doors to the sanctuary. He was wearing a beautifully cut gray suit and an elegant blue tie that matched the color of his eyes. And looked dazzling. Scanning the sanctuary, he found us seated toward the back and quickly headed to the vacant seat. He breathed a quick hi to my father and me before sitting down. His warm breath heated my cheeks.

"Put this on," I whispered to him. I handed him a white satin yarmulke, thinking that he probably wouldn't have thought of putting on this mandatory skullcap. He adjusted it atop of his silky hair and I quirked a smile; God, he looked adorable. "Now wrap this around you." I handed him a tallis, a fringed silk shawl. As he adjusted it around his broad shoulders, I couldn't help thinking how handsome my guest looked. He gazed into my eyes, with an expression that asked: is this okay? The little nod I shot back at him was his answer. Beneath my solemn black A-line dress, my heart was hammering.

Reaching into the pocket of the seat in front of his, I

handed him a prayer book. "You can follow along; there's an English translation as well as a transliteration, and the rabbi is pretty good about telling us what page to turn to."

"Thanks," he said softly with an adorable dimpled smile as the service began with the traditional Kol Nidre cello solo. Silence fell over the sanctuary.

I loved this opening cello piece. One day I hoped to choreograph it. The melody was so, so beautiful. And haunting. It never failed to send chills down my spine and tug at my heartstrings. Sadness surged inside me as I thought about the indignities suffered by the Jews over the centuries. And then my mind jettéd to my mom. Later in the service, I would say Kaddish, a mourning prayer for the dead.

The service was long, but I enjoyed it. I didn't go to temple often nor did I consider myself a very religious or spiritual person. But when I did go, it was an emotional, otherworldly experience that got me both out of myself and in touch with myself. The beauty of the sanctuary with its stained glass windows and high Romanesque ceilings also awed me. It was one of the oldest in the city. Generation after generation had worshipped here, including my grandparents on both sides. My Nana, my only remaining grandparent on my mom's side, unfortunately wasn't here tonight as she didn't live in the city. Or socialize with my father.

In the middle of the service, the rabbi gave a moving sermon on forgiving and forgetting, fitting for this

Day of Atonement. His profound words sank into me. Would I ever be able to forgive the man who had brought me to my knees? Brought me deep into an inferno of lust and despair. And would I ever be able to forget? A shiver shimmied through me.

The Mourner's Kaddish came near the end of the service. Everyone in the congregation rose. I mumbled the words in Hebrew. Ryan followed along with the transliteration. He, too, had someone to mourn. As tears poured down my face in memory of my mother, I gripped my father's thick calloused hand. He gave mine a squeeze. There wasn't a day that my father didn't miss or mourn my mom. I jolted when my other hand was suddenly also occupied. Without looking my way, Ryan had taken it in his. His hand was soft and warm, the grip steady and firm. Maybe he didn't want to grieve alone.

"Oh seh shalom," concluded the rabbi. The cantor, with his rich, operatic voice, began to sing, repeating the word "shalom" over and over. Tears continued to spill down my face. *Oh, mom!* How I missed her and wished I could right the wrongs.

The choir and congregants joined in, including both my dad and myself.

Shalom. Yes, peace is what I was seeking. In the world. And in myself in the year to come. As the hymn ended with an "Amen," Ryan squeezed my hand. I held back a sniffle, but heard my companion inhale deeply through his nose. Unbeknownst to him, I turned to look at him, and saw a tear running down his magnificent profile. He was in mourning, profoundly affected by this service. I squeezed his hand back and then felt his thumb rub the side of my wrist. The magical connection between us at this moment couldn't be put into words.

At the conclusion of the service, everyone filed out the back doors of the sanctuary. Since we were sitting in the back, we were amongst the first to exit. Pop and I said hello to many congregants we'd gotten to know over the years, some of whom frequented his deli. Ryan stood awkwardly by my side; he must have felt like such an outsider. Women of all ages stared at him, many shooting him seductive smiles. I'm sure some even recognized him from his fame and fortune. His Waspy gorgeousness was definitely a head turner and a force to be reckoned with. Even men, gay and straight, held him in their gaze. I inwardly laughed as congregants sauntered up to us to wish us a *Shana Tova*. A Happy New Year. Something I so needed after the past six turbulent months.

Before leaving, my father told me had to use the "little boys' room," and left me alone with Ryan in the synagogue lobby.

We stood awkwardly facing each other. I was a petite five foot four, and even in my three-inch heels, I was a lot shorter than he was.

"Did you enjoy the service?" I asked nervously.

"It was beautiful. Thank you for letting me come." He neatly hung up the tallis on a stand and set the yarmulke into a nearby basket.

"My pleasure." Sheesh. Couldn't I come up with something less mundane? Worse, the word "come" was whirling around in my head, playing crude mind games.

His cornflower-blue eyes gazed into my pickle-green ones—my "deli eyes" as Pop called them. I didn't know what next to say. Thankfully, Ryan spared me from coming up with something.

"Would you like to go out for a drink? There's a really great wine bar that's not far from here."

Dammit, that sounded good…so good…exactly what I craved after the emotionally draining service. But I couldn't.

"I can't. I'm fasting."

"Oh." The infamous little word when you didn't know what else to say. His voice and face registered disappointment.

Before my heart sank, I had an idea. "Why don't you come tomorrow night to my dad's deli. He hosts an open house break-fast for the neighborhood—and any one who doesn't have one to go to."

Ryan's face brightened. "I'd love to."

The word "love" danced around in my head.

"Do I need to dress up?"

"No, it's totally casual."

"Great. I'll see you tomorrow night."

As he loped out the front doors of the synagogue, my heart was racing.

He could show up in his birthday suit and I wouldn't care.

FIVE
Willow

At sundown on Saturday, the deli was packed with people young and old. There were families with children and babies, grandparents, young professionals as well as college kids and some local street people. Every table and seat was taken and the noise level was high. My father was in his element, hopping from table to table, to see if everyone had enough to eat. Trust me, they did. There was nothing my father loved more than to feed people. And watch them enjoy eating his food. There was a word in Yiddish for my big-hearted father: a *mensch.*

Dressed comfortably in black leggings, an oversized sweater, and ballet flats, I was helping the staff lug platters of lox and bagels to the hungry patrons. One eye stayed on the front door—anxiously awaiting Ryan. It was going on eight o'clock. Maybe he had changed his mind and wouldn't show up.

Then, as I lowered a platter onto one of the tables, a warm breath dusted the nape of my neck. I whirled around. My heart did a grand jeté at the sight of the man facing me. Ryan! A Cheshire grin lit up his beautiful face.

"Hi."

I don't know how long my mouth stayed open in shock before I said "hi" back. My heart thudded as goosebumps popped along my arms. God, he was gorgeous. He was wearing faded black jeans that molded to his thighs like a second skin and an open charcoal blazer. Beneath his jacket, his chiseled chest peeked out from the V of his pale blue T-shirt. He looked so damn sexy!

"Would you like a bagel and lox?" I asked, not yet having eaten a thing myself.

"Sure." He grabbed one and bit into it. I watched as he swallowed. He licked a smidgeon of cream cheese off his sensuous lips.

"Wow! This is good."

"Thanks. Mel's has the best Nova in the city."

"Nova?"

"As in Nova Scotia Lox…smoked salmon." I smiled, charmed by his naiveté.

"Right." He grinned back with embarrassment.

My eyes stayed on him while he finished the sandwich. His fine upbringing was evident by the way he gracefully held the bagel in his elegant, long-fingered hands and chewed his food quietly.

When he was done, there was still a drop of cream cheese on his upper lip. With my thumb, I wiped it away, relishing the softness of his velvety lips. Hot tingles bombarded me as he shot me a grateful smile. There must have been over one hundred diners in the restaurant, but I only had eyes for one.

"Good to see you here, Mr. Madewell. Have yourself another bagel."

I spun around. Coming our way was my father with a wide smile broadcast across his face. He, too, was carrying a large tray of bagels and lox.

"Thanks." Ryan helped himself to another bagel and bit into it.

"How's my daughter treating you?" asked Pop.

With the chunk of the bagel and lox masticating in his mouth, he couldn't say a word. Nodding, he gave Pop a thumbs-up.

"She's a beauty, isn't she? Just like her mother, may she rest in peace."

Ryan's twinkling blue eyes met mine as he swallowed. He nodded again. "Totally."

I felt my cheeks flush. Did this gorgeous, talented Adonis really think I was beautiful? Or was he just placating my father?

Then suddenly, I felt lightheaded. Everything around me became a messy blur, and the noise around me reduced to a din. Beads of sweat clustered all over my body as all the blood in my head rushed to my feet. It got worse. Like a swarm of bugs, little black dots clouded my vision.

"Pumpkin, what's wrong?" I heard my alarmed father say, but words stayed trapped in my throat as the black dots multiplied and I grew dizzier.

The noise drowned out as everything turned to darkness. And then my knees buckled. I was going down! Spiraling to the floor like a limp strand of spaghetti. Just before I crashed onto the hard wood, two strong hands caught me. I blinked my eyes open and the next thing I knew I was in Ryan Madewell's arms, blanketed against his buttery cashmere jacket.

My father brushed a few stray strands of hair off my forehead. "Pumpkin, you just fainted. Are you okay?"

"Yeah," I managed, finding my voice. But truthfully, I felt weak and queasy.

Ryan's eyes stayed fixed on mine. "Sir, I think she should lie down."

"I need to get back to work and help my father," I protested, feeling a tad stronger.

My father gazed at me lovingly. "No, Ryan's right. You need to get some rest." He looked at Ryan. "Would you mind bringing her up to her room?"

"It would be my pleasure, sir."

I loved the way he called my father "sir." It gave the always disheveled deli man dignity. Without making a fuss, I let Ryan carry me up to my room. He knew where the stairs were, having seen me bound up them last week to retrieve his book.

I wrapped my arms around his neck as he effortlessly mounted the flight of stairs to my room. His silky hair brushed against the back of my hand. I stifled the urge to run my fingers through the tousled locks. As I leaned into him, I could feel the hard muscles of his chest against me as well as those of his sculpted biceps. He definitely was in great shape. And I could hear his heart beat. It felt good to be so close to someone's heart…again.

The stairs led to a small, dimly lit foyer. A portrait of my mother graced the walls, and on the entryway table, there was a large vase of fragrant Asian lilies, my mother's favorite flowers. Not only did they remind me always of her, but they also deflected the pungent scent of the deli below.

"Which way?" asked Ryan.

"Down the hall to the right."

"You okay?" he asked as he strode to my bedroom.

"I'm fine." And I meant it. Being in his arms had restored my strength, but I felt like I was in some kind of dream.

The door to my bedroom was open. Stepping inside, he delivered me to my bed. He set me down gently, propping me against my pillows and covering me with the fuzzy blanket that was folded along the edge. After making me drink some water, he brushed vagrant strands of my unruly hair out of my face. The tenderness of his gesture sent a tingling ray of warmth all the way to my toes.

"Is it okay if I sit down on the bed?"

"Sure," I said breathlessly. A sudden wave of embarrassment and insecurity washed over me as he lowered himself next to me. Here I was in bed with

Ryan Madewell IV, the drop-dead, gorgeous bestselling author of *Undying Love*. Holy shit!

His eyes swept around the room, taking in every detail.

"Is this where you slept as a child?"

"Yes," I said diffidently. The room hadn't been redecorated for years. It still bore my white wrought iron canopy bed and the painted cottage furniture my mom had found at the 26th Street flea market. The pink floral wallpaper matched my bedspread and the curtains that hung on the window. It was so embarrassingly princessy. And next to me on one of my pillows was my favorite stuffed animal—a dilapidated little monkey.

"Who's that?" asked Ryan upon eyeing it.

"Baboo. I've had him since I was a baby."

Ryan's gaze stayed on him. "I had one of those. His name was Monk. But my mother threw him out when I was five. I think that was the beginning of all my fuckedupness."

"I'm sorry," I said with compassion, remembering what I'd read about his mother in his book. Eleanor Madewell. She was an icy alcoholic with narcissistic tendencies. So unlike my warm, loving mother.

His gaze moved to my nightstand. He studied what was on it.

"Is that your mom?" he asked, pointing his long index finger at a framed photo. It was a portrait of a woman in her early twenties with flaming red hair similar to mine. She held a little curly-haired redheaded girl in her arms. Me.

"Yeah."

"Your father is right. She was beautiful…like you."

"Thanks," I murmured, heating from the compliment.

Before I could say another word, his face brightened. "And you still keep a copy of my book on your nightstand?"

I felt my face flush and smiled shyly. "I like to re-read chapters before I go to sleep." I paused. "Thanks again for signing it."

"No, thank *you* for asking me." His eyes burnt into mine. I was having a hard time breathing and I didn't know what to say next. The heavenly scent of his light cologne drifted up my nose, making me feel heady.

His eyes surveyed the rest of the room. I'd read once that writers are observers.

His gaze fixed on the framed photos on my dresser—most of them of me, taken at various stages in my life, in leotards and tutus, some at recitals, others at classes. Then, he shifted his vision to the worn, pink satin pointe shoes that dangled from my headboard. They were my very first pair—I was only ten when I got them.

"Are you a dancer?" he asked.

My muscles tensed. "Yes." Or should I say was?

"Do you perform?"

I hesitated before responding. "No."

A half-truth. I hadn't performed for over six months and I wasn't sure if I ever would again. I didn't want to get into details about my recent past. Or think about Gustave …at least right now.

His eyes stayed riveted on the little pink slippers as he gave them a light tap. Tied to the bed by their frayed ribbons, they swung back and forth like a pendulum.

"Do you want me to go downstairs and get you something to eat?"

"Maybe in a little bit." The truth was I hungered only for him; I didn't want him to leave me. Not yet. As I soaked in his gorgeous profile, my heart thudded and a buzz of lust flooded my body. I longed to touch him. Run my fingers through his hair. For him to touch me. Trace my lips with his fingers. An awkward stretch of silence followed as he continued to play with my pointe shoes. Then, he turned to face me again, the expression on his face a mixture of hesitance and longing.

"Willow, I want to ask you something." He paused, holding me in his gaze. "Can I kiss you?"

My lips parted in shock, and my heart practically stopped. "Yes, please," I murmured. *Now!* I couldn't wait a moment more.

On my next rapid heartbeat, he cupped my cheeks in his hands, leaned down, and crushed his soft, warm lips against mine. He nibbled my upper lip, then deepened the kiss, gnawing and sucking. *Oh my God. Oh my God. Oh my God.* I'd never been kissed like this before. A heat wave spread through my body, setting every cell on fire. As a moan escaped my throat, his tongue parted my lips and found mine. They danced together, swirling and twirling, two strangers in the night discovering each other. The salty taste of the salmon lingered in his mouth and mixed with his sweet saliva, making him even more delicious. My fingers gripped his hair as our lips, tongues, and moans mingled. I had read about his kisses, but nothing had prepared me for the sensation of one. I thought I was leaving this planet.

Suddenly, heavy footsteps thudded in the near distance. For sure my father. Reality hit us fast and hard. I hastily pulled away from Ryan and caught my breath. While I tidied my mane of hair, he, in turn, jumped to his feet. Before standing up, he cursed under his breath and wiped my wet lips with the back of his hand. I could still taste him. Oh God, how I wanted more of him. To make matters worse, there was a sizable bulge between his thighs.

Pop lumbered into my room. I held my breath, wondering if my father would suspect what had just gone down between Ryan and me. I hoped his eyes wouldn't travel down my companion's torso. Oh shit! Then, on my next heartbeat, I was saved.

Huffing, Pop wiped a bead of sweat from his brow. Sheesh! Going up a flight of stairs undid him. He so needed to lose weight and get into shape.

"They ate me out of house and home," he panted, undoing his long, soiled apron.

I digested his words. That meant the grand break-fast was over, and my father had closed up. I glanced at my alarm clock—nine o'clock. Usually, he stayed open till midnight, but Yom Kippur was one of the few exceptions.

"How's she doing, Ryan?" he asked.

I inwardly breathed a sigh of relief. He obviously had no clue about what had transpired because my father, like my mother, was brutally honest, not one to hold back.

"Um, uh, I'd say she's completely recovered." Ryan stuttered, my father unconvinced.

"She looks flushed. Pumpkin, let me check your temperature."

"Really, Pop, I'm perfectly fine." I leaped out of bed and hugged him. My overprotective father.

"Did you at least eat something?" There was genu-ine concern in his voice as he shot Ryan a troubled look. "Sometimes my little girl doesn't eat enough."

"Don't worry. I did," I countered, realizing I had broken this year's fast with a delicious taste of Ryan Madewell. I turned my head to face him.

With suddenness, all of Ryan's color drained from his face. He fidgeted with the gold band around his ring finger and then bolted out of my room without saying goodnight.

SIX

Ryan

Holy Jesus! What had I just done? I kissed Willow Rosenthal. And couldn't get enough of her. I'd forgotten what it's like to kiss a woman you find insanely attractive in every which way. It was rough and raw, hot and addictive, and it totally turned me on.

My delicate deli girl tasted delicious. I completely lost myself in the kiss. But my ecstasy was short-lived. An ambush of guilt and remorse snuck up on me. In a panic, I fled, without thanking her or her father, leaving them both in a sea of confusion.

My cock throbbing and my emotions in turmoil, I jogged home. I felt sick to my stomach. As if someone had given me a punch to my gut.

As I slogged out the elevator that opened to my loft, a massive dose of guilt surged inside me. Fuck. There was Allee. Curled up on the couch as usual, this time wearing only one of my crisp cotton dress shirts. The top buttons were opened, exposing her eye-worthy cleavage. Once upon a time, I had placed my cock in that sexy chasm and let her rub her breasts against my shaft till I came all over them.

"I'm sorry," I muttered, hanging my head in shame.

"About what, Golden Boy?"

I slowly raised my head and met her gaze. After the awful discovery of her sordid "other" life and later the cancer, we'd vowed not to keep secrets from each other. Even if I tried to keep a secret, she would eventually pry it out of me. Sooner than later.

"I kind of had a date with a girl." Every word was a struggle.

Her reaction shocked me. A big smile spread across her luminous face. "It's about time, Madewell. You know you can't mourn me forever."

Allee's farewell letter flashed into my head. She had told me that she wanted me to meet someone new after she was gone. I didn't really believe her words when I first read them, but maybe she really meant them.

"So, what's her name?"

"Willow."

"Pretty. And two L's... a good sign." Allee had a thing for double "L's." She believed that Superman, her childhood superhero crush, had a thing for girls with double L's in their names. Like Lois Lane and Lana Lang. She had once called me her Superman though sadly I could not save her in the end.

"So, tell me, what does she look like?"

I described Willow in detail.

"So, a lanky redhead. That's a surprise. What's she like?"

I went on to tell her that she was the daughter of the deli guy we always ordered take out from. And then I explained how we met and told her about my Yom Kippur outing, not going beyond the synagogue part.

"So, she's Jewish?"

"Yeah, from the Lower Eastside."

"Oooh… your parents are really going to like her." Her voice was dripping with sarcasm…so very Allee.

"They're getting better." Seriously, they were. With the help of Dr. Goodman, I was slowly making amends with my father. Last year's major stroke—it happened while he was screwing one of his mistresses—had changed him. Partially paralyzed, he was now wheelchair bound, slightly more open-minded, and he was keeping his pants on. My mother, who should have left him, nursed him back to health, the good trophy wife she was. He was beholden to her though he'd never admit it and now disabled, he needed her more than ever. His dependency on her gave her power. Though the marriage was still strained by most standards, his forced newfound faithfulness had saved it. And my mother was drinking less. Okay. A little less.

Allee rolled her eyes while I dwelled on her snarky comment. What made her so sure I was going to introduce Willow to my parents? What kind of mind game was she playing with me? Before I could challenge her, she asked me another question.

"So, what exactly did you do with Willow on your

date?"

"Not much."

"You're bullshitting me, Madewell."

My stomach twisted; I couldn't fool Allee. I blurted out the truth.

"Allee, I kissed her." Suddenly, I was feeling miserable again, consumed by a horrific sense of betrayal. How could I have done that? I hardly knew her, and besides my heart belonged to another. When I thought about it more, it was my fault. I should have never touched my lips down on hers, but I couldn't help myself. To make things worse, she gave me a hard-on. Confession: I almost asked her to give me a blowjob. Guilt mixed with remorse.

"It's about time." To my shock, Allee gave me a thumbs-up. Her dark eyes sparkled as she smiled brightly. "Congratulations, Madewell!"

Actually, I was more than shocked. Her reaction hurt me. I mean, here was the woman I had loved—and still loved—with my body, heart, and soul. My wife, my lover, my light...the person for whom I would have given up my life...and she wasn't even jealous. In fact, she looked like she might do a happy dance. Christ. Allee was feisty. A fighter. And she wasn't fighting for me. Not one bit.

Miffed, I muttered, "I'm going upstairs. Are you ready?" On most nights, I mentally swept her off her feet and carried her up to my bedroom.

"Not tonight, Madewell."

"Fine."

Hey, Madewell, you gotta remember…" Her voice grew softer, the expression on her face more wistful. *"I can't do those kinda things with you any more."* She paused. *"Give Willow a chance."*

She had a point. It was no different from what Dr. Goodman or Duffy had told me. I was having difficulty letting go.

By the time I hit the sack, the throbbing between my legs had died down. I was exhausted but restless. I rubbed my eyes, tossed and turned, and kicked off the covers several times. Each time I managed to doze off, I would awaken, searching frantically for Allee by my side, her lovely limbs draped over mine. True to her vow, she never came upstairs.

Finally, God knows when, I drifted off. A dream claimed me.

I was in Paris wandering aimlessly through the Musée D'Orsay. Behind me, I heard footsteps. Those of a woman wearing heels.

"Can I help you?"

I recognized the husky, New York-accented voice immediately. Allee!

Spinning around, I gasped. "Allee, what are you doing here?"

She looked as stunning as ever. In fact, more stunning, wearing the little black dress I'd bought her.

"I work here now."

"No, you can't! You belong in New York with me."

"No, Madewell, I don't. I belong here now." She smiled. "I want to show you a wonderful new painting."

Reluctant and confused, I followed her to an adjacent wing. The paintings were more contemporary. Like they could have been painted only yesterday.

"Look at this masterpiece," she said, leading me to an exquisite, large erotic canvas of a man and woman making love.

My heart leaped into my throat. I recognized the setting. My bedroom. But the bed was different as was the woman who had her legs wrapped around me. Only her backside exposed, her long red hair cascaded down to her waist.

"Observe the impassioned expression on his face," said my analytic Allee. "The energy in his body."

I stared at the painting, my cock hardening as I did.

"Now, step into the painting. Experience it. Feel what the subject is feeling."

"What?" I murmured, mesmerized by the painting and the erotic high it was giving me.

Allee folded her arms across her chest. Her bossy stance. "Do it, Madewell. Do it for me. I'll be watching."

Mentally, as if in a trance, I did as she asked. Jesus. This lithe redheaded girl, sitting on my lap, felt incredible, her lightness of being contrasting with the strength of her thighs straddling mine. My cock fit perfectly into her sweet, tight pussy, and as I pumped her, she took me to the hilt, bucking me in perfect harmony, meeting every thrust. I clenched her slender hips while she gripped my shoulders and rode me with a skillful blend of grace and precision. Arching her back, the rosebud nipples of her pert tits brushed against my chest while the tips of her flaming hair skimmed my thighs. Ecstasy washed over her exquisite face as little moans, like musical notes, spilled from her lips. As I picked up my pace, the moans crescendoed as we came apart.

"Ryan, say *my* name!" she begged, her muscles shuddering around my cock.

"Willow!" I cried out, so ready to come. Then, like a gunshot, I exploded. My release met hers as Allee looked on, a contented smile spread across her face.

Suddenly, with Willow's name still on my lips, an alarm rung in my ears. I recognized it. My cell phone. My eyes snapped open, and in a cold sweat, I bolted upright to a sitting position. Grabbing the phone off my nightstand, I speed-dialed Dr. Goodman's emergency number. The one that was reserved for suicides, overdoses, and murder attempts. In my book, this was an emergency. I couldn't breathe, think, or function. Or get rid of my morning wood.

SEVEN

Ryan

I was fucking lucky Dr. Goodman had a last minute cancellation at 11:00 a.m. on Monday. I usually met with him on Thursday, but I couldn't wait that long. Stretched out on his couch, I felt like I was suffering from some kind of flu. My head was pounding and my stomach churning. Earlier, I'd even thrown up. That's how fucked up I was.

"So, Ryan, tell me what's going on," began Dr. Goodman.

"That girl I told you about…"

"Yes…"

I hesitated and then the words tumbled out. "I kissed her." I fidgeted with my ring. "And I more than enjoyed it."

"This is certainly no emergency. What's wrong with that?"

"Everything. I belong to Allee."

Dr. Goodman stroked his salt and pepper beard. "Allee is gone, Ryan. It's been almost five years."

"Only four and a half," I corrected. "I fantasize

about her every night."

"That's not uncommon. What do you fantasize about?"

"That she's still in my life. That things are like they used to be. She's always waiting for me when I come home." I paused. "Last night, after the kiss, I came home and I saw her. I told her about the other girl. What I did. I swear, she was happy for me. I don't get it."

Dr. Goodman adjusted his horn-rimmed glasses. "Ryan, Allee only exists in your subconscious. Last night, your subconscious was telling you that it wants you to let go of Allee. That it's okay."

I went on and told him about my dream.

"That's a very interesting dream, Ryan. What do you think it means?"

"That I'm fucked up."

Dr. Goodman chortled. "You're not as fucked up as you think, Ryan. What this tells me is that two women can co-exist in your life. That you're ready for a new relationship."

I processed what the Doc just said. Was I really ready to move on?

Dr. Goodman cut my mental ramblings short. "Ryan, you like this new woman, right?"

I nodded. I had to admit that there were many things I liked about Willow even though I didn't know much about her. She seemed smart, funny, and I found her attractive... make that sexy as sin.

"This is excellent. You have feelings toward her."

Okay, so he forced me to admit I had some feelings about her…something I'd not had toward a woman—or just about anything—in a long while.

"So, Doc, what should I do?"

"Get to know her better."

"O…kay." That I could do. "Then what?"

"Sleep with her."

Sleep. With. Her. The three words spun around in my head, colliding into each other like bumper cars. We may have fucked in my dream, but the reality of having her in my bed—the bed I'd shared with Allee—stabbed me in the heart. It was unfathomable.

"That's not possible."

"Why not?"

I fumbled for an excuse. "She lives with her father. I don't think it would be too cool to bang her while he's sleeping in the bedroom next door."

"I agree. That's not a good idea. But you have your own place and a bed."

My blood heated as I bolted upright. "There's no way I can fuck her in my bed! That bed's sacred. It was my wedding present to Allee."

"Then sell it and buy a new one."

His matter-of-fact words ripped into me. My fists clenched on my thighs. I was reeling.

He cast his eyes downward. "And it's time for you, young man, to stop wearing your wedding band."

My blood bubbled at his words. *Fuck him!*

Before I could utter a word—or punch him out which is what I really wanted to do—Dr. Goodman glanced down at his watch and announced that our session was over. Not thanking him for seeing me, I charged out of his office feeling worse than I had when I'd arrived. Therapy was supposed to help you—make you feel better—but a lot of the time it made you feel like crap.

Still simmering, I waited impatiently for the elevator. I needed to get the hell out of here. Blow off some steam. Maybe go for a run or take my bike for a ride. I tapped my foot as I anxiously rubbed the gold band on my ring finger with the pad of my thumb. What was taking so long? Finally, the elevator arrived, and when door slid open, my eyes almost popped out of their sockets. I was face to face with the person I least likely expected to see. Willow Rosenthal.

EIGHT
Willow

My heart raced as I lay down on Dr. Goodman's chaise. Why had I just encountered Ryan Madewell? He told me had an appointment, but not with whom. Yes, there were other medical personnel and professionals in this building—doctors, lawyers, dentists—but I positively knew he had just visited Dr. Goodman. How? Simple. I could smell the scent of his woodsy cologne.

A million questions whirled around my head as I waited for my psychiatrist to return from the bathroom. Had Ryan told him about me? What did he say? Should I tell Dr. Goodman about our relationship? And that's assuming there was one.

What happened last night had sent my emotions into a tailspin. Ryan Madewell had given me the most intoxicating kiss I ever had. It had sent me orbiting and everything indicated that he got off on it as much as I did. Then, shortly after my father showed up, he paled and took off like the wind with not as much as a goodbye. In a heartbeat, I'd gone from an incredible high to a terrible low.

Stinging with confusion and hurt, I called it a night, but no matter how much I tried, I couldn't fall asleep. Clinging to Baboo, I couldn't stop thinking about Ryan, the memory of him kissing me making it harder. Plus, the scent of him lingered. Sadly, as dawn approached, I came to the conclusion that I was just some kind of fling. Nothing more.

"So, Willow, let's pick up where we left off," said Dr. Goodman, snapping me out of my disturbing thoughts as he entered the room. Sitting down on an armchair close to me, he glanced down at a pad of notes.

"Why do you think you let Gustave control you?"

Gustave. Right now, he was the last person on my mind. I didn't want to think about him. Or talk about him. Someone else was all over my mind.

"I don't want to talk about Gustave today if that's okay."

"And why is that, Willow?"

"I met someone."

"A man?"

I nodded.

Knitting his brows, Dr. Goodman jotted something down on his notepad. "Do you want to tell me about him?"

"I think you can tell me more about him than I can."

"What do you mean, Willow?" His perplexed voice matched his expression.

"His name is Ryan Madewell."

For the first time ever, Dr. Goodman was speechless. His pen fell out of his hand. He quickly picked it up and persevered.

"So, you had some form of intimacy with him." It was a statement, not a question. Clearly, Ryan had told him.

My mother's personality shot through me. Not one to mince words. "I kissed him." *Oh, that kiss! That unforgettable kiss!*

"And…"

"He ran off. He didn't even say goodnight."

"How did that make you feel?"

"Like shit."

"As it should."

"Did he tell you what he thought about me?"

"My dear, you know I can't divulge that. Doctor-patient privilege."

I inhaled a deep, frustrated breath and then randomly asked, "Can two broken hearts find happiness together?"

Dr. Goodman looked straight into my eyes. "Yes, they can."

That's all I needed to hear. With forty-five minutes left to our session, I bounded out of his office.

NINE

Ryan

I nursed my caffè latte. A grande two percent. During my unexpected and unnerving encounter with Willow, I impulsively asked her to meet me at the Starbucks on Columbus and Eighty-First. While she agreed to it, I wasn't sure if she was going to show up. Especially after my dickish behavior last night. I alternated sips of my latte with glances at the entrance and nervously fiddled with my wedding band. Maybe Dr. Goodman was right…about everything.

It was weird that we'd run into each other at Dr. Goodman's office building. Maybe her dentist shared the same floor as my shrink. She told me she had an appointment, and I wasn't expecting her to show for another forty-five minutes, if at all, but on the next sip of my hot beverage, she dashed into the coffee shop.

Our earlier encounter was so rushed that I hadn't had a chance to soak her in with my eyes. She was again wearing black leggings, this time with a heavy, oversized rust sweater. Combat boots had replaced ballet flats, perhaps because of the cool autumn weather. No matter what she wore, she was still so waif-like, something that turned me on and made me want to hold her and take care of her. Her fiery red hair, almost the color or her sweater, was loose and cascaded wildly over her shoulders. Man, that mane of hair was insane. She looked ravishing.

Despite the place being packed, she spotted me right away and waved. Before joining me, she ordered something at the counter. After her name was called by a barista, she grabbed her order and sat down in the vacant chair opposite mine.

She sipped her coffee without ever taking her eyes off me. Her intense green-eyed gaze made me feel jumpy and heated at once. Each of us was waiting for the other to start a conversation. Finally, after another sip of my latte, I began.

"So you were visiting your childhood orthodontist?"

"Very funny. I didn't need braces."

She shot me a toothy smile. Her sparkling teeth were pearl-white and perfect. Cover-girl perfect. I fought back the urge to run my tongue over them.

"So, why were you there?" I asked.

"The same reason you were."

I processed her words. Holy shit. We shared the same shrink. My brows lifted to my forehead as I inquired. "Dr. Goodman?"

She nodded. "Yes, Dr. Goodman. I've been seeing him since I was a child."

"Me too. I'm fucked up."

"Headline news. I am too."

My eyes widened then softened. "What do you mean?"

"Listen, Ryan Madewell, your life is an open book, no pun intended. I know you hurt. But I hurt too. So, keep that in mind."

Tears leaked from the corners of her eyes. I had no clue what motivated them. An unrequited love? An untimely death? Or maybe I was the cause of them? My freakish behavior last night was nothing to be proud of; I owed her an apology. Whatever the source, I knew they were real. With my paper napkin, I dabbed them. They kept spilling down her high cheekbones. The words of Henry Wadsworth Longfellow flashed in my head. *Every man has his secret sorrows, which the world knows not.*

Allee had hers and obviously Willow did too. Maybe I was just attracted to fucked up girls, though my ex, Charlotte, who I hadn't seen in ages, definitely took the cake in the fucked up department. A total nutjob. But Willow was nothing of the sort. From what I could tell, she was sweet and unpretentious. I promised myself to be more sensitive. More caring. To listen more...starting right now.

"So, Willow, tell me..."

"I have self-esteem problems. I've been working on them."

"Did you lose someone?" I ventured.

"Yes. I told you. My mother. I never got to say

goodbye to her."

With love, there are no goodbyes. Allee's almost last words to me. "Maybe she didn't want you to."

Willow shrugged. "Maybe. But her death left me with terrible guilt."

I understood guilt. I was supposed to be Allee's Superman, but I couldn't save her. My guilt had morphed into various emotions from failure to anger. Even fear.

"How have you dealt with it?" I asked.

"I've inflicted pain upon myself."

Then silence.

I digested her words. Was she a cutter? Did she try to commit suicide? Starve herself to death? Before I could ask, and truthfully I didn't want to, she continued.

"I was in an abusive relationship."

"You let some guy hurt you?"

"It's complicated. Let's not go there yet."

"A boyfriend?"

"Please, Ryan. Drop it."

We shared a long stretch of silence until Willow broke it. "Maybe we should end whatever we started."

I jolted, for sure not expecting her reaction. "Is that what Dr. Goodman advised?"

She looked deep into my eyes and shook her head. We both broke into sheepish smiles at the same time.

I asked her out on the spot. She agreed.

Tomorrow night, we were having our first official movie and dinner date.

We finished our coffees when Willow's cell phone rang. She pulled it out of her backpack and answered it. Her face turned as white as chalk.

"Oh my God."

"Willow, what's the matter?" I asked.

"My father. He's had a heart attack!"

TEN

Ryan

My Fiat was parked just around the corner. I offered Willow a ride. She was more than grateful to accept it. Her father had been admitted to New York-Presbyterian on Williams Street in lower Manhattan, not far from his deli. Yet another hospital whose board my philanthropic mother sat on.

Sitting beside me in the small car, Willow was stone-faced. Biting down on her bottom lip, she didn't say a word as I drove down Fifth Avenue, expertly weaving in and out of the crazy lunch hour traffic, trying to get to the hospital as fast as possible. At a light at 34th Street, she burst into tears.

"Oh, Ryan!" she sobbed. "I'm so scared. What if he dies before we get there?"

Keeping one hand on the steering wheel, I gripped her hand with the other. It was cold as ice. "Butterfly, it's going to be okay." *Butterfly.* A term of endearment. I couldn't help it.

She squeezed my hand. I think she wanted to believe me. With quivering lips, she looked my way. Her misty eyes glistened like emeralds, making her more exquisite. There was a moment at the next light that I wanted to kiss her and make all her tears go away.

We parked the car with the valet and dashed into the hospital. She let me hold her hand as we headed to the information center. My distraught Willow was still in tears and could barely speak. "I'm looking for…" Her sobs didn't allow her to finish her sentence, so I did it for her.

"Melvin Rosenthal. He had a heart attack."

An attractive African American woman scanned his name on her computer. "Yes. He was just admitted. He's in intensive care."

"I want to see him!" cried out Willow.

"Sorry, Miss. No visitors allowed at this time."

"But, I'm his daughter," she pleaded desperately.

I hated to wield the power of my last name, but there were times it came in handy. I eyed the name card pinned on the woman's hospital uniform. "Sheila, I'm Ryan Madewell …my parents donated the…"

The woman's face brightened. "Of course, I've met your lovely mother. I think I can make an exception this time. She gave us visitor badges, which we clipped on to our sweaters.

Adjusting her badge, Willow gazed at me with her watery eyes, forlorn but full of gratitude. "Oh, Ryan,

I'm so glad you're here with me. I don't know how to thank you."

"You don't have to." I gently kissed the top of her head, inhaling the strawberry scent of her hair. Had this been a different situation, my lips would have consumed hers. And she would be thanking me in a different way.

I waited in the tenth-floor reception area while Willow visited her father. I tried to read a magazine but couldn't. Being in a hospital made me emotionally and physically ill. It made me think of Allee. Our last night together. An intense, nauseating sadness washed over me. I thought I would throw up when Willow reappeared. Her bloodshot eyes met mine. I leaped up from my seat.

"How's your dad?"

"He's going to be okay. His heart attack was mild, but they're going to keep him in ICU for a few days." Her face brightened. "He may be home early next week."

"That's great news." Drawing her into me, I gave her a hug. Her waif-like body felt so good in my arms. With a sigh, she leaned her head against my chest. I smoothed her hair and savored the warmth of body next to mine.

"Thanks again, Ryan, for being here for me." She

gazed up at me, with a small grateful smile and blinking back tears. I wiped them away. It felt good to be needed. It had been a very long time.

ELEVEN

Willow

I stayed at the hospital through the evening, never leaving my father's room in the ICU ward. He was attached to all kinds of IVs and beeping monitors, and he had a breathing tube up his nose. While he was weak, his great sense of humor was already shining through and he was already complaining.

Around eight o'clock, jovial Nurse Hollis, who reminded me a little of my mother with her curly reddish hair, told me visiting hours were over.

"C'mon," begged my father, his voice hoarse. "Can't she stay a little longer?"

"I'm afraid not, Mr. Rosenthal," she replied with a smile and a twinkle in her caramel eyes. "She can come back tomorrow morning."

My feisty father grunted, then he winked. "How 'bout you stay, beautiful, if I behave?" I swear if I didn't know better, he was flirting with the attractive fifty-something nurse.

"Sorry, I have rounds, Mr. Rosenthal."

"It's Mel…call me, Mel, sweetheart."

Nurse Hollis batted her eyelashes. Holy moly! She was affected by my father. Maybe my father's heart attack had given way to a little love attack. I silently chuckled. There was nothing I wanted more than to see my father get well again. Then after that, see him fall in love again. There had never been another woman in his life after my mother. He was a wonderful man, a *mensch*, who would make someone a wonderful husband.

Catching her breath, Nurse Hollis told my father she would come by one more time this evening to check on his vitals.

My father, his strength ebbing, smiled. "Yeah, all my vitals. I'd like that, Hollis."

With that, I rose from my chair and planted a good-night kiss on his forehead. "Night, Pop. You behave," I chided. "I'll come by tomorrow."

On my next breath, I followed Nurse Hollis out the door.

"Are you sure he's going to be okay?" I asked as we walked down the corridor, side by side.

"Don't worry, honey, he's going to be fine." Her voice was warm and comforting. "And I'll make sure he behaves."

I liked her. In fact, I liked her a lot.

To my great surprise, Ryan was still seated in the

waiting room. Putting aside a magazine, he jumped up as I approached.

"Ryan, what are you still doing here?"

"I didn't want to leave you alone. How's your father doing?"

"He's doing well. And he's in good hands."

He quirked a smile. "That's good to hear. What about you? You look tired."

I let out a breath that released a lot of my stress. "A little bit. More hungry I'd say."

"C'mon. Let me take you out for dinner."

"No, Ryan, it's fine. I'll just head home."

"No, I insist. And I'm starving too. Anything you're in the mood for?"

Your lips on mine. My heartbeat sped up, my body heated.

"Anything but deli. And a glass of wine would be great."

He wrapped an arm around me, naturally as if he'd done it a thousand times before.

"C'mon. I know a great little neighborhood restaurant."

Fifteen minutes later, we were sitting face-to-face in a small, dimly lit Indian restaurant, dipping Naan, a pita-like bread, into a yummy chutney sauce and sharing an order of tandoori chicken. The food was delicious and I ate ravenously, hungrier than I thought. I washed down the spicy food with sips of chilled rosé as did Ryan. My eyes stayed on him as he ate and drank, in awe of how elegantly he did thanks to his upper class upbringing.

"You eat the European way," he commented as I slipped a forkful of the tender chicken into my mouth.

Chewing, then swallowing the tasty white meat, I nodded. "I lived in Europe for a few years. Holding my fork like this comes naturally to me."

He took another sip of his wine. "Where did you live?"

"Latvia."

"Latvia?"

"Yes, it's a small country in northern Europe. Not that many people know about it. Riga, the capital, is often called the Paris of the Baltic."

At the mention of Paris, my companion's jaw ticked. I suddenly realized my faux pas. Paris was where Allee had died.

"I-I'm sorry," I stuttered.

"Don't be," he replied, his tone genuine enough to assuage my guilt. Reaching across the table, he swept his forefinger along my bottom lip. "You've got a little chutney on your mouth."

I let out an embarrassed giggle, his touch making my skin prickle.

His beautiful blue eyes stayed fixed on me. "What were you doing in Latvia?"

My giddiness gave way to an inward shudder. Even

with the wine, I wasn't feeling loose enough to talk much about my past.

"I was a dancer. A ballerina. I danced with a ballet troupe."

"Wow! Why didn't you tell me this the other night?"

I shrugged. "I don't like to talk about it that much."

"Why aren't you there now?"

I took another sip of my wine and then set the glass down on the table. "I needed to take a break. It was intense."

"How so?"

Gustave. My body tensed at the thought of him. Not wanting to take things any further, I quickly changed the subject and thanked him again for taking me to the hospital and staying with me. "My dad is my everything," I added, my eyes growing watery. "Except for my grandma, he's all the family I have. I love him to pieces. Maybe more than he loves me, if that's possible."

A wistful smile crossed Ryan's lips. "You're so lucky you have such a great relationship with him. Why does he call you Pumpkin?"

I laughed. "I was born on Halloween with a big head of bright orange hair. My dad thought I looked like a pumpkin and the name stuck."

Ryan laughed back. "That's funny. And by the way, you don't look anything like a pumpkin."

"Thanks."

"So, you have a birthday coming up soon."

"Yeah." My trick or treat birthday was four weeks away.

"IIow old arc you going to be?"

"A ripe old twenty-five."

He reflected on my words. "That's so young."

A tense silence followed. Intuitively, I knew what was going through his mind. Allee was just a few weeks shy of her twenty-fifth birthday when she died. I recalled that grief-ridden passage in Ryan's memoir. No, it wasn't fair that she died so young. I felt his sorrow as we both drank more of our wine. My mother wasn't that much older when God claimed her. We lowered our glasses back onto the table at the same time.

"How are things with your father?" I ventured, trying to keep our conversation going though knowing from his book that things had always been strained.

"A little better, but not great."

My eyes stayed on his. "Are you learning to forgive him?" In her farewell letter, Allee had urged Ryan to make up with his estranged father.

He took a long sip of his wine. "I'm learning to forgive, but it's hard to forget. I can never erase the memories of how he ignored me as a child, cheated on my mother, disowned my gay sister, and most of all, used and abused Allee."

"I'm sorry," I said again as he inhaled a fortifying breath.

"But, I'm trying. I owe it to Allee. My father suffered a major stroke last year and he's softened a bit. In his own way, he's trying to be a better husband to my mother and a better father to me. I think the stroke put a lot of things in perspective for him. That he isn't immortal. That he doesn't have a long time to live his life right."

"I'm glad to hear that." I caught myself. "I mean, about the two of you reconciling."

Ryan picked at the chicken. "It's not been easy. I still harbor a lot of anger toward him. But Dr. Goodman has helped a lot. I'm trying to let go of the past. Make up with him."

Memories of my mother flooded me. "You're lucky, Ryan. I wish I had the chance to make up with my mother. To tell her I loved her before she left us." The tears that had been building up behind my eyes broke loose. I could feel a couple trickle down my cheeks.

Ryan tenderly brushed them away and then clasped my hands. "Yeah, Willow Rosenthal, I'm lucky. Lucky that I met you."

I quirked a little smile. "I feel the same way, Ryan."

He smiled back at me. "C'mon, let's get the check. And I'll take you home."

TWELVE

Ryan

Over the course of the next week, I was needed in more ways than one. Well, maybe I wasn't exactly needed, but I volunteered my services: to help Willow run her dad's deli while he was convalescing at the hospital. It was a convenient way to spend time with her, but admittedly not the easiest. Making sandwiches and waiting tables. I sucked at hard labor. Mayflower-descended Madewells weren't made for it.

But as challenging as it was, it was the most fun I had in ages. And the labor-intensive work was validating, a feeling that had eluded me for way too long. Most of all, I loved being with Willow and her father's loyal, good-natured employees—the counter guys, waitresses, cooks, cashiers, and hostesses, who all embraced me like a son. I admit I didn't know a new pickle from an old one, but for the first time in my life, I felt like I was part of a loving family. Like I belonged.

I learned from Willow that there was an art to making a sandwich. And Mel's offered as many varieties of sandwiches as there were books in the New York

Public Library. Okay, not that many but still enough to fill an encyclopedia. And they each had their own unique name, some named after sections of New York like The Soho Double Decker, an oversized sandwich made with alternating layers of pastrami, corn beef, and coleslaw, while others were named after famous New York celebrities, many of whom had dined at Mel's like former Mayor Bloomberg and the late Pearl Bailey. No surprise that no one from my illustrious family was among them…

…Until one night Willow and I were alone, closing up the restaurant. It was almost midnight.

"How's your dad doing?" I asked, wrapping a huge roasted turkey in saran wrap. She'd gone to visit him earlier in the day, something she'd done daily since his heart attack.

Covering the tray of slaw, she smiled. "He's doing great. Complaining about the hospital food. They're going to release him early next week."

"Is he going to have to be on bed rest?" What I was really asking: Do you still need me to work here with you?

"Actually, no. He can resume working, but he's going to have to take it easy. No lifting heavy things…a definite nap during the day…that kind of stuff." She straightened up the plastic utensils bin. "Most im-portantly, he's going to have to watch his diet and do some exercise."

"That shouldn't be too hard."

Willow laughed. "Are you kidding? The doctor said he has to cut out pastrami. That's like telling a little kid he can't have candy."

I laughed too.

"And my father's idea of exercise is going to the bank, which is around the corner."

"Maybe I can get him to take up running," I said, still laughing.

"Fat chance. No pun intended." She adjusted her long white apron, bringing attention to her nipped waist. "I told him how helpful you've been."

"You think so?"

"I know so."

"It's been fun." That was an understatement; I loved every minute I'd spent with Willow. I hadn't felt this close to a woman in years. Or so alive.

"My father's really grateful. He wants me to name a new sandwich after you."

"Get out."

"Seriously. Let's create it now."

"What should we call it?"

"Duh. The Ryan Madewell."

"Thanks for leaving out 'The Fourth'."

"We can add it if you like."

"No, please don't." I actually hated my pretentious name and the fact that I had to share it with my father and his father before him.

"Let's start with the bread. Rye, right?"

She knew me well. "Yeah, definitely rye bread." I

watched as she reached for a loaf of freshly baked bread and sliced off two even-sized pieces.

"Watch your fingers," I urged.

"Don't worry. The last thing I want is another trip to the hospital."

I couldn't agree more, I thought as she set the two slices on the counter.

"Next?"

"Mayo."

"All right, but don't go overboard with it." She handed me the plastic mayo bottle. Holding it, I squeezed a generous amount of mayo on both slices of the bread, my cock flexing as I watched the creamy white condiment pour out.

"Okay, that's enough," said Willow, stopping me. A little bit of the mayo dotted the tip of the cap. It reminded me of pre-cum and made my dick grow thicker, especially when Willow wiped it off with her forefinger and sucked it off. Fuck. She was making me horny as sin.

"So, what's going into this sandwich, Mr. Madewell?"

"Let's keep it healthy in honor of your father. So he can eat it."

"No pastrami?"

I shook my head. Nope, no pastrami as much as I loved it too. About a year ago, I'd gone to California to meet with potential movie producers and recalled a delicious sandwich I'd eaten at a chic restaurant. It was filled with hummus, hand carved turkey breast, provolone cheese, avocado, and arugula. I was almost sorry I'd spread the mayo, but I thought it would still work. While I knew the turkey breast and hummus were available, I asked Willow if the kitchen stocked the other ingredients. Happily, I learned it did, but they were used mostly by the short order cook for omelets. While I unwrapped the turkey, Willow went to the kitchen to retrieve the other ingredients. In no time, she returned, her hands full. About to carve the turkey, I helped her set the remaining ingredients on the counter.

Her face was lit up, her expression inquisitive. "Ry-man, what do you have in mind?"

Fuck. I loved when she called me Ry-man. No one had ever called me that before. While it was close to my real name, it was different enough.

I tugged at her fiery red hair, which tonight was fixed in a long, loose braid. "Can you cut the avocado into slices?" I had no clue how to handle the green testicle-shaped fruit. My sister and I grew up with cooks, and with Allee, I ordered in most of the time.

"Of course," she replied with a sexy smile.

As I sliced thick pieces of the turkey, she cut the avocado. We were side by side. Totally in sync. Was this what sex with her would be like?

My cock twitching, I sneaked a piece of the turkey and then went back to slicing it. In a few minutes, we finished creating our culinary masterpiece.

"Let's try it," insisted Willow.

"Okay. You take the first bite."

I watched as her lips clamped down on the thick sandwich, wondering what they would feel like around my cock. I could feel my cock flex as she swallowed.

"Mmm," she moaned, the sound of her sensuous hum, turning me on more. "It's so good." Is that what she would say about my cock?

"Okay, your turn," she said, interrupting my dirty thoughts as she fed me the sandwich. I took a big bite. "Fuck, this is amazing. Even better than the one I had in California."

A big smile lit up Willow's face. "It's going to become our new bestseller."

Alternating bites, we devoured the sandwich. On my last bite, I closed my eyes and wondered: what would it be like to eat her? Savor her sweet pussy? Taste her on my tongue? It took all my willpower not to strip her of all her clothes and haul her onto the counter. I longed to kiss her again, too, but feared I wouldn't be able to stop there. My conscience told me to take things slowly, but my body didn't believe a single word. With my cock at full attention, I helped her clean up and then forced myself to go back to my loft. My only compensation—a delicious fantasy to get off on.

By the end of the next day, The Ryan Madewell Special was by far the most popular item on the menu. We couldn't stop making them.

"Everyone wants a taste of Ryan Madewell," Willow said flirtatiously as she loaded yet another sandwich onto a plate.

I chuckled. I, on the other hand, wanted a taste of only one woman. The beautiful and beguiling Willow Rosenthal.

THIRTEEN

Willow

Pop came home late Monday afternoon. His faithful staff and I had agreed to close the deli early—Monday night's were typically slow anyway—and give him a small welcome back party complete with balloons and a banner. My father was thrilled to be home, and I was thrilled that he was well on his way to a complete recovery. He'd even lost a little weight while in the hospital and I planned to make sure that more pounds would come off.

"This is some sandwich," he commented as he chomped into the new Ryan Madewell sandwich.

Ryan smiled proudly. "And it's totally healthy."

"Just don't eat three of them," I jumped in, knowing damn well my father could easily do that.

"One and a half?" No holds barred, my father reached for another half of sandwich. "They starved me in that damn hospital!"

"NO! Put it back." Stopping him with my hand, I watched my father make the face of a reprimanded child as he reluctantly put the overstuffed sandwich back down on the platter.

He looked to Ryan for moral support, but Ryan shrugged sheepishly.

"Sorry, sir."

"She's a tough cookie, my daughter."

Ryan laughed his adorable laugh. "Yeah, but I've gotten her to crumble a couple of times."

Oh, had he! In fact, right now, he was melting me with his presence. But with my father back home, I wasn't sure where things were going.

FOURTEEN

Ryan

At the end of the week, Willow and I finally went on our movie date, with her father's urging and blessing. At six p.m., I picked her up at the deli. While she was nervous about leaving her dad alone for the first time since his return, Mel assured us both he would be okay and the staff promised they would watch him like hawks... making sure he didn't snitch any pastrami—not even a *schnitzel*—and that he went to sleep early. Mel was getting stronger and thinner each day.

It had been a really long time since I'd been on a movie date with a girl. Well, except for my four-year-old niece Violet, whom I'd taken to some animated movies, but that really didn't count. I couldn't help but think of my first movie date with Allee. I'd taken her to see *Camille,* which little did I know at that time foreshadowed her untimely death. The movie had reduced her to tears, and that night we made love for the first time in my loft. I was a little nervous, but whatever tonight's outcome, I didn't think Willow would sleep with me. I wasn't ready for that yet. And I still wondered—would I ever be?

"What are we seeing?" asked Willow as we headed west by foot to Ludlow Street. The early October air was crisp and we walked briskly, holding hands.

"It's a surprise." Knowing she was a ballerina, I'd fortuitously found a dance movie festival at the nearby Metrograph theater. The popular cinema was renowned for playing Hollywood classics. Among the movies playing were *Black Swan, The Turning Point, Flashdance, Shall We Dance,* and *An American in Paris*, definitely not a flick I could stomach. Plus the one that was playing tonight.

"*The Red Shoes*?" asked Willow, when we arrived at the theater, which was housed in a former brick warehouse. Her voice sounded tenuous.

"Yes, I thought you'd like it." The photos in her bedroom along with her toe shoes flashed into my head.

She drew in a sharp breath. "Cool…" Her voice trailed off as we entered the theater and I handed the ticket-taker the reserved-seat tickets I'd purchased online. As we walked through the lobby, I was a little anxious. I thought she'd be way more enthusiastic about my movie choice.

"Willow…we don't have to stay if you don't want to. We can just go out for dinner somewhere."

"No, it's fine."

"You sure?"

"Yeah, I'm sure. I loved this movie when I was a kid. I watched it with my mother on TV."

Oh, so that was the connection. Now, I understood her reservation.

"Have you ever seen it?" she asked.

"No." In fact, I knew little about the movie except that it was inspired by the Hans Christian Anderson fairy tale of the same name. I'd foolishly not taken the time to read the movie description online. For all I knew, it was a comedy.

"It's considered the best ballet movie ever made," she said.

"I'm looking forward to seeing it." Maybe it would give me more insight into Willow, who was still very closed-mouth about her past. "Do you want something to eat or drink?" The theater housed a top-notch gourmet restaurant as well as a bar in the lobby.

"How 'bout some wine and popcorn?"

"Perfect."

Five minutes later, we were in our seats toward the back, each with a glass of red wine, a Cab for Willow and a Pinot Noir for me. We were sharing a large bag of popcorn, which I set on the tray table between us.

A geeky-looking attendant took center stage in the small but elegant theater, welcoming us to the film festival before going into some history of the movie. It had originally been released in 1948, almost seventy years ago, and garnered two Academy Awards—one for Best Original Score and the other for Best Art Direction. Without further ado, the lights dimmed, the red velvet theater curtain rose, and the opening credits began to roll on the screen.

It didn't take long for me to discover that this wasn't a comedy. It was an intense drama about a young, rising ballerina named Vicky, caught in the age-old battle between her career and love. Dominating the story was a heated love triangle between her Russian ballet master, Lermontov, and her lover, Julian, the composer of the ballet she was starring in—*The Red Shoes*.

Throughout the movie, especially the dance scenes, Willow breathed heavily. She stopped eating popcorn and drinking her wine.

"Are you okay?" I whispered as the beautifully filmed *Red Shoes* ballet sequence culminated with Vicky, under the spell of the evil Shoemaker and unable to stop dancing, nearing death from exhaustion. As a priest removed the cursed red shoes and Vicky took her last breath, Willow gasped.

"I'll be right back," she murmured, leaping up from her seat before I could say another word. Jesus. What had gotten into her? It was only make-believe. A movie about a fairy-tale inspired ballet.

A few minutes later, Willow returned.

"Are you sure you're okay?"

"Yeah," she rasped.

Trying hard to believe her, I took her hand as the movie continued. It felt cold and clammy. A big part of me wanted to split, but Willow insisted we stay. Her eyes stayed glued on the big screen as the plot thickened with Vicky choosing her career over her lover after marrying him. Returning to the company to dance in a revival of *The Red Shoes*, she encounters Julian on opening night. Again torn between her love for him and her need to dance, she can't decide what to do. Poor Julian, realizing that he has lost his true love, departs for the railroad station. Just as she's about to take the stage, Vicky, wearing the red shoes, decides to pursue him and rushes out of the theater. At the train station, Julian spots her and runs toward her. But not fast enough. To his horror, Vicky jumps from the balcony and falls in front of an approaching train. Even I gasped at the dramatic turn of events.

While sniffles abounded around me, Willow began to sob. So loudly I could barely hear Lermontov deliver his final line before the performance: "Miss Page is unable to dance tonight—nor indeed any other night." Willow's sobs grew louder as the movie culminated with the dance company performing *The Red Shoes,* a spotlight on the empty space where Vicky would have been, and then cutting back to the train station where a battered Vicky, lying close to death on a stretcher, asks her beloved, distraught Julian to remove the red shoes, just as in the end of the ballet.

While the teary-eyed audience exited the movie theater, Willow stayed in her seat, paralyzed and sobbing. A sickening sense of déjà vu washed over me. It was almost as if I were reliving Allee's hysterical reaction to the tragic ending of *Camille.* An ending that paralleled her own tragic one. Fuck. What had I done? Why did I have to pick this movie? Was it some sign that I was destined to lose Willow? My stomach twisted as this dark thought lodged in my brain and morbid fear seeped through my veins.

After the credits rolled, the lights came up. We were the only two moviegoers left.

"C'mon, baby. We should go."

Her face soaked with her tears, her eyes red and swollen, Willow staggered to her feet. I gave her a helping hand and then wrapped an arm around her.

"I-I'm sorry," she stammered, swiping at her tears.

"It's okay. Do you want to talk about it?" I asked softly.

She shook her head as tears continued to fall. "Ryan, I don't feel well. I need to go home."

"Sure." I didn't feel well either. Fate was a bitch. And she was fucking with me. Willow Rosenthal was hiding something, and deep inside my heart, I knew it was going to be my undoing. A chill ripped through me. It frightened me.

FIFTEEN
Willow

Following the movie, I didn't see Ryan all weekend. Having given him my cell phone number, he texted me on Saturday, but I told him I was still feeling ill. I lied saying it was some kind of bug, but I knew better. The movie had aroused in me my great need to dance, something I'd managed to suppress since I'd come back home. It also rekindled my great fear of going back to the thing I loved most. The world of ballet. The all-consuming world that had made every molecule of my being feel alive but had almost destroyed me. My insides felt shredded, my crippling anxiety gnawing at me. My father, God bless him, let me stay in bed all weekend, and believed I actually had come down with something since I spent a good deal of time in the bathroom on account of my upset stomach. The homemade chicken soup he kept bringing me did nothing for my aching soul. Though he was getting stronger every day, he was the last person with whom I wanted to share my condition. There was only one person I wanted to talk to.

Dr. Goodman. On Monday, I had my standing appointment with him and dragged myself out of bed, trying to make myself look as presentable as possible. Even after a hot shower, my reflection in the bathroom mirror looked gaunt and haggard. Dark circles orbited my eyes and my complexion was pasty. Tossing and turning at night, I hadn't slept much and the sleep deprivation only added to my malaise.

"So, what's been going on?" asked my therapist as I fidgeted in a chair facing him. I'd decided to sit in a chair rather than lay down on the couch because I feared I might conk out.

"I think I had a set back." My voice was small and uncertain.

His brows rose slightly. "Tell me about it."

"I went to see a movie—*The Red Shoes*."

A smile flashed on his kind face. "Ah, that's one of my wife's favorite movies. Moira Shearer, right?"

I nodded.

"What made you see it?"

"Ryan took me. We went on a date."

Stroking his beard, he nodded approvingly. "That's good."

"No, it wasn't good." My voice grew stronger. "It made me really upset. I burst into tears. Uncontrollable tears. I was sick to my stomach all weekend."

He listened intently. "I see. And why do you think the movie had that effect on you?"

Of course, he knew why. He'd treated me for almost ten years. He just wanted to hear me articulate the reason.

"It made me feel sad."

"It's a sad movie," he commented. "But that's not really why it had that effect."

My stomach crunched. Dr. Goodman was so damn smart and somehow he was going to get me to face the truth.

"Did you tell Ryan why the movie affected you?

I shook my head again. "No, I simply told him I was sick. I made him take me home."

"Does Ryan know anything about your recent past?"

I shook my head again. "Not really."

"Why haven't you told him?"

"I hardly know him. I don't feel comfortable yet confiding in him."

Dr. Goodman refocused on the movie. "Willow, let's backtrack. Why do you *really* think the movie had that profound effect on you?"

I spewed the answer. "I identified with the heroine. Her burning need to dance. It made me miss ballet, but at the same time it made me feel very afraid."

"Afraid of what?"

"Afraid of falling." I meant that literally and figuratively. Of falling flat down on my face. And of letting myself fall for *him*.

"Willow, do you want to dance professionally again?"

"I don't know. There's an emptiness in my heart that's eating at me, but I don't know if I'm ready." My voice grew small again. "Dr. Goodman, am I?"

Dr. Goodman lifted his glasses to the top of his head and pinched the bridge of his nose. He did that out of habit whenever he didn't have a clear-cut answer. Generally, whenever that happened, he responded to my question with another question. Sure enough…

"What do you think?"

"I don't know. I'm scared." My final months with the Royal Latvia Ballet whipped around my mind like a wicked rollercoaster. The ups. The downs. My final free-fall from the stage after Gustave's betrayal. My wasted body. My wasted life. My head pounded. Trying to assuage the pain, I squeezed my eyes shut and pressed my temples with my forefingers.

"Willow, take a couple of deep breaths."

I did as the good doctor asked, inhaling and exhaling sharply through my nose. My mind calmed down as he continued.

"You know, Willow, there are other ballet companies."

He was trying to say I shouldn't go back to Gustave. But the truth was he was my master and always would be. After all the other company directors had rejected me, he was the one who'd cherry-picked me. The one who had driven me to new heights. The one who believed in me. Saw in me what no one else had. Okay, I'd fucked things up. I'd gotten involved with him. Let him fuck my brains out. But I was better now. Physically stronger. More in control of myself. And there was someone else…

As if Dr. Goodman had read my mind, he stroked his beard again and said, "Willow, let's talk a little more about your relationship with Ryan before our session ends."

This time, at the mention of his name, my heart skipped a beat and my body heated. I squirmed in my chair.

"What do you want to know?"

"How do you feel about him?"

I couldn't deny my feelings. "I like him a lot." Okay, I wasn't totally being honest. I more than liked him a lot. I was crazy about him. Insanely attracted to him both emotionally and physically. "I feel bad about Friday night. I haven't returned any of his phone calls."

"Why is that?"

"I just couldn't talk to him."

"Understandable." Dr. Goodman lowered his glasses back on his nose. "Do you want to see him again?"

My lips twisting, I squirmed again in my chair. "Yes. But I don't think he'll want to. I'm too fucked up. I'm not what he needs."

"Willow, why do you say those things? You're a beautiful, bright, young woman with the whole world at your fingertips."

Swallowing hard, I processed his words. I obviously still had major self-esteem issues, or at least, I'd regressed.

"I honestly don't think he'll ask me out again."

A wry smile flashed on Dr. Goodman's face. "I think he will."

My brows lifted. "How do you know that?"

His smile widening, he pointed a knowing finger at me. "Because, my dear, I'm going to make him. He's going to invite you to his place for dinner."

And with that and my hopeful heart in my throat, our session ended.

SIXTEEN

Ryan

I was eager to see Dr. Goodman. Willow had snubbed me all week, telling me she was sick. But I didn't believe a word. I'd even called his office to see if he could fit me in early, but he was totally booked. So, I had no choice but to wait for my regular Thursday morning appointment.

For the first time since Allee's death, I sat in one of the chairs facing him. I was wired up.

"Ryan, you seem unusually anxious," he began, sitting in a chair angled to me, his hands folded on his lap.

"I am."

"What's going on?"

I blew out a breath and then got straight to the point. "What the hell is up with Willow Rosenthal? What's her story?"

He met my gaze. "Ryan, you know I can't tell you. Doctor-patient privilege."

A combination of frustration and anger rose in my chest; I silently cursed under my breath. "What should I do?"

"Maybe you should consider couples therapy."

"We're *not* a couple." I was growing edgy. "Any advice?

"Do you want to continue the relationship?"

Jesus. Sometimes, despite all his wisdom, this mind guru could drive me crazy. Answering a question with question. My blood curdling, I hurled back the answer.

"Fuck, yes." This was the first time I'd ever said the F-word to his face.

Dr. G. twitched a smile. "Good. Then invite her to your place for dinner."

"Fine." And with this four-letter F-word, I bolstered myself up from the chair and marched out the door. Our session was over.

SEVENTEEN

Willow

D r. Goodman worked his magic. Sure enough at the end of the week on Friday, things took a giant step forward. Ryan invited me to his loft for dinner. He asked me what kind of food I wanted. I told him anything but deli. Not that I didn't like deli, but enough was enough.

Around six o'clock, I got a call from him. He told me he was stuck in traffic, but that I should head over to his loft early and make myself at home. He gave me the code to get in.

"Should I bring anything?"

"Just bring yourself."

"What should I wear?"

After asking that question, I regretted it, but Ryan told me to dress casually. I felt relieved. I wanted to feel comfortable. So leggings and an oversized sweater was what I had in mind. And my favorite lace-up boots.

Stopping by the local Korean market to buy some flowers, I headed over to Ryan's place down the street. I walked fast, my heart racing as I did. I was as nervous as I was excited. While I'd walked by his loft numerous times in the past, this was different. When I got to his loft on Hudson, I followed his instructions and punched in the code to get in. The huge elevator opened, giving me a jolt. I got into the massive carriage, which was big enough to hold a concert grand piano, pushed the up button, and the metal door slammed down. Slowly, creak by creak, the elevator ascended and the door re-opened letting me out in Ryan's loft. Every nerve was buzzing, much the way they did when a theater curtain rose and I was about to leap onto the stage for the first time and dance.

Hesitantly, stepping out of the elevator, I soaked in his place. It was exactly as he described it in his book, except it felt much bigger with its sparse leather furnishings, high ceilings, and floor-to-ceiling windows. On one wall, I eyed a large built-in bookcase filled with art books and literary classics, and in the corner, the winding stairs that lead to his bedroom. *Their* bedroom. The bedroom he shared with *her*. His beloved, stunning Allee. Everywhere I looked, I saw her…them…taken in the short happy time they spent together. They looked so much in love. I could actually feel her presence…as if she had eyes on me and was watching my every move. A ripple of insecurity ebbed through me. Could I ever measure up to Allee? Could Ryan ever love another as much as he loved her?

The sound of footsteps cut into my mental ramblings. They were coming from the kitchen, which was set off by a partition. Was Ryan home? I heard what sounded like a refrigerator door open and close.

"Ryan, are you there?" I called out.

No response.

"Ryan?"

Grabbing a vase, I padded toward the kitchen to fill it with water and the flowers I'd bought. With the anticipation of seeing Ryan, my heartbeat quickened, and then I stopped dead in my tracks when a tall, blond woman appeared. Chicly dressed in a sleeveless black sheath, she was holding a glass of champagne in one hand and a monstrous red leather designer bag in the other. She stared at me with her icy blue eyes.

"Who the hell are you?"

"I'm a friend of Ryan's," I stammered.

Madness flickered in her eyes. "His latest slut?"

Her words cut into me. Who was this woman? Did Ryan have a secret girlfriend? Her venomous gaze stayed on me.

"Get the fuck out of here. Ryan belongs to me." Without warning, she hurled her glass of champagne at me. Splintering on the concrete floor, it narrowly missed me.

"Who are you?" I dared to ask as she dug her manicured hand into her handbag. For the first time, I noticed the initials monogrammed on the front of it. *C. V.* A light bulb went off in my head. Of course, it must be Charlotte Vanowen, Ryan's former deranged girlfriend.

"You're Char—"

Unable to get out the second syllable of her name, my jaw dropped to my stomach as my thudding heart leapt into my throat.

Oh, my God. She was pointing a gun at me!

"Please don't hurt me," I pleaded. "I-I'll leave."

"Shut up, cunt!" Grabbing a photo of Allee off a console table, she hurled it at me. It crashed on the floor at my feet. Wildly, she threw another and another.

"Please stop!" Shards of glass were scattered everywhere on the floor.

"One more word and you're going to be as dead as that whore."

"Please…" My legs like Jell-O, I began to take tiny steps backward toward the elevator, still clutching the vase and the flowers as her face darkened with fury.

"What part of shut up don't you understand?"

Then as she clicked the trigger, the elevator door slid open behind me.

EIGHTEEN

Ryan

Jesus fucking Christ. What kind of nightmare had I just stepped into?

Fucking Charlotte was here and she was pointing a gun at Willow. My mind raced a thousand miles a minute and so did my heart; one wrong word, one wrong move could set her off. She was fucking insane. *Stay calm*, I willed myself as the elevator door closed behind me. *Stay calm.*

I carefully lowered the plastic bag I was holding, filled with cartons of Chinese takeout, to the floor and straightened up, my eyes never straying from the psycho bitch. "Charlotte, what are you doing here? I thought you were in Europe with Max." Maxwell Wentright III was her mega-wealthy banker husband whom she'd married after she ditched me.

"Things didn't work out with the dick. But I'm getting a very nice divorce settlement that will easily support your writing career."

"That's good," I murmured, studying her. While she was still striking by most standards with her chiseled features, her beauty had diminished. Her shoulder-length blond hair was dull and disheveled, her body bloated, and her complexion blotchy. From the glazed look in her eyes, she must either be drunk or on something. Or maybe a combination of both. The smell of champagne drifted up my nose and my eyes shifted to the shattered flute on the floor, the crystal shards scattered in a puddle of the golden liquid.

She caught me staring at the mess. "So nice, you remembered my favorite champagne. Dom Perignon. What a lovely welcoming present. I saved you a glass."

Fuck. She'd consumed almost the entire bottle. She was definitely drunk.

"How did you get in here?"

With a smirk, she flung her head back. "A piece of cake. Your cleaning lady let me up. She was delighted to see me."

Damn the new cleaning service.

"What do you want, Charlotte?" My voice grew harsher, more demanding.

She let out a haughty, shrill laugh. "Oh, puh-lease, darling, must you ask? I want you."

My jaw tightened; my body tensed. What should I say? Do? I took a step forward so that I was standing beside trembling Willow. I so longed to take her in my arms and comfort her. Make this bad dream go away.

"Don't make another move," Charlotte barked out, the gun still aimed at Willow.

I remained frozen, weighing my options.

"You've always been the one for me, Ryan. Such a shame you fell for that lowlife whore."

Fury rose in my chest at her words. It took all I had not to lash back at her.

"And such a pity about her death." She tutted. "I'm sorry I didn't send you a condolence card. But maybe a congratulations card would have been more in order." She laughed again wickedly.

My blood was bubbling, my cheeks heating. My fists clenched so tightly I could feel my nails digging into my palms.

Her intoxicated eyes narrowed, zooming in on Willow. "I must say, with the exception of me, you have the worst taste in women. This little redheaded shrew is so beneath you. I think it's time you say goodbye to her."

I tried to make sense of her words. What did she mean by goodbye? *With love, there are no goodbyes*. I wasn't ready to say goodbye to Willow. Not now; maybe never. My mind went into overdrive. I *had* to placate her.

"Yes, Charlotte, you're right. Why don't you put the gun down and let her leave. Then, it'll just be you and me. The way it's supposed to be."

Instead of lowering the gun, her other hand joined the trigger-happy one. The expression on her face grew more furious, more determined, more irrational. Madness flickered in her eyes.

"This time I'm eliminating the competition right up

front. Taking no chances."

She steadied the gun in her hand. Fuck! She was out of her mind. Out of control. Without overthinking it, I darted in front of Willow. I held Charlotte fiercely in my gaze.

"If you kill her, you're going to have to kill me first."

Charlotte's face hardened. "Get out of my way, you idiot."

"Shoot me!" I yelled back.

"Oh God, no, Ryan!" I heard Willow whimper.

"DO IT!"

The gun shook in the psycho bitch's hand as her nostrils flared. My heart was beating like a jackrabbit's, not knowing how this was all going to play out. Her lips pinched, her breathing grew labored. The gun stayed pointed.

Think, Madewell, think! Stealing a glance at Willow, an impulsive idea flashed into my head. Facing life or death, I had to take a chance. I had no choice.

"Catch!" I shouted at Charlotte.

"Huh?" she mumbled as I grabbed the vase Willow was holding.

With my best little league pitch and all my force, I flung it at the insane bitch. I held my breath as it— *SMACK!*—hit her hard in the head. YES! Dropping the gun, she crumpled to the floor, unconscious. On my next breath, I whirled around and lifted the now sobbing Willow into my arms.

"It's okay, baby." I smoothed her hair and kissed her scalp as she clung to me, her arms and legs wrapped around me. Like I was her lifesaver. I was.

"Ry-man, you would have taken a bullet for me?"

"Baby, I would take a knife to my heart if I had to."

And at this very moment, something changed. I felt something toward Willow that I hadn't felt in many years. The word was in my heart and on the tip of my tongue, but I wasn't able to say it. At least not out loud. No, I wasn't falling in love. I already had and didn't want to lose her.

Ironically, fucking, blackmailing, sicko Charlotte, who had almost destroyed my relationship with Allee, had cemented my relationship with Willow.

I couldn't save Allee. But I saved Willow. I was her Superman.

As I held her in my arms and smothered her with kisses, I looked up once, and I swear I saw Allee heading toward the elevator.

She gave me a thumbs-up. "Nice job, Madewell. Fuck the bitch."

I smiled. She was never one to mince her words.

"Oh, and don't forget to eat dinner. Chinese is the best... make sure to open your fortune cookies."

And with that, she disappeared.

NINETEEN

Ryan

Thank God for my sister, the brainiac in the family. The rational one, who could solve any problem. After knocking out Charlotte, I bound her hands and feet with some old silk ties, then immediately called Mimi and told her what had happened. My sister despised stuck up Charlotte almost as much I did. "Should I call 9-1-1?" I asked her, not really wanting to do that. Mimi advised against it, feeling as I did that police involvement and an arrest would likely end up all over the news and the Internet—the last thing either of our prominent families would want. Charlotte was mentally ill and needed help, so Mimi arranged for her to be discreetly committed to an asylum in Westchester where she could be treated. When Charlotte came to, I read her the riot act, giving her two options: either she agreed to go to the asylum or I would call the police and press charges, not only for breaking and entering, but also for attempted murder. I took photos with my phone of the mess she'd created in her rampage and collected her gun. Charlotte had a melt down, screaming and cursing, throwing obscenities at both Willow and me, but she had no choice. Forty-five tense minutes later, four burly medics arrived from the asylum and forced her into a strait jacket while she kicked and screamed, then strapped her onto a gurney before carting her away.

Afterward, Willow helped me clean up the mess in the living room.

"I'm sorry she destroyed so many of your photos of Al—"

I cut her off before she could say her name. "Don't be. Just the picture frames are fucked up; they can be replaced. The photos are fine."

Picking up one of them from the floor, she studied it. "Allee was beautiful."

I forced a smile. "Yeah, she *was.*" I reflected on my response. My emphasis on the word "was." The past tense. Now, I had to focus on the present. Willow.

"C'mon, let's eat," I said. "I'll heat up the food."

Fifteen minutes later, we were sitting side by side on the floor around my coffee table. Cartons of Chinese food were strewn on the glass surface along with a bottle of sake. Some jazz was playing in the background.

"What if Charlotte escapes?" asked Willow as we fed each other lo mein straight from the carton with our chopsticks.

"She won't," I said after slurping some of the tasty noodles. "The facility is like a prison with barricades and twenty-four hour surveillance."

"Are you going to tell her family?"

"My sister is going to handle that along with all the paperwork."

"Mimi?"

"How do you know her name?"

Willow shot me playful smile. "Duh. Remember…I read your book."

I smiled sheepishly back at her. "Right."

"She sounds like an amazing woman."

"She is." I told her more about my sister, her spouse, and their four-year-old daughter, Violet. "They're going to be here at the end of next week. Violet is going to stay with me while Mimi and Beth go to Antigua for a long weekend to celebrate their tenth wedding anniversary."

"I'd love to meet them."

"I want you to." My relationship with Willow was moving forward at breakneck speed. That I was ready to introduce her to Mimi was an excellent sign. And perhaps soon, I would introduce her to my parents though I internally shuddered at the thought.

"Hey, let's open our fortune cookies," I said, eager to see what our future might hold.

"Okay," Willow replied brightly as I reached inside the take-out bag for the two plastic-wrapped cookies.

"Pick one," I told Willow, holding them out in my palms.

"I'll take this one," she said, reaching for the cookie

in my right hand.

"You open yours first."

My eyes stayed on her as she unwrapped it and split the cookie in half. She plucked out the fortune and read it.

"What does it say?"

"It says: 'You will be blessed with many children.'"

Her fortune made my stomach clench, and I couldn't help but think of the three embryos I'd created with Allee's eggs. My voice unsteady, I asked, "Butterfly, do you want to have kids?"

Her face lit up. "Yes. In fact, lots. I hated being an only child. I even want to adopt a few. What about you? You want kids?"

My voice grew more edgy. "Yeah, I think so." On the verge of telling her about the embryos, I stopped when she insisted I open my fortune cookie.

Putting the cookie to my mouth, I bit off the plastic and then tore the cookie apart. I read my fortune.

"What does it say?" she asked eagerly.

"'You will be going on a life-changing journey.'"

"That's interesting. I wonder what that means."

I had no clue. We exchanged fortunes as my eyes roamed the loft.

There was no doubt in my mind that Allee had something to do with them.

TWENTY

Ryan

Well, my fortune turned out to be true sooner than I expected. The next day was Willow's grandmother's eightieth birthday, and she asked me if I wanted to go up to the Catskills with her to celebrate the occasion. After our harrowing experience with Charlotte last night, getting out of the city and going on a relaxing ride felt like a good idea. So, I agreed.

It had been a long time since I'd been in the country. While my mother persistently invited me up to our family estate in Connecticut, I consistently declined. It held no fond memories for me. Just more of the same of what it was like to grow up with my parents. They were both never there. My mother played tennis and lunched with her socialite friends at the exclusive country club, showering herself with so much champagne that our driver had to take her home and carry her into her room where she passed out. And my father, well, he was pretty much absent too—playing golf with his cronies and screwing all the club waitresses. Mimi and I hung around, bored out of our minds. And totally neglected.

The year they sent the two of us off to a posh summer camp in the Berkshires was one of the best ones of our lives. A relief. An escape.

The drive up was beautiful. The mid-October air was unseasonably warm, likely in the low-seventies; there wasn't a cloud in the sky, and the trees, with their topaz, citrine, and ruby leaves, shimmered in the sun like magnificent jewels. I kept the top of my Fiat down and played lots Frank Sinatra and Ella Fitzgerald. Thanks to her grandmother, who grew up in the era of these greats, some of whom had even stayed at Gettinger's, the fabled grand hotel that she and her late husband owned, Willow knew all these classic songs. She sang along, her pitch perfect voice something else I found so attractive about her. She kept her hand on mine, which was on the gearshift, while I fantasized about it between my legs on another big stick. And grew hard.

I learned a lot about Willow's family during the ride, especially when we stopped at a roadside diner for coffee. This was her maternal grandmother she was visiting; her other grandparents had passed away. Her name was Ida. Combining their savings and a few loans from friends and family, she and her late husband, Harold, built Gettinger's Hotel from the ground up just after the second World War, and in no time, it became the place to go among wealthy New York Jews. The five-star resort was known for its elegant décor, luxury accommodations, fine Kosher cuisine, and its nightly entertainment, attracting every major star from Dean Martin to Jerry Lewis. Ida and Harold were legendary, beloved for their hospitality, generosity, and joie de vivre. They were also accomplished ballroom dancers, and while spending summers with them, Willow had developed her passion for dance. Sadly, ten years her senior, Harold passed away in his sleep when Ida was sixty, and soon after, she sold the hotel for a small fortune to a Club Med-like organization that turned the family-hotel into a swinging singles' mecca. The once thriving hotel went downhill quickly and in 2001, it burned down, likely an insurance-motivated fire set by the bankrupt singles' organization. It made Ida sad, but in a way she was glad it was over. She still resided in a guesthouse on the grounds.

Shortly after lunch, we reached our destination. We drove through a long tree-lined entrance, the ground thick with colorful fallen leaves. In no time, a sprawling gray-shingled residence with white wraparound terraces came into view. It finally dawned on me that Willow, like me, came from wealth.

"Bubula, you're here!" A chic, petite woman with cropped silver hair and big owl-like black eyeglasses breezed out the front door as I parked the car in the circular driveway. I could already tell she had amazing energy and warmth and was in every way much younger than her years.

Willow jumped out of the car to give the woman a big hug. "Happy birthday, Nana!"

They broke their embrace, and Ida's attention shifted to me. Her crinkly hazel eyes lit up, and she began to fan herself.

"Bubula, you brought me a hot young man for my birthday?"

I felt myself blush. Willow laughed. "Next time, Nana. This is my friend, Ryan."

She studied me. "Wait, I know you! I saw you on *Good Morning America* a couple of weeks ago."

Cringing with embarrassment, I let Willow's grandmother continue.

She jutted a finger at me. "You're Ryan Madewell, the writer! I loved your book."

Willow's eyes grew as round as saucers. It was her turn to be mortified. Or at least shocked. "Nana, you read *Undying Love*?"

Her grandmother dismissively waved her veined bony hand. I noticed the beautiful art deco diamond ring she still wore on her ring finger. It reminded me of the ring I'd given Allee.

"Of course! Such a beautiful love story!!"

"Thanks," I said humbly.

Without further ado, she invited us inside. But not before long, Willow and I were back outside on a tour of the beautiful property while her grandmother fixed lunch.

Inhaling the clean country air, I took in my surroundings as Willow led me through the estate. It was almost out of a fairy-tale with acres and acres of land that bordered on a small lake. Willow told me that in the spring a symphony of bugs buzzing, water gurgling, birds chirping, and frogs croaking filled the air. Today, however, as we traversed the bucolic grounds, the crunch of gem-colored leaves sounded beneath our footsteps. The snap, crackle, and pop was invigorating.

"Where are we going?" I asked my beautiful guide, holding her hand. We were both wearing lightweight sweaters over jeans and boots.

"You'll see soon."

Close to the lake, a huge tree came into view. A majestic weeping willow all by itself that seemed to rule the grass like a queen. As we neared it, Willow broke into a jog, tugging at my hand.

Following her lead, I felt so connected to her. Almost inseparable. What was most amazing was that I didn't feel Allee's presence anywhere. Not hidden in the trunk of a tree, a blade of grass, or a leaf. It was just Willow and me.

When we got to the noble tree, Willow hugged it.

"This is where my father proposed to my mom," she said, brushing her cheek against the bark. "My parents named me after this tree."

"Wow!" I responded, at a loss for words.

"Look. Here's their inscription." She pointed to a carving in the middle of the thick tree trunk. It was a heart with a Cupid's arrow etched through it. At either end was a name: Bel on the bottom and Mel on the top. *Bel & Mel.*

"That's your mom's name on the bottom?"

"Yes, it's short for Belinda. That's what my dad called her."

"How did they meet?"

"Here. At the hotel. He worked as a busboy in the dining room during summers while he saved up to open his own restaurant."

"Why isn't he here today?" I asked.

Willow inhaled a deep breath. "It's complicated. My grandmother wants nothing to do with my father. She feels he destroyed my mother's life."

"What do you mean?"

"My mom was only nineteen at the time. To my grandma's horror, she dropped out of Vassar and eloped with him. Shortly after moving to the city, she got pregnant and I was born."

In my head, I did some math. So, if her mother died ten years ago when Willow was fifteen, that meant her mother was only thirty-five at the time. About the same age I was. That seemed so young, yet oddly, I sometimes felt so old. I listened intently as Willow continued.

"My father's not the kind of man she fathomed for my mother. She envisioned a rich lawyer or doctor. Not some poor busboy from the Lower Eastside."

"But your father turned out to be successful."

"Not successful enough for her. And then when she was fatally hit by a taxi, she blamed my father."

"I'm sorry," I said, not knowing what else to say.

"Don't be. It is what it is. I've managed to navigate the line of love and hate."

I had too. We had something in common.

Silently, Willow traced the heart with a fingertip. I followed suit, the deep outline of the heart almost scraping my forefinger. It must have been made with a Swiss Army knife, like the one Marcus had once given me as a birthday present as a kid. I still always carried it in my pocket.

I studied the massive tree, taking in the depth and breath of it. From a huge jutting branch hung a swing. The old-fashioned homemade kind composed of two strands of thick rope and a plank of wood. Willow caught my eyes on it.

"Yeah. It's been here forever. It dates back to the forties. My grandpa installed it. I spent a lot of my childhood on it. Want to go for a ride?"

A few moments later, we were on the swing. Our entwined fingers gripping the ropes. Willow straddled on my lap facing me. Anchored on my cock. Pumping rhythmically with her long, supple legs. As forcefully as mine. Her face, her breath, her smile in mine. Her flaming red hair blowing in the warm wind with each pump. And with each pump, my cock growing harder. Her body arching back. Her eyes looking up to the sky. My head tilting to follow her gaze. The tree's leafy green boughs shrouding us like curtains. My cock thickening with each pump. Each pump more powerful. To make us go higher. Higher and higher. Shooting into the sky.

I was getting a high in more ways than one. So turned on, I wanted to stop the swing, zip down my fly, and make love to her. Hold her in my arms. Let her ride me. Give the birds and bees a show.

"Look at me," I shouted out to her on the next exhilarating pump. As my long legs straightened taking us sky-high, her radiant face met mine, her green eyes holding me fiercely, an inviting, wicked smile on her face. She was beautiful. A temptation. As the wind captured her hair, I leaned in to her and captured her lips. It wasn't premeditated; just pure savage need. Something I couldn't help.

Without slowing down the momentum of the swing, our lips stayed locked. I nibbled and gnawed on them, then consumed her mouth. My tongue darted inside and tangled with hers. Just like the dancer she was, her tongue whirled gracefully and purposefully with mine. Blood rushed to my cock. She tasted delicious. So sweet. So good. As I deepened the kiss, her moans mingled with the sounds of nature. The chirps. The breeze. The rustling leaves. Without losing contact with her mouth, I stopped pumping my legs and the swing slowed down. As it came to a near halt, I touched down my feet to the ground and jumped off with Willow's legs wrapped around my hips and her hands cupping my face, still devouring my mouth. We couldn't get enough of each other.

Briefly, she broke away, her breathing frantic. "Fuck me, Ryan. Please fuck me."

Jesus. As much as I wanted her, she wanted me more. She was begging me. My desperate cock was throbbing. It was time to give her what she wanted. What I wanted. She lowered her feet to the ground and returned her mouth to mine as we began to feverishly disrobe each other. It was broad daylight madness, each of us fumbling to get the other undressed, a clash of wild hands and hungry kisses wherever possible. In no time, we were bared to each other, my arms wrapped around her taut dancer's body, my cock hard against her flat belly. Together, we fell to our knees, the soft, warm grass our bed. Willow's tender breasts brushed against my chest, calling out for my touch. As she tugged at my hair, my hands cupped them. Not too big, not too small, they filled my palms perfectly. As I massaged them, I could feel her pert nipples harden into little pebbles. More moans escaped her throat, these much louder.

"Baby," I whispered against her swan-like neck. "Are you on birth control?"

"Yes," she managed, planting kisses all over me.

"I don't have a condom…" My voice trailed off.

"It's okay."

"I'm clean. I haven't been with anyone since—"

She cut me off before I could say Allee's name. "I believe you. Please fuck me, Ryan. I want you so badly."

I felt the same way. I wanted this fiery redhead beauty, who could whip a man up a sandwich and probably dance circles around him, in the worst way. On my next heated breath, I clasped her shoulders and lowered her to the grass. She circled her legs around me as I stretched out, anchoring myself with my hands on either side of her. My face hovered over hers...hers so impassioned.

"Ryan, please let me put you inside me. I want to feel you every way I can."

Without a word, I let her curl her slender fingers around my cock. It felt so fucking good. Squeezing the base, she inserted my hot, rigid length into her entrance, inch by thick inch.

"Jesus," I moaned out as I pushed inside of her. "You're so fucking hot and wet, my little butterfly."

"Oh, Ryan, you feel amazing!" she breathed out, clenching her muscles around me, intensifying the pleasure if that was possible.

I slid halfway back down and then began to pummel her. There was no foreplay. No tender lovemaking. Just hard fucking. My cock had been bereft for too long, and this was the way I was making up for lost time. My breathing grew ragged as she clawed at my back, her hips bucking to meet each fast, furious thrust. Whimpers spilled out of her mouth as my eyes stayed trained on her enraptured face. She looked and sounded like she was about to come, and I quickly put one hand to her soaking wet pussy, rubbing her clit to coax her to climax. Her whimpers morphed into sobs. She was close to coming, and as I felt my balls contract and thigh muscles pulse, I knew I was too. I was determined to take us over the edge together. With a grunt and one final powerful deep thrust, I felt her shudder all around me and heard her cry out to God as I met her orgasm head on with my own explosive one. As she continued to judder around me, the blast of my release bathed her until there was no more to give. My heart beating fast, my body heated, I collapsed on top of her, burying my head in the crook of her neck. Her sobbing subsiding, she silently stroked my hair. Right here, right now, there was no one else in this world but Willow Rosenthal. Beautiful just fucked Willow.

We stayed in this position until our breathing and heartbeats calmed down. Then, I repositioned us so she was snuggled in my arm, her head resting on my chest as the sun beat down on us. We didn't talk about what we had done—or about how amazing it was—but rather of sweet nothings. As we studied the billowy clouds, reflecting on what their shapes reminded us of, I picked a dandelion, left over from the summer, and blew on it. The furry little spurs scattered upon us.

Willow giggled. "Do you know when you blow on one a wish comes true?"

"Really? I didn't know that. I didn't make one."

A look of disappointment washed over her face. She frowned. "Then, I'll pick one and make a wish for the both of us."

I watched as she reached for another one of the fuzzy flowers and then pursed her lips, blowing on it. Again, the spurs fell all over us.

"What did you wish for?" I asked.

Laughing, she flicked the tip of my nose with the stem. "I can't tell you. If I do, it won't come true."

"Well, I hope it was a good one."

She looked up as the last of the spurs floated in the air. "Yeah, it was." A dreamy smile spread across her face as she caught one. "Hey, we better head back. My grandma is probably wondering what happened to us." She sat up.

As much as I could have stayed here in this euphoric state forever, I helped her to her feet and we both put our clothes back on. It was time to say farewell to the weeping willow, but there was something I wanted to do before we left. Reaching into my jeans pocket, I pulled out my trusty Swiss Army knife. I switched it open as Willow watched.

"What are you doing?" she asked as I put the sharp blade to the thick trunk of the stately tree and began to carve into it.

A few short minutes later, there was another heart gracing the tree just above the one carved by her father. Except this one was bigger and on either side of the arrow were two initials. *RM* on the bottom and *WR* on the top.

Willow flung her arms around me. I passionately

kissed her once again.

It was official.

I, Ryan Madewell IV, long time suffering, fucked-up widower, celibate for four years, had a girlfriend.

I was officially in love with a girl named Willow.

Bending down to pick another dandelion, this time I made a wish before blowing on it, hoping this love would last forever. Like the heart on this tree that eternally connected us. Love had no goodbyes.

TWENTY-ONE

Willow

"**M**ake a wish, Nana," I said after singing "Happy Birthday" to her with Ryan. A gourmet cook, she'd prepared a wonderful pasta primavera lunch, made with fresh vegetables she grew in her yard. Now, her homemade buttercream cake occupied the center of the dining room table along with an open bottle of champagne.

Hovering over the cake, she took in the many candles. "I only wish your grandfather Harold was here standing next to me and could see how beautiful you are."

Every year, the same wish. My grandma had never loved another man after my grandpa passed away. He was her everything, childhood sweethearts who grew up together in Brooklyn. Gettinger's Hotel was their life dream and they'd built the resort together, starting off with small bungalows and expanding it to the once grand hotel it'd become.

Every molecule of my being was tingling as Nana inhaled a deep, fortifying breath. The aftershocks of my out of this world orgasm rolled through me, my inner thigh area still vibrating madly. Standing next to each other, Ryan and I clapped our hands as my strong, fiercely independent grandma blew out all the candles with one breath.

Removing the candles, I immediately sliced, plated, and doled out three huge portions of the mouthwatering cake, giving the first one to my grandma. Nana loved cake and never said no to a slice. She was a hearty eater, who somehow had managed to maintain her svelte figure though she'd shrunken a few inches in height over the years. She was built like me and my mother, whose genes I'd inherited.

"Wow! This is delicious!" said Ryan, shoving another hefty helping of the homemade cake into his mouth.

"My darling, only the best," laughed Nana, shaving off the thick creamy frosting with her fork. "My cholesterol will likely shoot through the roof and my doctor will give me hell. Whatever!" She waved a hand dismissively. "You know what, bubula? You only live once. You might as well live your life to the fullest."

Ryan twitched a small smile. "Yeah, isn't that the truth?" He said it as if he meant it, and in an instant, I realized that my grandma's words had made him think of Allee's short, unfair life. Despite our amazing day, a shudder pulsed through me. There would always be Ryan's great love. The incredible woman he immortalized in his book. More than anything right now, I wanted to talk to my grandma… get her take on things. I could always count on her honesty. She had no filters and always told it like it is. Just like my mom.

Just at that moment, Ryan's cell phone rang. Pulling it out of his jeans pocket, he glanced down at the caller ID screen.

"It's my agent," Ryan said as the phone rang again. "Do you mind if I take this? It'll give the two of you some time to spend together alone."

"No, prob," I replied. "Why don't you take the call in the living room. I'll meet you there in a bit."

Once Ryan was gone, I took another bite of the scrumptious cake and washed it down with the bubbly champagne. Nana did the same. I also gave her the present I'd brought along—a small antique music box I'd found at a local antiques store. She collected them, the songs often reminding her of her ballroom dancing days with my late grandpa. To my delight, she loved it and gave me a thankful hug.

"You look good, bubula" she said, sitting back down.

"Thanks, Nana." Truthfully, I was beginning to feel a little uneasy. I'd fucked Ryan's brains out, but was now having second thoughts. Thoughts of regret. Before I could overthink things, my inquisitive grandma asked me another question. An unsettling one.

"So, tell me, when are you going back to dancing?"

My body tensed. Even my grandma, whom I confided in, had no clue about the extent of my breakdown.

She, like my father, believed it was exhaustion-related. My relationship with Gustave It was the only thing I ever hid from her.

"I don't know, Nana." At least, I was being honest with her. To be more honest, my desire to perform again had been tugging at my heartstrings ever since I'd seen *The Red Shoes* with Ryan. Gustave's didactic words, "Once a ballerina, always a ballerina," danced through my mind like a series of bourées.

To my relief, my grandma changed the subject. "So, how's your father?"

Still harboring anger toward my father, who she never could accept, her inquiry caught me off guard. I took a sip of my bubbly before responding.

"Actually, Nana, he's better."

"What do you mean?"

"Nana, he had a heart attack. A minor one, but nonetheless, it was a wakeup call."

Contemplating her next words, she set down her flute. "I'm sorry to hear that."

Her voice was devoid of emotion, but it could have been dripping with sarcasm, or worse, her response could have been plain out mean and heartless. Something like: "He deserves it." Even though she was estranged from my father, she knew how much my father meant to me. How much I loved him. Hence, she tempered herself.

"You know, Nana, it would be nice if you saw him. It's been a long time. Maybe you could come to the city or invite him up here. I think he'd like that."

"I'll think about it." She took several long sips of her champagne and then changed the subject again. "So, bubula, let's talk about something else. Forget that I'm your grandma and tell me everything."

As she flicked flakes of dried up leaves from my hair, I almost choked on my next sip of champagne. "What do you mean?"

Of course, I knew what she meant. My sex-charged grandma wanted to know *everything* about Ryan.

Over another glass of champagne, I told my beloved Nana about how I'd met Ryan and what had transpired, including the details of our afternoon. She hung on every word, convinced that Ryan Madewell IV was in love with me.

"Nana, I'm scared."

"Why, darling?"

"I don't think I can ever be *her.*"

Nana shot me a reassuring smile. "No, my bubula, you can never be her. You can only be you. And you are special."

God, how I loved my grandma.

"But what if he freaks out? Lets me go? Breaks my heart?"

There was no doubt in my mind that he was still fucked up. Still in love with another. A woman who was timeless. Written on his soul with words that had touched a million hearts.

My grandma took another bite of her cake and then

lovingly brushed her fingertips along my jaw.

"My dear, there are no what-ifs when it comes to love. Only what is."

I digested the wise woman's words.

"But, Nana, you never found another man like Grandpa." Nor did my father find another woman like my mother, I added silently.

"Darling, it hasn't happened yet. But it will. I'm eighty years young."

I couldn't help but laugh before my insecurity manifested itself again. I knew that love could be all consuming. It could put you in a blender, twist and turn you …shred you to pieces.

Then, Ryan returned with all his virile glory, love written on his face. My fears evaporated. Hope filled me. I'd love him from page one. Maybe we could get to the end together.

TWENTY-TWO

Ryan

The next week went by quickly. After fucking Willow at her grandmother's house, I couldn't get enough of her. It wasn't easy. In fact, it was next to impossible. One time we snuck into the women's room of her father's deli and while a customer banged on the locked door, I did some other form of banging against the door. The woman, who was with a young child, gave us a dirty look as we giddily clambered out of the small, cramped room. We tried to have a tryst at a local hotel—in fact, any hotel, but every room in the city was sold out because it was Fashion Week. We both skirted the issue of sleeping together—that is, in her bed or mine. On Thursday, I discussed my progress with Dr. Goodman, who was pleased but concerned that Willow staying over at my place was still off limits. Once again he urged us to seek couples therapy and told me that sooner or later I would have to get over my inability to share my bed with another woman, let alone let one stay over. He was convinced this hang up was connected to my writer's block. Since Allee's death, I hadn't written anything new. Not a single word.

Dr. Goodman's words gnawed at me all day. I just wasn't sure if I could make it to the next step. Though I loved Willow, sharing my bed with her was something I wasn't sure I was ready for. Fortunately, she wasn't pushing me and seemed content with the arrangement we had. Which was a lot of stolen kisses and a few more encounters in the restroom of her father's deli. Maybe I should look into renting a fuck pad, some small furnished apartment with a bed that had no meaning to me. No emotional attachment. Dammit. I wished I could have drinks with my love guru Duffy, but he'd left for California. His wedding, which I was attending, was next weekend. Man, it was hard to believe it was just around the corner. Time had gone by so quickly, perhaps because I now had Willow in my life.

On Friday, I had little time to dwell on my predicament. My four-year-old niece was coming in the late morning to stay for the weekend. I hadn't done shit to get things together and I had to admit I was freaking out. This was the first time the little girl was sleeping over and I wasn't even sure where she was sleeping. My loft technically only had one bedroom—mine—and it wasn't what I'd call kid-friendly. Thank God for Willow. She came up with the perfect solution. Her childhood sleeping bag—a plush pink and white satin-quilted bag, which was shaped like a ballet slipper and came with a matching pillow. I gave her a hug when she brought it over. Violet was going to love it, and I could place it on the area rug in my room.

Willow insisted on accompanying me to the nearby Whole Foods on Seventh Avenue to stock up on food for my niece. Of course, my obsessive-compulsive sister had sent me a list of everything my niece required. It might have been the longest email I ever received. What was with this kid—organic almond milk, flax seed muffins, and kale for making smoothies and fresh veggie chips? And that was just for starters; attached were recipes. Was my sister out of her fucking mind? She knew damn well I didn't cook. In fact, I almost burned down my parents' kitchen when I was eleven trying to make pizza. I showed the list to Willow and shared my childhood cooking fiasco. She burst into laughter and continued to laugh as I showed her the second attachment: a minute by minute breakdown of Violet's activities from the minute she woke up to the time she went beddy-bye. Holy Jesus. I was never going to survive this weekend. Nonplussed Willow told me not to worry as we drove to Whole Foods. Leaving the posh supermarket with three bags worth of stuff, we made another stop at the Gristedes around the corner and left with a bag of groceries that weren't on the list. Then, on the way home, we made a final stop at her dad's deli.

Stocking my kitchen cabinets and fridge with Willow's help, I was getting more and more anxious by the second. My sister Mimi and her spouse, Beth, would be here any minute with Violet. Over the years, I'd seen them numerous times, both here in New York and Boston, where they lived. They'd both been so supportive, especially in the months following Allee's death. I was beholden. So, when I found out that the two workaholics were flying to the Caribbean for a long weekend to celebrate their tenth anniversary, I offered to take care of Violet at my place while they were away. Now, I was having second thoughts. While I adored my niece and was also her godfather, I had no idea how to take care of a little girl. Fuck. What was I thinking? My stomach knotted, I scurried through my loft making sure everything was childproof while Willow remained behind in the kitchen preparing lunch. This was the first time Mimi would be meeting Willow...the first woman in my life since Allee...and this also made me nervous as shit. My brilliant sister-the-lawyer was very judgmental, and I worried if she would like Willow...even a fraction of how much she adored Allee. Allee, indeed, was a hard act to follow.

Then, suddenly out of nowhere, Allee appeared...sitting cross-legged on the couch.

"Relax, Madewell, you've got this."

"Allee!" I gasped. *"I'm freaking out. I don't know the first thing about kids."*

She laughed. *"Madewell, you'll do just fine. I always thought you'd make an awesome father."*

A sudden cloud of sadness fell upon me. The memory of that fateful day in Paris drifted into my head. That moment I learned about her frozen eggs, harvested in college before receiving her first cancer treatments. The eggs that I'd fertilized and were still waiting for a surrogate to bear them. Since becoming involved with Willow, I hadn't thought about them. Guilt mixed with the sorrow. Remorse.

Allee smiled at me. It was a wistful smile. A smile that gutted me.

"I know what you did, my Superman."

"You do?"

She nodded. "One day, you will be a fine father, Ryan Madewell." She emphasized the word "will." Then, her smile brightened and she shot me her signature eye roll. "And stop worrying about what your sister will think about Willow. She's gonna love her."

The intercom sounded, and with that, she disappeared.

My emotions in a jumble, I ran to answer it.

"Uncle Ryan, we're here!!" a sweet raspy voice shouted. Violet. My spirits instantly lifted. I was excited to see her as well as Mimi and Beth. I hit the intercom button and let them in.

A few minutes later, my adorable niece was in my arms while her moms set down her small suitcase and a doll. She rubbed my face.

"Uncle Ryan, you grew a beard!"

I laughed. God, she could even make me laugh in all the dark times. "Do you like it?"

She rubbed it again with her little hand and then

scrunched up her face. "It's very scratchy. I liked you better before without it."

Frowning, I faked a sad face. "Does that mean you don't love me anymore?"

"Of course not, silly!! You're my *bestest* uncle." She gave me a delicious hug, kissing my thick stubble. "Eeww!"

While I chuckled, my sister chided her. "Violet, that's not nice. Tell Uncle Ryan you're sorry."

My stubborn niece hedged and hawed. She reminded me in ways of my bullheaded Allee. "Hey, don't worry about it, kiddo." I affectionately tugged at one of her long braids. "Beards are an acquired taste."

"They taste yucky, Uncle Ryan."

I chortled at her literal interpretation. She'd likely tasted my cologne or the remnants of the soap I used to wash my face. Then behind me, I heard footsteps and a familiar voice. With Violet still in my arms, I spun around. It was Willow, holding a tray with food and beverages.

"Hi, everyone. I hope you're staying for lunch. I've made some sandwiches and hot dogs."

"YAY! I'm starving!" shouted my niece. "And I love hot dogs with mustard and ketchup!"

A big smile beamed on Willow's face while my sister frowned.

"Since when do you eat hot dogs, young lady?" she asked her daughter.

"Marta buys them for me all the time from the hot

dog man in the park."

Marta was their nanny. Mimi and Beth exchanged what-the-fuck looks while Willow waltzed up to us.

"And, sweetie, I also made you chocolate milk."

"Wow!! I love chocolate milk. My mommies never let me have it."

My strict as hell sister shot me a guilty as charged look. Holding back a laugh, I introduced Willow to everyone.

"Guys, this is …" I paused, not quite sure what to call Willow before continuing. "… *my new friend,* Willow." I then introduced her to my sister, Beth, and Violet.

"You're SO pretty!" gushed my niece. "Like a Disney princess."

Thanking her for the compliment, Willow blushed, but indeed she was as beautiful as any princess. In fact, that was an understatement. She was exquisite with her fine-featured porcelain-skinned face and her riotous red hair that was held back with a headband. My eyes stayed on her lithe, fuckable body as she set the platter down on my dining table. A few moments later we all sat down to eat. To my relief, conversation flowed, and though my sister was asking Willow lots of questions, the kickass trial lawyer that she was, the mood was relaxed. And my stunning companion was handling the interrogation well.

"So, Willow, what do you do?" asked my sister.

Willow set down her sandwich. "I'm a dancer."

"You mean like Angelina Ballerina?" asked wide-eyed Violet.

Willow smiled. "Yes, I'm a ballerina, but I'm not a mouse."

My niece burst out into laughter. Her laughter was contagious and we all followed suit.

Calming down, Violet sipped her chocolate milk through a straw and then said, "When I grow up, I want to be a ballerina just like you."

"We'll see about that." My sister rolled her eyes. Knowing my ambitious sister, she probably had plans for Violet to become come President of the United States. I silently laughed. How ironic that my lesbian sister would give birth to the girliest of girls. My mother's genes must have slipped in there somewhere.

A connection, however, was forming between my niece and Willow. Chatty Violet fired one question after another at Willow, who answered every one.

"Willow, can you teach me how to do ballet?"

Willow winked at her. "If you eat your whole hot dog and finish your milk, I think I can do that."

"YAY!" Eagerly, my niece took a couple of big bites of her hot dog, finishing it, and then depleted her milk. My sister glanced down at her watch.

"Ryan, our flight departs at four o'clock. We need to leave soon."

Beth offered to help Willow clean up. My niece, already so attached to Willow, tagged along, leaving my sister and me alone.

"I really like her," began my sister, wasting no time to give her opinion of Willow.

I smiled with relief. I valued my sister's opinions, and it wasn't easy for her to approve of someone.

"Where does she dance? Is she part of a company?"

"She was."

"Which one?"

"Some company in Latvia.

"Latvia?"

I nodded. "She doesn't like to talk about it much. She's on some kind of sabbatical."

My inquisitive sister persisted. "Haven't you Googled her? Gone on Facebook? Or Instagram?"

I told my sister that I couldn't find anything about her on social media. Truthfully, I'd kept away.

Narrowing her eyes with suspicion, Mimi dragged the pad of her thumb along her lips. "That's odd."

I came to Willow's defense. "Not everyone is an open book."

"Says the man who wrote a tell-all memoir."

"Says the woman who keeps secrets."

Just like when we were kids, my sister and I were at each other. Verbal sparring.

Then, my sister's expression turned solemn. "Ryan, I just don't want to see you get hurt again."

I twitched a small smile. Even though we had our moments—and what siblings didn't?—my sister had my back. She always had...even when we were growing up with our dysfunctional, inattentive parents.

And if it hadn't been for her, I don't know how I would have gotten through those god-awful months following Allee's death. She'd even offered to be a surrogate and carry Allee's baby if that helped, but I didn't want her to bear that responsibility nor was I ready. After taking a sip of my cream soda, I responded.

"We're taking it slowly, day by day."

"Are you sleeping together?"

My muscles tensed. How should I answer that question?

"Well?"

"It's complicated. We've fucked, but we haven't spent the night together."

Mimi cocked a brow. "Why is that?"

"She's living with her father. He owns the deli around the corner. Their apartment is above it. Her bedroom is right next door to his. That's pretty awkward."

"So, why doesn't she stay over here?"

"I can't have her sleeping in the bed I shared with Allee."

Mimi leaned back in her chair. "Little bro, I know how much that bed means to you, but maybe it's time to get rid of it. And move on."

I tensed. It was like she and Dr. Goodman were in cahoots with one another. "I'll think about it." My laissez-faire reaction to her comment was a far cry from the outraged one I had in my shrink's office a few weeks ago.

Then, another thought entered my mind. "And besides, I don't think it would be good for Violet to see her uncle in bed with a woman he wasn't married to. I don't want to give her the wrong impression."

My sister's reaction surprised me, though it shouldn't have, given how liberal she was.

"Actually, I wouldn't have a problem with that. Vi has only seen two women sleeping together in bed. For her, that's the norm. It would be healthy for her to see how the heterosexual population lives, especially since she's already a little boy crazy."

"She already likes boys?"

Before my sister could reply, Violet's sweet voice filled our ears. Sporting a bright smile, she came skipping toward us. Willow and Beth trailed behind her.

My eyes stayed on the adorable little girl as she curled her tiny hand on the back of one of the chairs around the table.

"Guess what!" she said excitedly. "Willow taught me how to do a plié in first position. Watch!"

Our eyes stayed on her as she put her heels together, forming a V, and then bent her knees so that she was almost squatting. She held out her other slender arm gracefully. A smile formed on Willow's face as she looked on.

"Bravo!" I clapped.

"That's wonderful," chimed in my sister, though I wasn't sure if she really meant it. My sister's plans for her daughter likely included passing the bar, not doing pliés at the barre. I inwardly chortled.

"Mommy, Willow says she's going to teach me more ballet. Maybe a whole dance."

Having no clue about my sister's career plans for my niece, Willow kept smiling.

"Violet's adorable. I can't wait to teach her more."

Before my sister could say a word, her cell phone rang. It was their driver. He was here, waiting downstairs to take her and Beth to JFK. They quickly gathered their belongings as they rattled off do's and don't's for my niece. Sheesh. After that five-page email, as if I didn't know. Willow and I stifled our laughter.

Her roller bag by her side, my sister lifted Violet into her arms, and after kissing the top of her head, said, "I'm going to miss you, Vi-baby." Her voice was a little watery. This was the first time she and Beth were leaving Violet alone for an extended period of time. It was Violet's first sleepover, and for the first time in my adult life, I saw a softer, more vulnerable side of my sister. It was refreshing.

"Me too," echoed Vi.

My sister smacked another kiss on her daughter's scalp. "I love you from here to the moon and back."

"I love you, too, and Mommy Beth. Don't forget to bring me back a present!"

I watched with a tinge of envy as Violet gave her mommies farewell hugs. Maybe one day, I would have a little girl who would shower me with love and affection. I met Willow's wistful gaze and wondered if she was thinking the same thing.

Confession. I had no clue what I was getting myself into when I volunteered to take care of my niece Violet for three days. While I'd spent considerable time with her, I'd never spent 24/7 with her. She was a handful. A non-stop bundle of energy. Sometimes, I wanted to curse my sister out for not warning me. The kid didn't even take naps.

Thank goodness for Willow; she was a blessing. Unlike me who'd grown up with absentee parents—a cold, ruthless father, who'd rather fuck his latest mistress than tuck in his son, and an equally cold, alcoholic mother, who'd rather go to a benefit for the zoo than take her children there—Willow grew up with loving, attentive parents and knew all the fun, kid-friendly city attractions to take Violet to. It also helped that she was a girl and knew what little girls liked. I had no clue; growing up with my rebellious sister, who was more like four going on forty-four, was no help.

Okay…another confession. I was having the best time I had in years. Each jam-packed day was full of fun, adventure, laughs, the unexpected…and love. We did things I'd never done before—like riding the sky-high tram to Roosevelt Island, ice skating at Chelsea Piers Sky Rink, and taking a ferry to the Statue of

Liberty. We also went to the Museum of Natural History, where Vi showed off her encyclopedic knowledge of dinosaurs, and to a matinée performance of *Wicked* on Broadway. We all loved it and came out of the theater singing the songs before heading over to legendary Rumplemyers for ice cream sundaes.

Everywhere we went, people fawned over us and told us we were a beautiful family. It wasn't surprising. Throughout our excursions, Violet, who looked a lot like me, with her light brown hair and baby blue eyes, stood between us holding our hands. Rather than correcting them, I simply thanked them. This was my first taste at what being a family was like and I more than enjoyed it. Interestingly, Willow never said a thing to the contrary either. I wondered why.

The fun we had together during the day spilled over into the evenings. In the early hours, Willow spent some secret "girl time" upstairs in the apartment she shared with her father and afterward we ate dinner at her father's deli. Mel, with his big, loveable personality, wrapped Vi around his finger, making special treats for her like hamburgers with funny faces, spoiling her with extra desserts, and even letting her ring the cash register. The joy I got from watching them together couldn't be put into words. Violet had never met my father as my sister couldn't and wouldn't forgive him for disowning her when he found out she was gay. A big part of me wished they would make amends, but given how bullheaded they both were made that unlikely. Chances were my sweet niece would never have a grandpa.

Following our first dinner together, Violet, who'd grown incredibly attached to Willow in less than a day, begged for her to come back to my place to watch some TV and put her to bed. She would not take no for an answer, cajoling us with pretty pleases and tears. On top of being too adorable for words, the kid was a great actress. I gave in.

The first night was awkward. Not for Violet, but for Willow and me. Watching Nickelodeon together was easy, but putting Vi to bed was a whole other story. The overactive child refused to go to sleep unless Willow tucked her in and read her a story. Again, the pretty pleases and the crocodile tears. Gutting me, the sucker that I was, I had no choice but to acquiesce. And since Violet was sleeping in my room, it meant that for the first time in our relationship Willow would be stepping foot in the bedroom I shared with Allee.

"Are you sure you want me to do this?" Willow asked as we wound up the stairs, me carrying an overjoyed Violet piggyback on my shoulders.

"Yeah…unless you want to pull an all-nighter cartoon marathon." There was no doubt in my mind that this child could stay up all night and just the thought of entertaining her 24/7 was exhausting.

"Okay," mumbled Willow as we entered my bedroom.

The antique four-poster bed that I bought as a wedding present for Allee practically smacked you in the eyes upon stepping foot in the sparsely furnished room. To my relief, Willow made no mention of it though she couldn't stop staring at it. Yes, it was spectacular and I'm sure conjuring a lot of emotions in my companion. After I set Violet down, Willow hastily got my niece settled into her ballet slipper sleeping bag, which was parked on the rug near my bed. Violet loved it, especially after learning that Willow used to sleep in it as a child.

Once tucked in, Violet studied my bed. "That's like a princess bed!" she exclaimed. "Do you sleep in it all by yourself, Uncle Ryan?"

I swallowed hard, searching for an answer. I wasn't sure how much Violet knew about Allee. My niece wasn't even born when Allee passed away. Once when I visited her in Boston, the inquisitive child asked me why I wasn't a daddy and my sister told her it was none of her business. After that, any related discussion had never arisen. Nor had any questions about her sperm donor conception or the fact that she had a twin that didn't make it. My sister uneventfully lost the second baby early on in her pregnancy, but I was sure one day when my niece was older she would explain everything to her.

"How come you're not answering my question?" persisted Violet, definitely inheriting my sister-the-lawyer's interrogation skills.

One pathetic word at last spilled from my lips:

"Yeah." *I sleep it in alone.*

Cocking her head, my niece shot me a puzzled look. "How come doesn't Willow sleep in it with you? There's lots of room. And it's so pretty!"

My stomach twisted. This is exactly what I was afraid of. I exchanged an awkward glance with a flushed Willow, neither of us knowing what to say. Finally, Willow broke the ice.

"Because, sweetie, I have to go home and take care of my daddy."

"Don't you have a mommy that does that?"

Willow's voice softened. "I used to, but she's in heaven now."

"Like my Auntie Allee? She's in heaven too."

At the mention of Allee's name, my heart squeezed. So, my sister had told my niece about her. Not commenting, I saw discomfort wash over Willow's face.

Violet's twinkling eyes stayed fixed on Willow. "I bet they know each other."

Willow twitched a smile as she straightened Violet's long pigtails. "I bet they do."

"My mommies told me that people in heaven are called angels and they watch over us."

Willow's smile widened. "I believe that too. Now, sweetie, you should go to sleep. We have a big day planned for tomorrow."

"Can you read me a goodnight story first?"

"Sure. What book do you want me to read?"

A few minutes later, we were both seated on the

carpet, cross-legged, as Willow read her one of the many *Angelina Ballerina* picture books she'd brought along.

By the end of the book, Violet was fast asleep. Five minutes later, Willow was out the door, leaving me bereft.

And so a routine began. A full day with Violet in the city…Willow and Vi's secret girl time…dinner with Mel… television and bedtime.

With each passing day, my feelings for Willow grew. I loved how comfortable she was with my niece and how much Violet adored Willow. My new girl was naturally maternal. One day at lunch, my inquisitive niece asked her if she wanted to be a mommy. Convincingly, Willow told her what she'd told me—she wanted to have lots of kids, and after Violet asked her how many, she counted on her fingers, deciding on ten. Though I didn't really believe that number, her heartfelt words resonated with me, and once again, I painfully thought about the embryos I'd made with Allee's eggs. At some point, I was going to have to deal with them. Make a decision.

Putting Violet to bed at once became my favorite and least favorite part of the day. It meant saying goodnight to Willow too. While I was increasingly tempted to fuck her anywhere but my bed—on the kitchen counter, the dining table, the couch, and even the floor, she didn't give me the chance. Once Violet fell asleep, she gave me the excuse that she had to leave and help her dad. Though I didn't believe her, I didn't argue. Fucking Willow while my niece was here probably wasn't a good idea anyway. I shuddered at the thought of her waking up and finding us bared to each other, entwined on the floor, panting and moaning. At the same time, that image made my cock ache. It had been over a week since I'd fucked Willow. And I wanted her badly. So badly I had to jerk off behind the locked door of my bathroom before I got into bed. My sad, empty bed.

On Monday, the final day of Violet's stay, I had a long-standing lunch with my literary agent. Having canceled on her too many times, I had to meet her. Over breakfast with my niece at Mel's, I explained this to Willow.

"Ry-man, don't worry. I'll take care of Vi. There's one thing we haven't done—and that's go shopping."

"Yay!" chimed in my exuberant niece, devouring one of Mel's specialties—a thick wad of challah French toast smothered in maple syrup.

With a relieved smile, I reached into my jeans pocket for my cardholder and slapped my American Express card on the table.

"Here, baby. Use this."

To my surprise, Willow shoved the card back at me.

"I don't need it. This is all on me. Just try to be home by three...when your sister and Beth come to pick up Vi."

"Are you sure?"

"Yes, I'm sure."

Slipping the card back into my pocket, I had the feeling that a surprise awaited me.

My literary agent, Paula Friedman, had agreed to meet me downtown for lunch at trendy Balthazar. I owed Paula my success. While the manuscript for *Undying Love* was initially rejected by agent after agent, all saying no one wanted to read a book with a sad ending, Paula fell in love with it and managed to sell it to a major publisher, getting me a nice advance. Little did anyone know that Allee's farewell love letter would go viral and the book would go on to become a major bestseller. A shrewd, don't-fuck-with-me negotiator, Paula had been instrumental in getting me a shitload of money for the film rights as well as a subsequent three-book deal, this time with an ungodly, unheard of advance.

Over roasted beet salads, we chatted about the literary world as well as the movie version of *Undying Love*. I told her I was going out to LA on Wednesday to meet with the producer and some of the cast. Then, she cut to the chase.

"Ryan, I'm getting a lot of pressure from your publisher for your next book. What's going on?"

Every muscle inside me tensed. Since writing *Undying Love*, I'd suffered from major writer's block. I'd been dealing with it with Dr. Goodman, who told me it was likely attached to my inability to let go of Allee. "Emotionally stuck," he called it. Playing with my greens, I faltered for words. Okay, one word...

"Nothing." I hung my head in shame.

"Ryan, look at me." Her voice was soft but firm.

Slowly, I lifted my head and met her gaze.

"Listen, Ryan, I know what you went through, but you've got to get out of this funk. You're a brilliant writer; you're wasting your talent. Maybe the trip to LA will do you good or you need another change of scenery..."

A change of scenery. As she rambled on, offering remedies for my problem, those four words reverberated in my head. Suddenly, I knew what I had to do. A writers' retreat wasn't the answer. But another type of retreat was.

Right after lunch, I hurried to a nearby antiques store on Broome Street. The one where I'd purchased my bed. My heartbeat quickened with each rapid step. Stopping in front of it to take a steeling breath, I swung the front door open. A bell chimed as I stepped foot inside, the scent of expensive furniture polish and potpourri wafting up my nose. Upon hearing the ding-ding-ding, the proprietor, a stocky aristocratic-looking fellow, made his way through the clutter of antiques, heading toward me. Though it had been almost five years, instant recognition flickered in his eyes.

"Ah, Mr. Madewell, good to see you again," he beamed, extending his hand. "How have you been?"

"Not bad." He didn't need to know all the grief I'd been through nor the turmoil that was making my stomach churn as I shook his hand.

"I saw you a few weeks ago on *Good Morning America*. Congratulations on the movie."

I thanked him politely, eager to change the subject.

"So, what brings you here today?"

I inhaled another fortifying breath and then spit out the words before I changed my mind. "I'd like to sell the bed I bought from you. Perhaps, I can put it on consignment or exchange it for something else."

The dealer adjusted his half-moon glasses. "Actually, you're in luck. A client of mine, who runs a small decorative arts museum upstate, has been looking for a bed much like the one you have. With its provenance, I'm sure he'd be willing to pay a hefty sum for it."

My pulse in overdrive, I digested the dealer's words. *A museum?*

"Sir, actually, I don't want the money. I'd rather donate the bed on one condition." A commemorative plaque. I told him how I wanted it worded.

Gift of Ryan Madewell IV
In Loving Memory of Allee Adair Madewell
July 14, 1988–June 10, 2013

After one phone call to the curator, we had a deal. And my Allee was going to at last have a tombstone of sorts. RIP, my beautiful angel. The bed was scheduled to be picked up tonight by the dealer's movers. An unexpected peacefulness washed over me. Maybe it was just the proverbial calm before the storm and I'd made a terrible mistake I'd regret. Second thoughts flooded my head, but there was no going back. As my father always said, "A deal is a deal."

The elated dealer broke into my thoughts. "You're going to need something to sleep on. We just got a new shipment from Europe. Take a look around and let me know if there's anything you like."

Aimlessly, I meandered through the store. Nothing struck my fancy until I came upon a regal queen-size bed that had a tufted pale pink satin headboard. The upholstered fabric and color reminded me of the toe shoes that dangled from Willow's childhood bed.

"What's the story with this bed?" I asked the dealer, who was standing beside me.

"Rumor has it that it belonged to a famous ballerina who danced for the Ballet Russe. She supposedly wrote her memoir in it and then died peacefully in her sleep at the age of one hundred, surrounded by her loved ones."

Holy shit! "I'll take it."

Adding that it came with a brand new high-end mattress, the dealer beamed. "Let me show you something else that belonged to this ballerina."

Intrigued, I followed him to a jewelry case near the front of the store. Unlocking it, he slipped out a necklace from which hung a small pink-enameled pair of ballet shoes encrusted with diamonds. He set it atop a black velvet pad on the glass counter. Beneath the halogen lights above, the diamonds glistened.

"It is rumored to be a gift from her lover. It may have been designed by Fabergé, but unfortunately there are no markings."

I studied the dainty jeweled shoes. They reminded me a lot of the pink satin toe shoes dangling from Willow's bed. The dealer continued.

"Because you are an excellent customer, I can offer you the necklace at a very special price. It's an investment piece and would certainly make a wonderful treat."

Treat. The word reverberated in my ear. *Trick or Treat.* Everywhere I'd walked those words popped up somewhere. Even Balthazar was decked out with pumpkin decorations. Tomorrow was Halloween. Holy crap! Willow's birthday. In the nick of time, I'd just found the most perfect present.

"I'll take it." The words tumbled out of my mouth.

Five minutes and several thousand dollars later, I was out the door, on my way to Bed Bath & Beyond.

It was all meant to be.

Bursting with energy and carrying a bouquet of wild flowers that I'd spontaneously picked up at a local florist, I arrived home a little before three. My sister and Beth were already there, looking tanned and rested from their long weekend in Antigua. They were seated on my dining area chairs, which were now lined up like a row of theater seats. Some of the other furniture has been moved to the side, making way for a large empty space.

"Where are Willow and Vi?" I asked after chatting with them a bit about their trip. Luckily for them, Antigua was one of the few Caribbean islands spared from the wrath of recent hurricanes, and they had a fantastic time.

"Getting ready for the show," said my sister after sharing some photos on her cell phone.

My eyebrows lifted to my forehead. "The show?"

Mimi and Beth shrugged in unison. "Take a seat," instructed Beth.

I did as I was told and sat next to my sister with the flowers on my lap. A few short minutes later, Willow breezed down the stairs and joined us, sitting next to me. She was holding my remote.

"What's going on?"

A sly smile crossed her kissable lips. "You'll see in a few seconds."

My curiosity was piqued as she pressed the remote. On my next breath, a burst of classical piano music filled the room. I recognized the piece—it was some Tchaikovsky waltz that I'd once dance to with this creepy girl in Cotillion. The memory vanished as adorable Violet pranced down the stairs onto the makeshift dance floor. Wearing a pink leotard and tights, a lavender tulle tutu, and pale pink dance slippers on her feet, she looked like a little ballerina. Make that a beautiful little ballerina with her long hair gathered into a bun and a bit of shimmering makeup on her face.

For the next five minutes, the four of us sat silently, mesmerized by my precious niece's performance as she twirled, jumped, and leaped to the music. I was captivated by both her agility and grace. With her slender arms fluttering like wings, she looked like a delicate little bird. A bright smile lit her face as she continued to dance across the concrete floor. I now realized what Willow had bought on her shopping expedition and what she'd been secretly doing with Violet each evening. Giving my wannabe ballerina niece dance lessons. Watching her effortlessly and passionately perform, there was no doubt in my mind that she was born to dance. As she continued to glide across the floor, I dared to take Willow's hand. Without taking her eyes off her protégé, she gave mine a little squeeze.

When the piece ended, Willow hit the remote again,

turning off the sound system, and as Violet gracefully curtsied, the four of us leapt to our feet, giving her a standing ovation, applauding madly and shouting bravo. Wearing a proud, ear-to-ear grin, Violet skipped up to us.

"Did you like it?"

I was the first to chime in. "Kiddo, you were incredible." I glanced down at the flowers in my lap. "These are for you."

I handed her the bouquet. Though they were intended for Willow, the sparkle in my niece's eyes as she inhaled the fragrant flowers made my heart swell with joy.

"Thank you, Uncle Ryan. They're so pretty!"

"Sweetheart, that was amazing," said my sister, rarely one to give effusive compliments.

"Totally," echoed Beth.

"Willow taught me how to dance. She's the *bestest* teacher in the whole wide world."

Willow blushed; God, she was adorable when she did that, her pale face turning the color of Violet's ballet shoes. After swallowing a breath of air, she told us Violet was a natural.

Violet cocked her head. "What's a natural?"

"That means you're very good at something that's very hard. Ballet comes easily to you."

"Cool!" Her attention shifted to my sister. "Mommy, can I take ballet lessons when we get home?"

My sister hesitated, but then agreed to them.

Willow smiled. "I have a friend in Boston, who's a great dance instructor. I'll email you her contact info and will personally call her to recommend taking on Violet as a student. She has so much potential."

"Does that mean I could be as good as you and Angelina Ballerina?"

Willow winked at her. "Better."

A half hour later, my sister, Beth, and Violet, now proudly holding a quilted pink bag with all her new ballet gear, were on their way back to Boston. There were hugs all around, my niece unable to let go of Willow. The powerful connection between them filled me with a happiness I'd never known before. Willow promised to visit and told Violet to send her videos. Once they were gone, my loft felt so quiet and empty. For the first time, I realized how much a child could fill your life.

After putting back all the furniture, Willow and I ordered in pizza and shared a bottle of wine. I told her about my meeting with my agent and mentioned that I had a surprise for her. *Us.* As much as she nudged me to tell her what it was, I kept mum.

At close to seven o'clock, my intercom sounded. The movers.

A few minutes later, the elevator door creaked open.

"It's upstairs," I said.

"What's going on?" asked Willow as the four burly men wound up the stairs to my bedroom.

Deciding I really wanted this to be a surprise, I

searched the living room for something I could use as a blindfold. My eyes darting left and right, they landed on my plaid cashmere scarf that I'd left on the couch. I made a quick dash for it, and when I returned to Willow, I told her to turn around. I began to wrap the scarf around her eyes.

"What are you doing, Ry-Man?"

"What does it look like I'm doing? I'm blindfolding you."

"Huh!?" She squirmed.

"Don't move. You're making it hard." *Really hard.* I could feel an erection in the making, already straining against my jeans.

Upstairs, I could hear the movers dismantling my four-poster bed. A few minutes later, two of them carefully marched down the stairs, holding the bed on its side while the other two carried the mattress and bedding. I'd be lying if I didn't say there was a part of me that wanted to stop them. My stomach clenched as I blew out a steeling breath. Once downstairs, they headed toward the elevator. One of them pushed the button and the door re-opened. *To my shock, Allee was standing inside the carriage. She flashed an approving smile at me and I gasped.*

"Ry, is everything okay?" asked Willow.

"Yeah." My voice wavered as I watched the men cart the mattress, the bedding, and the bed into the elevator. *Then to my surprise, Allee gave me a thumbs-up and then blew me a kiss. I caught it with my heavy*

*heart and blew a kiss back. The door cranked shut, and
to be honest, my heart sunk to my stomach as the
elevator descended. My Allee was gone.*

"Can I take this scarf off now?" asked Willow,
bringing me back to the moment.

"No, not yet." Grasping the fringed ends, I pulled it
a little tighter.

Willow was getting impatient and annoyed.
"C'mon, Ryan, tell me what's going on."

"You'll see soon." I meant that figuratively and
literally.

Ten minutes later the elevator returned, and this
time the four men were carrying my new bed and the
mattress along with two large plastic bags filled with
the bedding and accessories I'd purchased at Bed Bath
& Beyond and had delivered to the antiques dealer.
Brand new pillows, sheets, a comforter, and a duvet
cover. And some candles. My pulse thudding, I
watched as they brought everything upstairs. Butterflies
flitted in my stomach. I hope I'd made the right
decision.

"This is absurd," protested Willow. Lifting her arms
behind her, she attempted to untie the scarf. I caught her
wrists in time and stopped her.

"You're being a really bad girl. One more bad move
and I'm going to have to spank you."

She giggled. But truthfully, the thought of giving
her tight little ass a little spanking that would make it
turn ballerina pink turned me on. My dick grew harder

and began to throb. I hoped the movers would assemble my new bed quickly with all the trimmings.

In no time, they were back downstairs and told me everything was done. Digging my hand into my jeans pocket, I pulled out my money clip and handed them each a twenty-dollar bill as a tip. They were beyond thrilled by my generosity and happily bid me good-night. Before leaving, one of the movers gave me a thumbs-up, hinting at the night ahead. My pulse quickened and I could feel it in my dick.

"Okay, baby, hold my hand," I anxiously told Willow, taking hers in mine once they were gone. Carefully, I led her up the winding stairs to my bedroom and when we got to the top, I took off the scarf.

"Oh my God!" she gasped, soaking in my, or should I say, our new bed. Having instructed the movers to make it up and place scented candles throughout the room, the antique bed with its shimmering pink upholstered headboard, thick white duvet, and fluffy pillows looked absolutely delicious.

"Oh my God!" Willow gasped again, her voice breathier, more in awe.

"Do you like it?"

"Oh my God! It's so beautiful. Honestly, the most beautiful bed I've ever seen."

Moving my hand to her lower back, I ushered her toward it. She ran her fingers over the plush Egyptian cotton duvet and then over the pink satin headboard.

"I found it today right after my lunch. It called out your name." This was my way of letting Willow know it was a bed for her. *A bed for us.* That I was ready to move on.

"I love it!"

"It belonged to some legendary Russian ballerina."

"Really? What was her name?"

"No clue." I hadn't asked, and now that I thought about it, maybe this clever antiques dealer had made up a story to make a sale. It didn't matter. Willow's eyes fixated on the bed and then zoomed in on the small whimsical pillow that was anchored in the middle against the pile of fluffy goose down pillows. She read the embroidered words aloud:

"Make love, not war."

While I'd almost bought one that said, "Dance until you drop," something told me that might upset her. Don't ask why, but I followed my gut instinct. So I bought this one instead, which was fitting in these politically trying times. It replaced the 'I'd-rather-be-in-Paris' pillow I'd given to Allee, which I'd torn up in a fit of rage right after her death.

I nuzzled the back of Willow's long neck. "So, what do you say…"

"Say what?" she whispered back.

"We make love."

TWENTY-THREE

Ryan

Despite how aroused I was, I wanted to take things slowly. Make every second count. As tempting as it was, I didn't want to jump straight into bed. I wanted to choreograph each move. Make this a production I would never forget.

Kissing her everywhere I could, I removed Willow's clothing piece by piece, her helping hands and soft moans telling me she was as eager as I was to claim each other. Between heated breaths, she clawed at my T-shirt and worked at the button of my jeans. Tossing her top to the floor, I massaged her perfect breasts before unhooking her lace bra and slipping it off. Her ballerina-pink nipples erect, I sucked and nibbled them, intermittently swirling my tongue around the delicate puckered buds as I slid down her leggings. Kicking off her ballet flats, she stepped out of the stretchy pants. My beautiful ballerina girl was bared to me, her flaming red hair cascading over shoulders like a theater curtain. Not taking my eyes off her, I disrobed like a madman, unable to control my pace. That's how great my need for her was. My cock was already giving her a standing ovation and was so fucking ready to take her. To dance with her pussy. Lead her to an orgasm. On my next feverish breath, I lifted her into my arms and carried her to the waiting bed.

I set her down, her head on a pillow, and I couldn't stop staring at her, marveling at her inhumanly beautiful body. Her chest heaved up and down, her full lips quivered, and her waist-long hair fanned out across the bedding. Her porcelain skin shimmered in the glow of the candlelight as did the contours and defined muscles of her taut dancer's limbs. If I were a painter, I'd paint her. This thing of beauty. This work of art.

"What are you doing, Ryan?" she whispered, her dreamy eyes looking up at me.

"Just looking at you." It had been so long since I had a woman in bed. If only I could paint her with words. "You're so fucking beautiful."

"I want to make it perfect for you," she breathed out.

My beautiful ballerina. The pleaser. The perfectionist.

"Bend your knees, my butterfly. Then spread your legs."

Silently, she did as I asked. I climbed onto the bed, sitting back on my knees between her V'd legs. My eyes lingering on her glistening pink pussy, I ran my hands over her long, lean sculpted limbs, relishing their silky smoothness, feeling every sinewy muscle. Then, I put one hand between them and stroked her soft, delicate folds. I hissed. She was soaked, so slick with wet heat.

Arching her back, she let out a moan.

I continued to caress her, my thumb finding her clit. "My beauty, you're so fucking wet for me." My thumb rubbed her sensitive bud, making circles, pressing harder, picking up speed.

"Oh, God," she spluttered as she bucked against my touch. I could feel her hypersensitive clit harden beneath the pad of my digit. Sexy whimpers filled her throat, the sounds of her arousal growing more and more impassioned. I fucking loved how responsive she was. I hungered for more of her. I wanted to stroke her, touch her, eat her, fuck her. I wanted to own all of her. This was my kingdom. My bed.

Removing my thumb from her clit, I put it to my mouth and sucked it. Fuck. She tasted delicious. So sweet and pure.

"Ryan, please. I need more."

I fucking loved that she was begging for me.

Hungrily, I splayed my hands on her tight inner thighs and spread her legs further. Keeping my hands in place, I leaned forward and buried my face in her pussy. I inhaled through my nose. Oh, God, she smelled intoxicating. I couldn't wait to get another taste of her. On my exhale, my tongue darted out and I began to flick and lick her swollen clit. Fuck. So, so good. I wondered—is this what ecstasy tasted like? I'd never done drugs, but if love was a drug, I'm sure it tasted like this incredible woman. I was addicted. I couldn't get enough of her, and she couldn't get enough of me. Writhing, she bucked her hips up against me again as an exquisite cry escaped her lips. The only downside of going down on her was that I couldn't see the expression on her face. Yeah, I could have gazed up, but I didn't want to stop my ministrations, break this magical spell of pleasure. The insane pleasure I was giving her. The insane pleasure she was giving me as I sucked and kissed her, bringing her closer and closer to the edge. So I used my imagination, picturing in my mind the expression of tortured ecstasy on her beautiful face. Her neck arched, her eyes squeezed closed, her lush lips parted allowing her to breathe and moan.

"Oh God, you feel so amazing."

I was surprised she was able to speak.

"Please don't stop."

I wanted to tell her not to worry. But I wasn't about to stop what I was doing. The wordsmith that I was, I nonetheless knew actions spoke louder than words.

Going at her with my tongue and my mouth, I was going to redefine "amazing." Give her an orgasm of epic proportions she'd never forget. Never be able to put into words. On her next frantic breath, I plunged a finger into her fiery entrance, without losing oral contact with her clit.

She let out another desperate cry as I began to pump her and suck her dry. Her cries became screams as I brought her to climax.

"Oh my God, Ryan, I'm going to come. Oh, oh, oh…"

Yes, *my beautiful ballerina girl, come. Come all over my face. Come!*

"OHHHH!" And as if she heard my command, she exploded, her sweet pussy juddering all over my face, her inner thighs trembling, her body quaking.

Slowly, I pulled out my finger and lifted my head, glimpsing her expression as her body went limp. It was one of pure ecstasy.

"Oh, Ryan, that was so, so, so…"

Cutting her short, I put my drenched finger, the one that had been inside her, to her lips, gently hushing her.

"Shhh. It's okay. You don't have to say anything. We're not done."

Her glistening eyes widened.

"It's time to christen this bed. I'm going to make love to you now. Are you ready?"

Feverishly, she nodded. I loved that she was insatiable. Still on fire. Dripping with desire. Gripping the base of my thick, rigid erection, I rubbed the wide crown along her slick heat, coating and lubricating it with her hot juices. Then I grabbed her slender ankles, slid her down the bed closer to me, and threw her legs over my shoulders. A new position. Like in a ballet. We were perfectly lined up. My cock at her entrance. Still holding the base, I slowly inserted my dick, inch by thick inch, feeling her expand to accommodate my width. As I pushed inside, she let out a soft groan.

"Baby, am I hurting you?"

She shook her head. "No, it's just that you're so big."

"And you're so fucking perfect. So tight. So hot. So wet."

Deep inside her, I repositioned myself, planting my palms on either side of her torso, and straightened my body until I was hovering over her. Her dainty tits grazed my chest and her warm breath heated my face. I slid my cock inside her until it could go no further. Slowly, I slid halfway down and then slid it back up. I continued these controlled movements, getting into a steady rhythm. Like I said, I was going to take it slowly and break in this new bed. We had all night. And for the first time, we had tomorrow. Willow didn't know it yet, but she was spending the night.

As we came blissfully together and I held her in my arms, I realized that if life was a book, I was starting a new chapter.

TWENTY-FOUR

Willow

I stretched my legs and pulled the heavenly covers up over my chest.

Mmm. Just five more minutes.

The sound of a soft raspy voice drifted into my ears.

"Hey, sleepy head."

I blinked my eyes open. Hovering over me was the epitome of virile perfection. The man who'd made incredible love to me last night. The man who'd whispered sweet nothings to me all night long. The man who'd spooned me with his spectacular body. The man whose beautiful bed I'd shared.

Ryan.

"Hi," I murmured, my voice groggy. Pulling the covers up higher, I sat up and smiled at him. Dressed in sweats and a V-neck tee, he was holding a tray with a blueberry muffin and a container of coffee. The muffin had a pink candle in it. Also on the tray was a small trick or treat bag with a pumpkin face.

"You went out?" I asked, my voice growing stronger.

"Yeah. I went to the Coffee Bean around the corner. Breakfast in bed. Happy Birthday, my beautiful butterfly."

"You remembered my birthday?"

"How could I not? There were pumpkins all over town, Miss Pumpkinhead."

Embarrassed, I tried to fix my wild mane of hair. It was futile. I was a bedhead, plain and simple, so I giggled. How sweet of him to remember. Sitting down on the bed, he planted a soft kiss on my lips and then handed me the tray.

"Make a wish," he said, after lighting the candle with his gold lighter.

I knew what I wanted. I wanted this moment to never end. I wanted more of him in the worst way. Pursing my lips, I blew out the candle.

I drank the coffee and ate the muffin. Ryan then set the tray on his nightstand after handing me the trick or treat bag. Taking off his shoes, he repositioned himself so that he was sitting cross-legged and facing me.

"What's inside this bag?" I asked.

"A treat." A mischievous smile curled on his lips. "Go ahead. Take a look."

Some candy?

Hesitantly, I reached inside, and to my surprise, the touch of velvet met my fingertips. A small rectangular box. I slipped it out.

"What is this?"

"Your birthday present."

"Ry-man, I don't need a present. Waking up to you is the best present I could ask for."

"Open it," he ordered, jutting out his chin. It was an order. A dominant side of Ryan I'd never seen before. I more than liked it.

Doing as I was told, I snapped open the lid. My breath hitched and my eyes grew wide. Inside was a magnificent necklace with a sparkling diamond-encrusted pendant. A pair of pink enameled pointe shoes.

"Oh my God, Ryan!"

"Do you like it?"

"I love it, but you shouldn't have. It must have cost a fortune."

"Just a small fortune. But you had to have it. It belonged to the ballerina who owned this bed."

"Really?"

"Yeah, really. Let me put it on you."

My skin prickled as he expertly hooked the breath-taking necklace around my neck.

He smiled, his eyes drifting down from the pendant to my half-exposed breasts.

"It looks beautiful on you. Go take a look in the mirror."

My eyes darted around the sprawling room in search of one. And then I found it. Hung above a set of drawers in the far corner. On the chest were dozens of photos of Allee and Ryan. Having not noticed them before, my throat constricted as a sudden rush of insecurity overcame me.

"What's the matter?" asked Ryan, sensing my un-ease.

"Ry-man, I can't accept this gift."

"What do you mean?"

"You still belong to her." My watering eyes stayed fixed on the photos.

Following my gaze, Ryan muttered, "Shit. I should have put those photos away."

"No, Ryan, I understand. If my father married someone new, he could never hide the photos of my mom nor the portrait of her in our entryway. Nor could I."

Ryan's anguished expression softened. He stroked my face, brushing away the few tears that had escaped. "Willow, Allee will always be part of my life. She lives in my heart. Dr. Goodman told me that's why love never dies. Please try to understand that."

Undying Love. Biting down on my bottom lip, I nodded. Ryan's blue orbs burned into mine.

"Willow, what can I do to prove that you're the only one for me now?"

I shrugged. How could I ever replace Allee? My eyes stayed on him as he glanced down at his hands. He drew in a sharp breath, and then to my shock, he tore off his wedding band.

"Ryan, what are you doing?" I gasped as he set it on the nightstand and gripped my bare shoulders. I trembled at his touch as he held me fiercely in his gaze.

"I'm no longer married to Allee. I want to move on. Be with you. Wake up to you and go to sleep with you. Hold your body against mine. Smother you with kisses. Taste your lips on mine. Make love to you every way I can."

I couldn't help but burst into soft sobs. Ryan took me into his strong arms and held me until they subsided. He gently tilted up my chin.

"You okay, butterfly?"

I nodded.

"Say it. I need words."

"I'm good."

"Good." His gaze dropped to the trick or treat bag, still on the bed. "There's something else in that bag."

Curious, I reached my hand back inside it, withdrawing a plain white business envelope. A birthday card? It didn't look like one. Ryan confirmed that, apologizing that he didn't have time to buy one.

"Open it."

I unsealed the envelope and slipped out the folded sheet of paper inside it. I silently read the handwritten words: *Come fly with me, butterfly!* Below them was a drawing of a butterfly whose wings looked like two connected hearts. Perplexed, I unfolded the note. Again, my eyes grew wide.

"What is this?" I asked.

"A round-trip ticket to LA."

Stunned, I let him continue.

"I'm going to LA tomorrow for my best friend's

wedding. I want you to come with me."

Overwhelmed, I floundered for an excuse. "I-I can't. I need to look after my father."

"Don't worry. I called him this morning. Nurse Hollis will be at his beck and call.

"Nurse Hollis?"

"Yeah, your father invited her for dinner and she promised to keep an eye on him all weekend. He wants you to go."

Processing this news of my father's blooming social life, I fidgeted with the charm on my new necklace. As my hesitation slipped through my fingers, Ryan's hand met mine.

"Well, what do you say?"

"Okay…Yes."

Grinning, he yanked down the covers and tweaked my nipples. "And what do you say we fuck our brains out right now?"

"Oh, Ry-man. YES!"

A million times yes! Happy Birthday to me!

TWENTY-FIVE

Ryan

I'd been to Los Angeles several times before, but it was a whole different experience with Willow. Getting my meetings with the producer and director of *Undying Love* out of the way, I was able to spend the rest of my time with her. The Malibu Beach Inn, where we were staying and where Duffy and Sam were getting married Saturday evening, couldn't have been more idyllic. Our luxurious suite overlooked the Pacific, and we woke up and went to sleep to the sound of crashing waves. Rather than sightseeing, we spent lazy hours in bed making love and took long romantic walks on the sandy beach. The warm, sunny weather was a welcomed reprieve from the cold gloom that had befallen us back home. In the late afternoons, Willow took a long nap, and I just sat there staring at her, both bewildered and beholden that this beautiful angel had come into my life. Like a butterfly in winter. And it was during these times that I took out my notebook and jotted down my thoughts. Random words. I wasn't sure if they'd amount to anything, but it felt fucking good to be writing again.

The three days leading to Duffy's wedding went by quickly. At six o'clock on Saturday, we joined a small crowd on the beach to watch Duffy and Sam exchange their vows. Barefoot and in a suit as the wedding was far from formal, I sat next to Willow, holding her hand. She looked ethereal, almost like a bride herself, in a flowy ivory dress and a band of daisies circling her head. Her wild red hair hung loose, cascading over her shoulders.

Marching down steps that led to the beach, the procession began as a hippyish guitar-playing duo performed "Sea of Love." … *Do you remember when we met? That's the day...* On which I married Allee in Central Park. The memory hit me like a grenade. Pieces of shrapnel ripped through me, tearing me apart. Then, as Sam appeared on the landing with her father, the music changed. The guitarists began singing a song that totally undid me. "Endless Love." The beautiful face of my first love, with her jet-black hair and those expressive dark eyes, filled my head. She was every breath I took, every step I made. As we said our vows in Central Park, our lives had just begun, and just when we had it all, everything was taken away from us. As Duffy took his beautiful pregnant bride into his arms, nausea rose in my chest like a hot air balloon. My hands grew cold and clammy.

"Ryan, are you all right?" whispered Willow, turning to me.

"I've got to get out of here." Choking out the words, I leaped to my feet and ran toward the ocean. I didn't think Duffy or Sam saw me flee because they were both facing the reverend, about to exchange their vows.

I kept running and running and running. My feet sinking into the sand, the gentle waves brushing over my feet, the sounds of the ocean filling my ears, propelling me forward. The sun began to set; pink streaks lit the sky as it turned gray; and not before I long, the sky was pitch black lit up only by a full moon and a bevy of stars. The white crested waves glimmered in the darkness. I'd lost sense of time. I didn't know how long I'd run or how many miles I'd gone. It felt like a marathon. Breathing heavily, I stopped in my tracks, bending over to catch my breath. As I did, the ugly reality of what I'd done hit me like a giant wave crashing against a rock. I'd deserted my new girlfriend with no explanation and missed my best bud's wedding. A mixture of guilt and self-loathing pounded me. I felt sick to my stomach. Would they ever forgive me?

Conscious of time, I jogged back to the hotel, too emotionally and physically worn out to run any faster. It took me close to three hours. By my calculations, it must have been close to midnight. The wedding was over, the beach deserted. Staggering into the hotel, I passed some late-night partiers at the bar; neither Willow nor Duffy was among them. Desperately needing a drink, I didn't stop. In a panic, I sprinted to our suite wondering—what was I going to tell Willow?

That I'm too fucked up and you shouldn't be with me? Or maybe she'd throw those words at me first. If she wanted to break up with me, I couldn't blame her. A thousand knives stabbed at my heart. Was I about to lose the next best thing that had come into my life?

My breathing labored, I dug out my keycard from my breast pocket and unlocked the door. As I stepped inside, my heart almost stopped. There she was on the couch, one long leg crossed over the other.

"Allee!" I gasped. *"What are you doing here?"*

She folded her arms across her chest, looking not too pleased to see me.

"I'm always here, Madewell. I just don't always manifest myself. I hide in a corner of your heart. I like it there; it's my happy place."

"Why can't I always see you?"

"Only certain things make me appear. To be present. They played our song at the reception."

"I Won't Give Up?"

"Yeah. It's my favorite. I keep it on replay."

I, in contrast, never played it. I couldn't. It held too many sad memories for me.

"Madewell, why did you ditch Willow?"

"Allee, I fell apart watching Duffy take Sam into his arms. I couldn't breathe."

"You seem to be breathing just fine." Her voice dripped with her signature sarcasm.

"You don't understand. It was a trigger." Dr. Goodman had taught me that word.

"I get it. You regressed, but you gotta let go. You can never take me in your arms again."

My chest tightened and I felt weighted down by my two-ton heart. Allee was right. She was always right.

"Listen, Madewell, the A-For-Allee Plan didn't work."

It sure as fuck didn't. It was an epic fail. A tragedy.

"It's time for Plan B."

"Plan B?"

"Plan B as in B-E...Be. It's time to exist, Madewell. To live your life. Life isn't going to be here forever. Trust me, that's the one thing I know for sure."

My heart stuttered. I knew that too. Too damn well.

"Life passes by quickly, so don't waste it."

I processed her words. I was almost thirty-five and still floundering in a sea of grief.

"Willow...she's good for you. I really like her."

"You do?"

"Yeah, I do."

"What should I do? I fucked up big time."

"You're gonna do what I tell you to do."

My bossy Allee.

"Find her. Tell her you're sorry. And tell her the truth."

"Then what?"

A smile glowed on Allee's angelic face. How I wished I could still feel her lips...touch her skin... smooth her hair...

"I'm not giving up on you. Go on your journey to

happiness, Madewell. I'll be waiting for you at the end."

And with that, she magically disappeared.

Hoping Willow would be there, I returned to the crowded bar. My eyes darted in all directions in search of her. My heart sank to my stomach. She was still nowhere to be found. I, however, spotted Duffy, now dressed in casual jeans. I ran up to him.

"Duff, have you seen Willow?" Despair laced my voice.

"Hey, man, where'd you disappear to?"

"It doesn't matter," I stammered, grateful that he seemed too plastered to be pissed at me. "Willow…is she here?"

He took a chug of his beer. "To be honest, dude, I haven't seen her for a while."

"Hi, Ryan," came a familiar voice from behind me. I spun around. Duffy's beautiful bride, or should I say wife, strolled up to us. Like Duff, she was wearing jeans along with a tank top that showcased her baby bump.

"Sam, have you seen Willow?"

"Actually, I just saw her heading back to the beach. Is everything okay?"

Without responding, I flew out of the bar.

Confession. In my fucked-up state, panic gripped me by the balls as I hurried back to the beach. It crossed my mind that Willow might have done something crazy. Like drowned herself. And disappeared from my life forever. Thanking fucking God, my irrational thoughts were short-lived. Spotting her right away, they evaporated from my mind.

The sole person on the beach, she was by the shore-line, dancing in her bare feet. Leaping into the air and twirling, her slender arms fluttering like the butterfly she was, her rapid intricate steps making little splashes in the water, her sexy chiffon dress, blowing in the ocean breeze like a sail. I stopped dead in my tracks. I was mesmerized; in awe. I'd never seen her dance before. She was the epitome of grace, her moves precise and fluid, as if she were center stage and the whole world was watching her. The beam of the moon was her spotlight and the twinkling stars her stage lights. She shimmered beneath them. A sight to behold. Spectacular.

She had no clue I was here watching her. My gaze followed her as she sprinted ankle-deep into the ocean, held out her dress, and curtsied.

I clapped loudly and shouted bravo.

Startled, Willow whirled around. "Ryan, what are you doing here?"

"I've come to apologize." I ambled toward her. "I shouldn't have left you like that."

"Where did you go?" Her tone was cold.

"I went for a long run."

"I see. So, it was okay for you to abandon me … leave me alone with a bunch of people I didn't know. And miss the entire wedding."

"I know. It was a shitty thing to do." Bowing my head in shame, I kicked up a spray of sand.

"You hurt me, Ryan."

My heart was cracking. "Yeah, I hurt you. I'm sorry. I'll never do that again." I paused, meeting her gaze. "Come over here."

Silently, she took hesitant steps my way. My eyes never straying from her, I swept her into my arms and ran my fingers through her wild mane of hair. She gazed up at me. Sadness, not forgiveness, filled her eyes.

"Ryan, I can never be Allee." Her voice was small and watery.

I traced her soft lips with a finger. "I don't want to be her."

Her eyes searched my soul. "Ryan, what do you want?"

As I contemplated my response, music started playing in the bar. I could faintly hear it, but I recognized the song instantly. Jason Mraz's "I Won't Give Up." My nerves sparked through my bones. Allee was testing me! Taking a deep breath, I answered Willow's question.

"Willow, I don't want you to give up on me." And for the first time I said it: "I love you."

She didn't respond. Our eyes still locked, I cupped her shoulders. "What do you want?"

"I want you to dance with me." Exactly what Allee had said to me when I'd asked her that very question the night after learning of her imminent death. Except tonight, it wasn't raining; the stars above us were shining brightly. We had a lot to live for.

Silently, our bodies melded, my arms looped around her tiny waist, hers around my neck. I'd forgotten what if felt like to have another heart so close to mine. It felt good. So fucking good.

"You're a really good dancer, Ry-man," she said softly as I swayed her.

Cotillion. At least it was good for something. Lifting her off her feet, I spun her around and around. Then, I set her down and my lips captured hers, now only our tongues dancing, our moans mingling with the waves and creating a harmony of sorts.

I don't know how long we stayed locked in this passionate embrace until I finally broke the kiss.

"C'mon, my butterfly, let's head back to our room."

I kept my arm around her as we walked back in the direction of the hotel. At the steps leading up to the deck, she bent down and picked up a bouquet of white flowers.

"What's that?" I asked as she stood up.

"Sam's bouquet. With her eyes closed, she tossed it, and somehow it landed in my lap."

I laughed lightly.

"Why are you laughing?" she asked as we mounted the weathered wooden planks.

"Sometimes the way things work out is funny." There was no doubt in my mind that Allee had her hand in this. Wherever she was, she was watching over me.

Over us.

TWENTY-SIX

Ryan

In addition to my writing breakthrough, something else happened while I was in California. The white ring around my finger left behind from my wedding band tanned. There was no longer a trace of it. Upon my return to New York, Willow seamlessly blended into my life like the ring mark had done with my finger. She became a part of it. With her father recovering from his heart attack and spending more and more time with Nurse Hollis, she was more or less living with me. I woke up to her and went to sleep with her. We spent our days as lovers, exploring parts of the city we'd never been to… stopping for long wine-filled lunches…stealing kisses everywhere we could. Sometimes at my loft, she'd make me a wonderful dinner while I wrote on my computer. And night after night, she read all my favorite books to me, stark naked, before we made beautiful love. I couldn't get enough of her. We'd definitely broken in our new bed.

I now had to face the inevitable. It was time to introduce Willow to my parents. My mother knew about her from my sister and was eager to meet her. The perfect opportunity presented itself the third week of November. My mother was hosting a cocktail party and wanted us to come. It was far better than bringing Willow to a formal sit-down dinner. At least at the cocktail party, we could mingle with other people and escape inconspicuously without either of my parents noticing. My mother, in particular, was more interested in socializing with her highfalutin friends—the who's who of New York—than with me.

After all these years, my stomach still bubbled as our cab approached my parents' majestic apartment building on Fifth Avenue. I was already having second thoughts about attending my mother's event and introducing Willow to my parents. The cab pulled up to the curb, and George, one of the white-gloved doormen, instantly ran to the passenger door to open it. Willow gracefully slipped out, with me following her. George's face lit up at the sight of me as I wrapped an arm around my stunning date.

"Mr. Madewell, so good to see you again. You're looking well." Then, his twinkly eyes flitted to Willow. "And who might this beautiful young lady be?"

With a smile, I introduced Willow to George. She shook his hand.

"I've known this young man since he was a tod-dler," chuckled George. "Make sure he behaves."

"I will," laughed back Willow. "He can be very naughty."

I felt myself blush. Oh, could I. Well, at least, George had lessened my anxiety and put me in an upbeat mood. I hadn't been here for over a year. Not since my father's stroke. This apartment where I'd grown up held no fond memories for me. In fact, it was hard not to think about all the bad memories, especially that horrific dinner where I'd introduced my parents to Allee after which my father vilified her and forbid me to see her. Yeah, I'd forgiven my father for all his asshole acts, but that was one I couldn't forget. As I ushered Willow into the elegantly appointed lobby toward the elevator, an unsettling feeling again washed over me. A shiver ran through me, the past mingling with the present and an uncertain future.

"I'm nervous about meeting your parents," Willow said, her eyes glued to the spinning floor dial as the elevator ascended. We were passing the twentieth floor, one floor away from my parents' penthouse.

I gave her a squeeze. "Don't be. My mother doesn't bite and my father is bound to a wheelchair and can barely make himself understood." Then, I pecked her cheek. "And besides, you look gorgeous. And I'm here with you."

She twitched a tentative smile as the door pinged open. The elevator took us straight into the grand foyer of my parents' twenty-room duplex. A white-gloved attendant immediately met us and took our coats. Then another offered us each a glass of champagne and led us into the stately living room where the cocktail party was in full swing. We were fashionably late.

Willow's eyes grew wide as she sipped her champagne and took in the high-ceilinged art-and-antiques-filled room. It hadn't changed much since I'd been here last—maybe a few new Old Master paintings, which my parents collected, and new ivory silk drapes, which puddled onto the floor.

"Oh my God, this place is amazing," murmured Willow.

"It's okay if you like living in a museum."

With a laugh, Willow almost choked on her champagne. I loved that she loved my sense of humor. Loosened up a bit, we made our way deeper into the crowd, snagging some delicious hors d'oeuvres along the way, which were being passed around by white-gloved waiters. I recognized several of my mother's society friends, including her closest friend, Cici Holdsworth. The last time I'd seen her was at the opening for the Madewell Wing at The Met.

Already snockered, the matronly woman greeted with me with open arms and an effusive kiss on each cheek.

"Why, Ryan, darling!! How good to see you! How have you been?"

"I've been good." Less was best.

She brushed her free hand along my stubbled jaw. "I like your new beard."

I swear she was hitting on me. Then, her eyes shifted to Willow. "And who might your stunning companion be?"

I introduced her to Willow. *My friend.* With as few words as possible.

"Lovely to meet you, my dear." She snagged a canapé from a passing waiter and stuffed it into her mouth before returning her attention to me. "Oh, by the way, Ryan, did you hear the news about Charlotte Vanowen?"

My blood froze. "No."

"Rumor has it she was put in the loony bin. I'm positive that's the reason her poor parents aren't here tonight."

"That's a shame," I muttered, wanting to get off the subject of Charlotte. Especially in front of Willow. Fortunately, the gossip-hound excused herself just in time to chase after a waiter who was serving champagne.

"Are your mother's friends all like that?" Willow asked.

I laughed. "Yeah, they're all peas from the same pod. Welcome to my world." I caught myself. "Rather her world."

My Willow rolled her eyes before they roamed the room full of bejeweled women in designer cocktail gowns and dapper sixty-something men in expensive dark tailored suits and ties. Then, her gaze landed on something, not someone, of interest.

"Oh my God, is that what I think it is?"

My gaze followed hers. Her eyes fixed on the original Degas ballerina oil that hung above the baby grand piano. The very painting that had mesmerized my impressionist-loving Allee. Why should I be surprised? Willow was a ballet dancer. The painting would grab her attention. I trailed her as she waltzed in its direction.

Standing behind her, my arms folded over her shoulders, I told her it was indeed an original Degas. My mother's favorite painting. Something she'd bought herself at an auction many years ago. She'd paid one hundred thousand dollars for it in 1980. God only knew what it was worth today.

"Well, hello, darling!" came a familiar breathy voice, cutting me short.

I spun around along with Willow. It was none other than my whippet-thin mother, holding an almost drained glass of champagne. As stunning as ever in a vermillion silk sheath, her collection of dazzling diamonds adorning her ears, neck, and hands. Beside her was my silver-haired father in his wheelchair, looking thin and frail in one of his custom-made suits, and with him, his caretaker—our former housekeeper, Maria. Maria's dark eyes brightened at the sight of me. I adored this big-hearted woman, who had literally raised me. The few grays interspersed through her jet-black hair were the only clue that she was now in her early seventies. Her toffee-colored skin was still as smooth as velvet. Not a line was etched in her face—no easy feat, having worked for my demanding parents for close to four decades. About to give her a hug, I held it back as my mother gave me her customary double-cheeked kiss.

"So glad you could come," she crooned, already giving Willow the once-over. My arm stayed wrapped around her as I introduced her to my parents.

My mother took another sip of her champagne and hiccupped. "Oh, so you're named for a tree?"

Inside, I was cringing, but Willow held her own. "Yes, actually, I am. A very special weeping willow."

At the memory of that indeed very special tree on her grandmother's property, I relaxed a little, even becoming aroused. My dick stiffened beneath the fabric of my suit.

"And, dear, what might your last name be?" My mother, the society doyenne, paid special attention to lineage.

"Rosenthal," Willow spouted proudly.

My mother's brows lifted. "Oh, like in Rosenthal China?"

Willow flashed a confidant smile. "Yes, like in the china."

I smiled too. So did Maria. Score one for Willow. She knew how to play this connect the dots game. Better yet, she knew how to cheat it.

My mother continued to study her. "You look very familiar to me, my dear. Have we met before? Or perhaps you've served on one of my boards?"

Before my Willow could respond, my father opened his mouth. The words took a while to form.

"You're Jeeeew…ish?" he slurred.

Mortification raced through me. Duffy was right. My bigoted father, who despised blacks, Jews, LGBTs, the homeless, and probably every person in this world who didn't descend from someone who had stepped off the Mayflower, held Willow in his vulturous eyes. They roamed up and down her sexy, lithe body, and for once, I was glad he was confined to a wheelchair and likely impotent. He deserved his fate.

Willow had read my book. We had discussed my parents before coming here. Her knowledge served her well.

With an air of confidence, she responded. "Yes, Mr. Madewell. I'd say I'm 'ish.' So nice to meet you." She extended her hand. Slowly, my father extended his good one. Okay, progress.

Sparing us from further conversation, one of the help rang a bell. The ping resounded in my ears as my mother made an announcement.

"Everyone, please welcome our guest of honor…"

As he strode into the living room, I heard Willow gasp, "Oh my God."

I turned to face her. Her complexion had turned ashen. Then, her hand grew cold in mine as my applauding mother tapped her champagne flute. Her voice boomed.

"Mister…"

TWENTY-SEVEN

Willow

"…Gustave Fontaine."

At the very mention of his name, I felt all the blood in my body drain and all the air leave my lungs.

It had been over six grueling months of recovery. I'd given him everything, all of me, but he had fucked me, literally and figuratively, shattering my heart, ego, and soul into a million pieces. Still holding Ryan's hand, I looked for a place to hide. But it was too late. Ryan's mother ushered him into the room and his eagle-like eyes made contact with mine. All eyes were on the dashing impresario with the shiny black cane as they headed our way.

"Ryan, can we leave?" I spit out the words.

"Willow, what's the matter?"

"I just want to leave."

"Do you feel sick?"

"Yes." Sick to my stomach. I felt like I might puke.

"Okay. Just let me say goodbye to my mother and a quick hello to her guest and we can split."

Too late. Oh God, no! There was no avoiding him.

No escape. Every nerve in my body on edge and my stomach a giant knot, I kept my head down as Ryan planted his hand on my lower back and ushered me toward the man I dreaded seeing again. His mother was beaming.

"Ryan, darling, I'd like you to meet, Gustave Fontaine. He's the artistic director of the ballet company for which I'm hosting a fundraiser tomorrow night at Lincoln Center."

"Nice to meet you." Ryan shook Gustave's hand as his mother's focus shifted to me.

"And this is my son's new girlfriend…Willow."

Gustave's hand took mine and lifted it to his smirking lips. My spine tensed like a tightrope as they touched down on my flesh.

"How sublime to see you, my *petite oiseau*." Pronounced *wha-zoh,* the word was French for bird. It was Gustave's pet name for me because when I leaped it was like I was flying.

His eyes narrowing, Ryan cocked his head. I could feel tension radiating off his body. "You two know each other?"

Gustave fired him a dirty look. "Miss Rose *was* one of the lead dancers of my ballet company. A rising star."

"Miss Rose?" The expression on Ryan's face told me he was putting two and two together. "And the name of your company would be…"

Oh, God!

"The Royal Latvia Ballet."

Ryan's jaw dropped to the floor, but before he could utter a word, his tipsy mother chimed in.

"Ah! Willow Rose! Of course! I knew you looked familiar. Darling, I'm sure I've seen you dance in Europe."

"I-I don't perform anymore," I stuttered, Gustave's presence suffocating me.

"It is such a pity. I have been trying to woo her back." He eyed me lasciviously, leering at the ballerina neckline of my little black dress.

Beads of sweat were clustering behind my knees and nausea was rising in my chest like a tempest. Gustave was getting to me. Already casting a wicked spell. I needed to get to a bathroom quickly.

"Excuse me, but I need to use the restroom." I was thankful that only words spilled out of my mouth.

"Willow, there's one down the hall." Ryan's concerned voice drifted into my ears as I dashed out of the packed living room, hoping to find a bathroom quickly in this sprawling apartment. Thankfully, I came upon one just in time. I raced inside and falling to my knees, I lifted up the toilet seat. Holding back both my long braid and Ryan's dangling pendant necklace, I wretched until there was nothing more I could throw up. My knees weak, I stood up and staggered to the sink, glimpsing myself in the mirror. I looked wretched, nothing like the glamorous woman who had arrived here only minutes ago. Turning on the faucet, I rinsed my mouth and then splashed cold water on my face, not caring if I washed off my makeup. How many times had he done this to me? That was his power. His invincible super power. To make me fall apart. Make me undone. Haphazardly twisting my braid into a bun, I made my way to the door on my Jell-O-like legs. Cranking it open, I got another surprise.

Mira Abramovitch. Or should I say Abramobitch, which is what the other dancers called her. My archrival. The girl who coveted every part I got and did her best to sabotage me. We'd competed against each other since we were in pre-school. Or more precisely, she'd competed against me. With the support of her wealthy, power-driven mother, who was set on her daughter becoming the world's foremost ballerina.

I literally froze, ready to puke again.

She was skinnier, blonder, and more intimidating than ever. Her platinum hair was tied back in a tight chignon and glittering diamonds dotted her ears. Her bony hands were splayed on her hips, which jutted from her body-hugging fuchsia dress. Every muscle and bone protruded. It was no secret in the ballet world that she was a major bulimic. Rumor had it she used laxatives to purge and could stick a finger down her throat deeper than a dick.

If she was surprised to see me, she didn't show it. Her predatory cat-green eyes met mine. A slow poisonous smile snaked across her face as she gave me the once over.

"Hello, cow."

Cow? Yes, recovered from my breakdown, I was at last back to a healthy weight, thanks to my therapy, nurturing father, and Ryan. But by most standards, I was still as thin as a rail.

"Moooooo!" she snickered.

Anger rising in me like bile, I tried to brush past her, but she blocked the door with her outstretched sinewy arms. I was too weak to jostle her.

"Hey, bovine, you look like you're ready for the slaughter house," she snipped.

"Please...I need to go," I rasped, my throat raw from vomiting.

"No bitch," she barked back. "You *need* to know I'm Gustave's girl now. He's cast me in the lead of *The Firebird. I'll* be performing it tomorrow night."

The part I always wanted to play. The role I was born to play. The role for which I'd endured tendinitis, shin splints, blisters, sprains, and sleepless nights. And last but not least, Gustave's wrath and passion. In one desperate heartbeat, I yearned to be a ballerina again. Gustave's ballerina. Gustave's puppet. Gustave's Firebird.

Another wave of nausea rolled through my chest as Mira continued to block the doorway.

"And by the way, *I* fuck him now. He's amazing."

My jaw dropped. I couldn't stop myself. On my next breath, a stream of vomit flew out of my mouth, landing all over Mira.

"Oh my fucking God!" she screeched, looking down at the damage I'd done. My puke was all over her bony chest and the bodice of her dress.

Still shrieking and cursing, she let go of the door-frame and dashed to the sink. Seeing my window of opportunity, I fled.

TWENTY-EIGHT

Ryan

My hand still reeling from his intense handshake, I studied him. Though I hadn't written a book in over four years, that's what writers did.

Gustave Fontaine.

Though several inches shorter than me at perhaps five ten, the man projected power and exuded sex. He was lean and swarthy, with a headful of unruly black hair and a dark layer of stubble dusting his face. His lips were full, his nose carved like a Greek statue's, and his eyes the color of steel, razor sharp beneath his dense brows. Dressed in a sleek, obviously expensive black suit that showcased his muscular build and a black high-collar shirt, he reminded me of a sleek black panther ready to strike. A mixture of madness and animal magnetism flickered in his irises as he tapped the shiny black cane he was holding. A tense silence filled the air between us. His gaze held me fiercely, and I'm sure he was likewise sizing me up. Without warning, he broke the ice.

"So, you fuck her."

A statement, not a question. I was taken aback. That sure wasn't something I was expecting from some asshole I knew for less than five minutes.

"Excuse me?"

He stabbed the tip of his cane into my shin. "You heard me. You fuck Willow?"

The indignity of him! Rage surged inside me like mercury. I could feel my blood heating.

"None of your fucking business."

A smirk crawled across his lips. As if I'd given him his answer.

"Do you give it to her hard? The way she likes it."

As his words whirled around in my head, he poked my shin again with his cane. "Do you fuck her in the ass? Slap it a few times to make it rosy pink? Bite her nipples until she whimpers? Pull out of her until she's begging you for more?"

Ready to explode, I clenched my fists by my sides so I wouldn't strangle him or punch him out. The last thing I needed was to get into some bloody fistfight with my mother's guest of honor in front of all her society friends.

"Excuse me, I need to find *my* girlfriend," I gritted out, putting special emphasis on the possessive adjective.

To my surprise, he laughed. "I'm surprised Willow is even attracted to someone as ordinary and vanilla as you."

Willow was all sweetness. A deliciously sensuous

fuck. What didn't I know about her? How could she ever be with a dick like this?

"She should be on the stage dancing, not wasting her time with some pedestrian prick. She's made for greatness. And for fucking greatness. She'll never stay with you. Never!"

Clenching my teeth, I saw Willow heading our way. She looked wan and disheveled, and her steps were unsteady. I wrapped a protective arm around her as she met me.

"Ryan, I want to go home."

Gustave held her hostage in his steely eyes. "Willow, *I* am your home. The ballet is where you belong."

I swear he had a hypnotic effect on her. Her eyes glazed, she swayed a little on her feet.

"C'mon, baby, let's go. I'll just say goodbye to my mother and I'll take you home."

About to whisk a dazed Willow away, a pencil thin but stunning blond woman intercepted us. A horrific smell permeated the air around her. Her catty eyes narrowed at my girl.

"Fuck you, Willow Rosenthal. You're going to pay for what you did to me."

Gustave wrapped an arm around the irate woman. "Calm down, my princess." Then, he focused his fierce gaze on us. "Perhaps, we'll see the two of you tomorrow night."

My nostrils flared and my muscles clenched. After Charlotte, Gustave Fontaine was the last person on earth I ever wanted to see again.

TWENTY-NINE

Ryan

It was Friday nights like this that I wished I still had my driver, Marcus. It was fucking raining, and everyone and their mother was hailing a cab.

Shortly after Allee's death, his daughter, the result of an affair in his special ops days, gave birth to a son. It was Marcus's first grandchild, and he wanted to be with them. When he asked for vacation time, I told him he should move to Michigan where they lived. Though my longtime driver and friend was one of my lifesavers during my darkest days, it was time for him to retire and take the hefty retirement package my family had put away for him. Reluctantly, he gave in, but we agreed to stay in touch, with me promising to visit him one day.

After a fifteen-minute wait, the doorman on duty finally got us a cab. In the backseat, I held Willow close to me. Her head resting on my beating heart, I stroked her hair as the cab wove in and out of the insane traffic heading downtown. It would likely take close to an hour to get to my loft if the traffic kept up. A ton of questions were burning on my tongue, but I asked her only one.

"Are you feeling better?"

"A little."

"Are you coming down with something?"

"No."

And then I got daring. "Does it have something to do with that asshole?"

She squirmed against me. "Please, Ryan. I don't want to talk about Gustave."

My heart squeezed. There was something between them, but she was shutting me out. Silence fell upon us as the cab hit Forty-Second Street and continued downtown.

Forty-five minutes later, we reached my loft. As I reached for my money clip to pay the cabbie, Willow lifted her head off my chest and scooted away from me.

"Ryan, I'm going to sleep at my place tonight."

"Why?" I challenged, my tone sharp.

"I need to be alone."

And dream about him? "Fine. I'll have the driver take you there."

"No, you can just get out here."

"No fucking way. I need to know you get home safely." Yeah, I was a gentleman, but this had more to do with me being a worrier. Allee's short life had turned me into one. Plus, there was more than Willow's well-being clawing at my mind.

"No, Ryan, please. I'll be fine. Let's just call it a

night."

Yeah, a fucked-up night. Reluctantly, I gave in and paid the cabbie enough to take Willow home. Opening the passenger door, I told him to watch after her and make sure she got inside her place safely. With the generous tip I'd included, he promised he would. Stepping onto the curb, I watched the vehicle head down the glistening wet street and turn the corner, disappearing out of sight.

The relentless rain beating down on me, I hurried to my loft and kicked the massive elevator door before entering the security code. Dammit, I shouldn't have let her go home. We needed to talk. I could tell she was still attracted to that arrogant asshat. He had a sexual power over her. A magnetic pull. It was so fucking obvious. Like acid rain, a toxic mix of jealousy and rage seared every cell of my body.

Furious with myself and soaked to the bone, I pounded the corroded metal with my fist just before the door opened. As the lift ascended, my heart descended to the pit of my stomach. I'd learned a lot about Willow Rosenthal tonight. Professionally known as Willow Rose, she was a rising ballerina, who had some kind of kinky affair with her prick of a headmaster, which had ultimately derailed her career. I wanted to know what had gone down between them. Tomorrow, I was going to Google both Willow and the fucker and find out everything there was to know about them. There was still a part of me that was an investigative journalist.

Tonight, however, I was going to drown my sorrows with some whiskey. I was going to get drunk and hope that I wouldn't leave my place to pick up a late night sandwich at Mel's Famous. Willow needed her space, and I needed mine.

THIRTY
Willow

The cab let me off in front of my father's deli. With the rain, I dashed inside. Not yet nine o'clock, it was still open and would remain so until midnight. It was a favorite hangout for the downtown after hours hipster set. While my father used to stay until it closed when I was younger, he no longer did, letting the business run smoothly in the capable hands of his loyal staff.

Usually when I was out late, I hung out a bit with the gang and grabbed a late night snack. But not tonight. I was drenched and chilled from the rain, and still shaken from my encounter with Gustave. Making excuses that I was tired, I headed to the back stairs. Taking off my wet shoes, I quietly crept up the steps, hoping not to wake up my father who might be sleeping.

When I got to my room, I immediately stripped off my soaked coat and then the rest of my clothes. Skipping a hot shower, I slipped into my bed, stark naked, and still shivering, snuggled under the covers.

Turning off the light, I glimpsed Ryan's book, which was still on my nightstand. Usually I read a few passages, sometimes even chapters, before I went to sleep, but tonight I couldn't focus. Seeing Gustave had made my heart, mind, and body unravel. Physically and emotionally torn me apart. And damn Mira had only added to my misery. Poor Ryan had no clue.

I closed my heavy eyes, hoping sleep would claim me. But that was wishful thinking. Tossing and turning, I couldn't get my encounter with Gustave out of my mind. Memories of my life as a ballerina swirled around in my head. Heated my skin like a fever. Consumed my being like a plague. Drenched with sweat, my heart beating in a frenzy, I threw off the covers and hopped out of bed. Turning the light back on, I darted over to the one bag I'd never unpacked. The one bag whose contents I couldn't bare to look at until now. I threw it onto my bed and then with my shaking hand unzipped it. The grating sound of the zipper sent a rush of goosebumps to my flesh and I could hear my pulse thrumming in my ears. Hastily, piece by piece, I removed the contents and laid them out on the bed.

My black leotard.

My pink tights.

The roll of tape.

The toe pads.

And lastly, my peach satin pointe shoes.

Sitting down on the bed, I began the familiar ritual.

I taped my toes.

I slid on my tights over my legs and then slipped on the leotard.

I stuffed my shoes with the gel pads.

And then I coddled my square-toed shoes in my hands, as if they were a rare treasure, relishing the feel of the smooth satin and their elegant form. The shimmering ribbons slivered over my fingers like streamers. Every cell in my body fluttered. It had been a long time. Too, too long.

One by one, I slid them on my feet and wrapped the ribbons around my ankles. Rather than feeling alien to me, they felt so natural, like I was born wearing them. Like I'd never taken them off. And my tights and leotard fit like a second skin. With my heart in my throat, I stood up on my toes and bourréd my way over to my full-length mirror. At the sight of myself with my messy bun and long, sinewy legs, I let out a gasp. Yes, I was a little fuller, but that was me, the *real* me, standing before the glass. Involuntarily, I rubbed the sparkly ballet shoes charm hanging around my neck. Then, I smiled at my reflection, and my reflection smiled back at me.

Lowering myself to my heels, I grabbed the water bottle off my nightstand and with the turned-out gait of a dancer, I headed back downstairs, this time to the basement.

The brick building, which housed both the deli and our apartment, was built in the thirties, a time when city dwellings were built with basements. Originally, my father used it solely for storage, but when I took up dancing, he divided the large space into two rooms—one still for storage and the other he turned into a dance studio where I could practice. I hadn't been down there since I'd come home. Not even with Violet. It held too many memories for me. But now, I was ready. In fact, as I descended the rickety stairs, it was if a magnetic force was pulling me to it.

The studio was exactly as I remembered it. Shiny, blond hardwood floors, recessed lighting, and mirrored walls. Affixed to one of the walls was a barre, where I'd practiced countless times. In the corner was a small table. On top of it sat an old fashioned, needle drop stereo player that had once belonged to my mother. Under the table was a box of albums, all classical pieces that I'd danced to. Wasting no time, I pranced over to the table, and after setting my water on it, I crouched down and sorted through the albums. They were arranged alphabetically by composer. I knew exactly what I was looking for. Quickly, I found both the Liszt disc and the Stravinsky. Carefully, I slipped out the Liszt one and set it on the turntable. I turned the stereo on, then gently dropped the needle onto the first groove. *Liebestraum*—his famous *Love Dream.* As the melodic strains of the piano piece filled the room, I began to stretch my torso and limbs in every direction I could. After several minutes, I was already feeling warm and loose so I made my way to the barre and started my very methodical exercise routine: a combination of pliés, tendus, degagés, and frappés. Grasping the cool, smooth wood with my left hand, I performed the mandatory exercises at different speeds, focusing on nothing but my turnout, posture, lines, and movement. It was if I were in a hypnotic trance; ballet and the concentration it required did that to you. From time to time, I glimpsed myself in the mirrors to check my form. As the piano piece ended, I concluded my workout with a grand battement, surprised by how limber I still was and how high I could kick up my leg.

Stretching my legs on the barre, I was warmed up and ready. Taking a break, I returned to the table. After taking a sip of the water, I lowered the Stravinsky album onto the turntable and dropped the needle to the center of the disc. The dance of *The Firebird*— the part where the Firebird takes center stage and performs a solo. I quickly moved to the center of the studio, and at the sound of the first familiar chord, my heart leapt into my throat. I swallowed hard. While I hadn't danced to this piece in months, I knew every move like I was born dancing it. Every nerve in my body buzzed with excitement as if I were about to dance in front of The Queen.

My nerves calmed with the pitter-patter of my pointe shoes as I glided across the wood floor, working my feet and arms. Every step was like a word, communicating my feelings and emotions. Transforming me into the magical bird, who was both a curse and a blessing. Much like Gustave.

As I performed the intricate dance, I felt Gustave's presence. His hawk-eyes scrutinizing me, his ubiquitous cane tapping against the floor like a metronome. The cane that would come crashing down on the barre if I failed him, filling my eyes with tears of disappointment and frustration.

"You need to shimmer more," I heard him bark in my head as I threw my head back and smoothed my imaginary feathers.

"Work harder."

"Faster!"

"More emotion!"

Oh, how I wanted to please him! Such burning desire! As the electrifying music played, every move fell gracefully into place. My arms fluttered like a bird's wings, and with every leap, I felt like I was flying. I lost sense of time and space. Right now, I was The Firebird. I owned The Firebird and it owned me.

Suddenly, a husky familiar voice broke into my mindset.

"Willow?"

Coming down from a sauté, I landed on my feet and pirouetted around. It was my father, wearing his pajamas and a robe.

"Pop!" My voice registered shock and surprise. As much as I loved him, he was the last person I wanted to see right now. Though he didn't know the extent of the damage, he knew that ballet had been a destructive force in my life. He didn't make it a secret that he never wanted me to return to that world.

"What are you doing down here?" I asked, my heartbeat slowing down.

"I heard some music playing. I thought maybe I'd left the TV on. What are you doing down here?"

"Dancing. I couldn't sleep." I kept things as simple as possible, not wanting to create a conversation that would stress him out or raise eyebrows.

To my relief, my father didn't question me further. "It's late, pumpkin. You should go back to bed."

I twitched a small smile to placate him. "Okay, Pop. I'll be right up."

He nodded. "I'll see you in the morning."

"Night, Pop."

And with that, he lumbered out of the studio. The music still playing, I could hear him thudding up the stairs. He still wasn't in good shape and that worried me.

A few minutes later, I was back in my room. Untying them, I slipped off my pointe shoes and next peeled off my damp tights and leotard. I put them all back neatly in my ballet bag and then put on my PJs. Hopping into bed, I removed the tape from my toes and massaged my aching feet. My eyes jumped from a photo of six-year-old me performing in a lilac tutu to the cover of Ryan's book.

Undying Love… Was ballet *my* undying love? Dancing had awoken me. I felt more alive than I had in months. Enervated. Yet, at the same time, I felt more conflicted. My chest constricted as a torrent of emotions whooshed around inside me. My eyes stayed on Ryan Madewell's beautiful face. My heart was torn. I wasn't sure if I belonged to him, but I knew I belonged to dance. Was I ready to return? Should I? Would Gustave take me back? And if he did, would that be the best decision of my life or the biggest mistake?

Overcome with anxiety, I clutched my little plush monkey, Baboo, and gazed at the ceiling. Thank goodness, I was seeing Dr. Goodman on Monday. Maybe he could help me figure things out. With so many unanswered questions bombarding my mind, it was a miracle sleep claimed me. I was dancing in my dreams.

THIRTY-ONE

Willow

Pop wasn't feeling well the next morning and I urged him to stay in bed. Trudging down to the basement last night and then back up two flights of stairs to our apartment must have taken a toll on him. I felt guilty that I'd woken him up. Despite a protest, he agreed to rest upstairs while I minded the store with the help of his loyal crew.

As always, Saturday business was brisk. People came in early to pick up lox and bagels for Sunday morning brunch, and throughout the day, families frequented the restaurant for our special weekend lunch. I was playing hostess, taking care of the long line of regulars waiting to get seated.

Despite how busy I was, I couldn't get last night out of my mind. My encounter with Gustave haunted me as much as my need to dance. I couldn't get *The Firebird* music out of my head. It was in my bloodstream, in my bones, and in every cell of my being. And in my heart and in my soul. Breathing and reliving it. While I plastered a smile on my face as I greeted customers, inside my guts were twisting. And that wasn't the only thing that had my stomach in knots.

It was late afternoon, and I hadn't heard from Ryan. Admittedly, last night ended badly. To be honest, it was a disaster. I owed him an explanation. I had to let him know how my unexpected encounter with Gustave affected me and assure him that there was nothing between us. That my heart belonged only to one man—to him. Ryan Madewell. With business calming down a little until the dinner crowd came in, I decided to call him. No answer. It went straight to his voicemail. Rather than leaving a message, I ended the call and texted him instead.

Are you okay? I need to see you. xo

As I typed the letters, a chill swept over me. Maybe he didn't want to see me anymore. That whatever we had was over. Then, my back to the front door, a familiar tap, tap, tap, tap resounded in my ears, each tap getting closer and louder.

"*Oiseau...*"

Almost dropping my cell phone, I whipped around. Gustave! My mouth formed an "O" and my eyes widened. He was wearing pleated black wool slacks, a tight black pullover, and expensive black leather loafers with no socks—his uniform. The one he always wore at practices and rehearsals. The manic look in his eyes frightened me and I inwardly shuddered.

"G-Gustave. What are you doing here?"

Without warning, he pulled me into him, squeezing

my shoulders. His hot breath licked my cheeks like flames. "I need you back…"

"Gustave, let go of me." He tightened his grip, relentless desire darkening his eyes.

"I need you to dance."

Oh, God. He wanted me back. My heart hammering, I turned my face away from him. With a pinch of my jaw, he jerked my head forward.

"P-please, Gustave. I'm not sure. I don't know if I'm ready. I need more time."

His fiery gaze burnt a hole in mine, holding me captive. "There is no time. I need you to dance for me…tonight at Lincoln Center."

"What do you mean?"

"Mira sprained her ankle during the rehearsal. She can't perform."

"W-what about Frederica or Odette?"

"Frederica is playing the part of the lead princess." Then, he snorted. "And Odette dances like a pathetic sparrow."

My emotions in a whirlwind, I didn't know what to say. I chewed my lip. I was torn, fractured. Part of me wanted to scream out yes while the other part of me wanted to run as far away as possible. The push and pull was excruciating.

He gripped me tighter; his gaze grew fiercer. "Only you, my *petite oiseau*, can dance the part. Only you can be The Firebird."

He impatiently tapped his cane, the taps synchronizing with my rapid heartbeats. *Tap. Tap. Tap. Tap. Tap.* I stood as still as a statue, paralyzed, afraid to move or say a word. My heartbeat accelerated as he moved in closer to me, his lips a breath away.

"Willow, you must do it for me. The company is facing bankruptcy. Hundreds of thousands of dollars in funding are contingent on tonight's performance. It's the only thing that will save us. I shall not leave until you say yes."

And then, he began to nibble my neck. His wet kisses sent a shiver down my spine.

My muscles clenching, I squeezed my eyes shut. "Please, Gustave. Don't taunt me like this."

He ignored my plea. He flicked the area behind my ear before sucking the lobe.

"You belong on the stage, my *oiseau,* not here."

"Please, Gustave. Let me think about it." Maybe I could reason with him, though any form of rational thinking was flying out the door. Fiddling with the ballet slipper charm around my neck, I felt myself giving in to the magical power Gustave had over me. Submitting to him. What I'd always done.

"There is no time to think about it." Anger rose in his voice. "I am giving you the opportunity of a lifetime. To dance in front of New York's elite. Tomorrow morning, you will wake up and you will be a star. *My* star. Pack your bag and grab a gown. My driver is waiting for us."

I didn't move.

He leaned into me. "Will this convince you?"

I quickly jerked my head away, avoiding a kiss. "Don't do that, Gustave." I swallowed a deep breath. I'd made up my mind.

He eyed me lustfully. "I shall not take no for an answer."

"I will dance tonight. Not for you, but for the company."

Five minutes later, I met Gustave back in the restaurant, my dance bag with my necessities slung over my shoulder and a garment bag with a cocktail dress and heels folded over my arm. With a victorious smirk, he snatched my free arm, hooking his through mine, and whisked me to the front door. On the way out, I told my father's staff that I'd be back later, not telling them where I was going or what I was doing. They looked at me quizzically as I asked them to tell my father that I'd call him later. I didn't want my father to know what I was up to. It would upset him. Worse, kill him.

A shudder shimmied through me. I was having second thoughts, but I told myself it was just a one-night thing. A good thing. Fingers crossed I could help save The Royal Latvia Ballet from going under. Save the careers of the dancers who had become my family. Well, except for one. Fucking Mira.

With these positive thoughts in my head, Gustave swung open the front door. I stopped dead in my tracks. A gorgeous man, dressed in jeans and a leather jacket, stood before me.

"Ryan!" I gasped, my eyes wide.

His eyes, as wide as mine, ping-ponged from me to Gustave and then back me. "Willow, where the hell are you going?"

"I-I'm…"

Gustave finished my sentence. "She's going with me."

"What!?" A cloud of shock, rage, and confusion fell over Ryan. With my heart in my throat, I watched as Gustave shoved him out of the way.

"Get your fucking hands off me!" Ryan snapped.

"Then get lost, peon. Willow's going where she belongs. On the stage."

"What!?" Ryan repeated.

My heart stuttering, I filled him in. "Ryan, Gustave has an emergency. His lead dancer injured herself, and he needs me to fill in at tonight's performance of *The Firebird* at Lincoln Center."

As Ryan processed my words, Gustave, to my horror, whacked Ryan's shin with his cane.

"Jesus Christ," he cried out in pain.

"Oh my God, Ryan! Are you okay?"

Grimacing, he bent down to rub his sore leg, but before I could join him, Gustave grabbed my elbow.

"Gustave, what are you doing?"

"Let's go. We cannot waste time."

On my next heartbeat, he hauled me away to the waiting limousine and shoved me inside. Looking out the tinted window, I watched as Ryan hobbled to the car, trying desperately to yank open the locked passenger door. Tears burned my eyes as a sharp pang of guilt shot through me.

"Fuck," Ryan shouted, still clinging to the door as we pulled off the curb. "Open up, Willow. Don't go."

It was too late. On my next painful breath, the limo sped off and we were heading uptown.

THIRTY-TWO

Willow

Everything happened so quickly. It was like life had whooshed by. One minute I was playing the role of the hostess at my father's deli, the next I was about to play the role of The Firebird at Lincoln Center.

While I'd never been backstage at Lincoln Center, the renowned arts complex where every dancer dreamed of performing, it was not much different than the others I'd hung out in. In the hallways, already costumed and made-up dancers were stretching and practicing their moves. Many stopped when they saw me and ran up to me to give me a hug. I was overwhelmed by their warm reception, several saying how much they missed me and how good it was to have me back. Gustave, however, didn't give me any time to enjoy my welcome back.

"Allez!" he snapped at my fellow dancers as he whisked me away. "There is no time. The performance starts in less than one hour."

At his command, the dancers scuttled off like mice. A few moments later, I was seated in the dressing room in front of a wall-length lit up mirror. Scattered across the long counter were tubs of eyeshadow, blush, and powder, tubes of lipstick and mascara, hairbrushes, lash curlers, bobby pins, and elastics. The remains of the other dancers who were here before me. Not many outsiders knew that ballerinas did their own hair and makeup. Even the greatest ones. It was our job to make ourselves beautiful.

I stared at my makeupless face in the mirror, meeting the reflection of Gustave, who was standing behind me.

"*Oiseau*, I want you to shimmer tonight," he purred. "Make sure you put glitter on your eyes and dust your skin with the sparkling powder."

Gustave knew exactly how he wanted his ballerinas to look. Perfect for him. He then raked his fingers though my unruly hair.

"And make sure you gather this despicable mess into a tidy bun. Not a hair out of place." Gustave was obsessed with hair. Or rather the absence of it—except for a solid little knot at the top of our heads or at the nape of our necks.

"You must hurry. The performance starts in forty-five minutes. Now, I shall leave you alone and get myself ready."

My brows shot up as I processed his words. "You're performing?" He'd choreographed *The Firebird* and rehearsed it with me countless times, but I'd never gotten to perform the ballet on stage with him. That fateful night in Vienna—the night I collapsed—had made that dream an impossibility.

A slow, smug smile met my surprised look in the mirror. "Yes, my *petite oiseau*. Tonight *I* am playing the part of Prince Ivan and at last you shall be *my* Firebird."

A shiver skittered through me. Every nerve in my body buzzed with trepidation.

"Don't we need to rehearse?"

"There is no time. I believe in you, my *oiseau*. Trust yourself to light up the stage and trust me to make you shine. I shall be your magic feather."

Again, he met my gaze in the mirror. His one of smoldering self-assuredness, mine one of crippling anxiety. A smirk crossed his lips.

"Just look beautiful for me, my *oiseau*." And with that he was gone.

My heart hammering, I began to put on my makeup, the familiar ritual coming back to me quickly. It was actually calming because I had to focus on getting every detail right. Finally, after applying the fire-red lipstick, I worked on my hair, pulling it back into a tight chignon that hit the nape of my neck with the help of a hair elastic and several bobby pins. I smoothed the top of my scalp, making sure every hair was in place. Then, I stared at my reflection.

I literally gasped. I almost didn't recognize myself with my glitter-lined, long-lashed eyes, full bright-red lips, and my hair tightly pulled back off my face. Still gazing into the mirror, I heard the dressing room door open … then a *tap, tap, tap, tap*. Gustave? Was he here to check on me? Craning my head to see who it was, I was in for a surprise.

"What the fuck are you doing in my spot, you bitch?"

Mira! Wearing some kind of fur coat, she hobbled in my direction with the help of crutches. Her right foot was taped up with an Ace Bandage.

"How's your foot?" I stammered.

"Why would you give a shit? Answer my question. What are you doing here?"

"I'm filling in for you. Gustave asked me to dance the part of The Firebird."

The expression on her face turned livid. "What!? That's impossible!"

"Think again, my lovely." Another voice. Gustave! Loping my way, he was dressed in his costume—a pair of beige tights that exposed every bulging muscle of his powerful legs and that huge package between his thighs…a sparkly belted tunic that opened at the neckline to reveal his sculpted chest… and on his feet, a pair of soft leathery boots that were made for dancing. In a word, he looked formidable. Every bit the part of Prince Ivan.

"You look beautiful, my *oiseau*."

Mira's jaw dropped to the floor with disgust. "You call that fat ugly bitch beautiful?"

Gustave furrowed his thick brows. "My princess,

watch your mouth. In fact, I'm going to ask you to leave. Madame Kapinski will be here any minute to help Willow change into her costume."

"*Her* costume? That's *my* costume!! It was custom made for me. It'll never fit the fat pig!"

My mother had always told me, "Sticks and stones will break your bones, but names will never harm you." Usually my nemesis's insults stung despite my mom's words of wisdom, but somehow at this moment my mother's bold, courageous soul came alive in me. I stood up and squarely faced Mira.

"Mira, I'm sure it'll fit just fine." I held my head up high, narrowing my eyes at her. "It's *my* turn. Now, please get out of here."

Rage washed over her face. "Gustave, how can you let her talk to me like that?"

Gustave grew angry. "Mira, if you don't leave, I'm afraid I shall have to call security to escort you out."

She scrunched up her face. "Fine. But trust me, Gustave, you're going to be sorry."

"Is that a threat, Mira?"

"It's just a statement." Pivoting on her crutches, she glared at me, venom pouring from her eyes. "And you, fat cow, break a leg. And I really mean it."

A few minutes later, I was alone with Madame Kapinski. She was the company's longtime wardrobe mistress. She was of French-Russian descent and in her late fifties. We all adored her, including me. She was like a mother to all of us. I was overjoyed to see her and the feeling was mutual. We exchanged hugs.

"My little bird, how good you are back. We have all missed you."

"I've missed you too."

"You look wonderful. The sabbatical has done you well."

"Really?" I asked, Mira's cruel words circling my head.

"Mais oui! You look like a beautiful woman in love."

I felt myself blush. Indeed, I was. Playing with Ryan's ballet slipper charm, I smiled wistfully. If only he could see me dance.

Madame Kapinski noticed the pendant. "A gift from your lover?"

Heating, I nodded.

"He has beautiful taste. That *eez* the reason he chose you."

I smiled again, thinking again about Ryan.

"Unfortunately, you cannot wear it during the performance. Monsieur F. wants no distractions."

Reluctantly, I let Madame take the necklace off me. She promised she would personally watch over it and hand it back to me once the performance was over. That made me feel a little better as she slipped it into a pocket.

Five minutes later, I was in The Firebird costume. It fit me like a glove. A stretchy fire-red body suit with an attached skirt composed of red and gold tulle fragments resembling the plumage of a bird. The skirt also included one genuine feather—the magical feather I would give Prince Ivan in my first scene.

"I'll get my pointe shoes," I told Madame Kapinski, already heading to my ballet bag. Pulling out a pair, I sat down on a nearby chair and began to put them on.

"Stop, *ma chérie*," said Madame as I began to coil the pink ribbons of the right shoe around my ankle. "Monsieur F. *eez* insistent you wear only *zee* red shoes."

The red shoes? The memory of that tragic, eponymous movie—my first real date with Ryan—flashed into my head. I shuddered. Would this ballet be my undoing?

"Are you okay, *ma chérie*?" asked Madame, sensing my malaise.

My stomach knotting, I floundered for an answer. "I-I don't have red shoes." My eyes flitted to a pair hanging from a hook on the wall. Most likely Mira's. "Should I borrow Mira's?"

Madame Kapinski shook her head, frowning in deep in thought. "*Non, non, non*, that *eez* not possible. She wears a size smaller than you, and even *eef* you were *zee* same size, they would fit you differently."

She was right. It took days to break in new pointe shoes. Days that often took banging the shoes and stretching them until they molded your feet. Everyone's feet and needs were different. Panic gripped me. "Madame, what are we going to do?"

After furrowing her brows, her face suddenly brightened. "I have a crazy idea, but I think *eet* might work."

So close to showtime, I was all ears. "Madame, what do you have in mind?"

Five minutes later, we were both seated at her seamstress table, each of us frantically coloring my pink pointe shoes with king-size red Sharpies like preschoolers doing an arts and crafts project.

"*Eet eez* working!" beamed Madame as any trace of pink rapidly disappeared. Within ten minutes, a pair of bright red pointe shoes graced the table.

"What about the ribbons?" I asked Madame.

Smiling, she slid open a draw beneath the table and then held up a pair of long red satin ribbons. "*Voilà! Ma chérie*, you stretch while I sew them on."

Fifteen minutes later, I was loosened up and in the red pointe shoes.

"Come, *ma chérie*. The industrious woman smiled again. "We have one final thing to do."

Following her to the full-length mirror, I stood as still as a statue as she put on my magnificent headpiece. A gold sequined band with layers of spiky red tulle and gold-dipped feathers. Motionless, I stood before the mirror in a state of shock.

I was The Firebird.

And I was ready to dance.

THIRTY-THREE

Ryan

There was no way I was going to miss Willow dance. Let me rephrase: there was no way fucking way I was going to leave Willow alone with that douchebag, Gustave Fontaine. After recovering from my hangover earlier in the day, I'd Googled him. Everything I read about him set off an alarm.

The guy was more than a douche. Or a prick. Or an asshole. He was a monster. According to Wikipedia, he was born in Paris, the bastard child of a destitute prostitute. In his youth, he pimped for his mother, only to be physically abused by one of her lovers. After his mother died from syphilis, her best friend, a former ballerina, took him in, teaching him how do dance. A long story short, he was very talented and won a full scholarship to the Paris Opera Ballet School, one of the most prestigious dance academies in the world. Upon graduating, he joined the city's top ballet company. He had an affair with one of the principal dancers, but she accused of him of rape. Forcing her to have sex with him without consent. The dancer's enraged husband bashed Gustave's leg and pressed charges but ultimately dropped them on the condition Gustave leave the country. Agreeing to the deal, Gustave moved to Latvia...with a cane. That cane that became his signature, though he didn't really need it, as he formed his own company and conquered the dance world—one beautiful ballerina—and patron at a time. With his dashing looks and partying ways, he became the bad boy darling of the dance world. *L'enfant terrible*. He fucked, he snorted, he shot up. And he conquered.

Thank fucking God, I hadn't thrown out the tickets to the gala that my mother had sent me months ago. I just had to remember where the hell I'd put them. Madly, I scavenged my loft, tearing it apart until I found the envelope in a pile of unopened fundraiser invitations. Inside was the invite and two tickets—shit, it was black tie. Eschewing my mother's events, I hadn't worn my tux in years. In fact, not since my wedding to Allee. Fingers crossed it wasn't eaten by moths or in need of major dry cleaning.

Showered and groomed with a bath towel wrapped around my waist, I tore through my closet in search of my tux. I found it tucked away among a bunch of suits I hadn't worn in ages. It was neatly hung in a garment bag along with my tux shirt, bowtie, and dress shoes. I unzipped the bag. Everything looked to be in good shape. Fingers crossed the suit still fit me. Since the last time I wore it, I'd grown buffer and broader from working out.

Slipping off the towel, I laid the ensemble on my bed and decided to go commando. I hastily slipped on the suit, beginning with the pants. They fit, but I had to say they were a little tight in the crotch. Next, the shirt and jacket, then finally the bowtie. As I knotted the tie in front of my mirrored armoire, I studied myself. I looked good to go. Grabbing my overcoat, I hurried out of my loft. I had less than an hour to make it to Lincoln Center.

Damn the fricking Saturday night traffic. Why was everyone in the world going uptown? Even if I had my car, which was in the shop for a tune-up, I'd be fucked in the butt. Any kind of car service was booked until eight p.m., including Uber, and not one taxi that shot by was vacant. Fuck. According to the program, the ballet portion of the gala started at 7pm following cocktails at six. I didn't give a shit about the cocktails, but I didn't want to miss one second of Willow's performance. I wanted to be there for her. And selfishly, I wanted to be there for me.

Anxiously, I glanced down at my watch as another cab whooshed by me. It was six fifteen. I had less than forty-five minutes to get myself uptown. I weighed my options. I could run uptown. I was a runner, having run the New York marathon in excellent time. I did the calculations in my head. If I sprinted, averaging a six-minute mile, I could be at Lincoln Center in about twenty-five minutes. That's if I could do a six-minute mile. While I was fit, I wasn't in marathon shape, and I was wearing my dress shoes, which wouldn't help. It was cutting things too short. The subway? With the way I looked, I'd probably get mugged. I had no other choice...

Five minutes later, I was on my Harley racing up Broadway, weaving in and out of the insane traffic. The bike was my first major purchase after Allee's passing. Dr. Goodman said it symbolized a death wish on my part. Maybe it did. But when I took it on trips out of the city, zooming down the Jersey Turnpike or a deserted rural road at some hell-bent speed, the roar of the motor soothed my soul. Numbed my pain.

I hadn't ridden it since the summer. With time of the essence, thank God, it was running smoothly. Stupidly, I wasn't wearing a helmet. In my strung out state, I just didn't bother. Fingers crossed I'd make it to Lincoln Center alive. And in time. If people were looking at some out-of-his mind madman running lights and cursing at vehicles in his way, I had no clue and didn't give a flying fuck. Several times I almost struck pedestrians, and more than once, ignoring all traffic signals, a cab almost hit me. I deserved every angry honk and curse I heard, but they meant nothing to me.

At 6:45, I made it to Lincoln Center. I desperately needed to find a place to park. Zipping around the block two times, I finally found one ...a small space between two cars parked on Sixty-Third Street, but just big enough for my bike. I angled my Harley into it and jumped off. 6:55. I had five minutes to spare.

Lincoln Center was across the street. With all the muscle power I had, I sprinted across Columbus Avenue and raced up the ramp that led directly to the Koch Theater where the gala was taking place. A guard was standing outside the entrance.

"I'm here for the gala," I panted out.

The burly guard narrowed his eyes at me with suspicion. "The doors are closed. I was given strict instructions not to let anyone in after six forty-five."

Jesus fucking Christ. I glanced down at my watch again. 6:58. The ballet was starting in two minutes.

"But the ballet doesn't start until seven," I pleaded. "And I have a ticket." I pulled out the ticket from my breast pocket and showed it to him.

He glanced down at the ticket and then met my desperate gaze. "Sorry. No entry. Strict orders."

Fuck. Fuck. Fuck. What was I going to have to do to take him down? Much bigger than me, he looked like he was straight out of the World Wrestling Federation and could knock me out in a single blow. Time to rethink.

"My mother, Eleanor Madewell, is the Chairwoman of the event."

With his brawny arms folded across his broad chest, the built like a brick shit house guard looked at me stoically. "Sorry, no exceptions."

Frantically, I dug my cell phone out from my coat pocket and speed-dialed my mother. The phone rang three times and then went to her voicemail. Shit. She must have it turned off.

Regardless, I left a message, my voice rushed and panicked. "Mother, it's me. I'm here. Come to the entrance of the theater and let me in."

The staunch, macho guard rolled his eyes at me, and I could feel him silently laughing at me. *Ha, ha, what a mama's boy; he's calling Mommy.* Jesus, what was it going to take for him to let me in? I had only a minute to get to my seat. Then, like a pinging light bulb, it came to me. What it always takes…

I reached back into my pocket and pulled out my money clip. Thank fucking God I always carried a wad of cash with me. I yanked out a crisp one-hundred dollar bill and dangled it in front of the asshole.

"Will this do it?" I gritted.

His eyes lit up as he snagged the bill out of my hand.

Yes!

Expecting him to unlock the door, my stomach twisted as he stood staunchly in front me, not budging an inch. A sly smile slid across his face as he lifted his index and middle fingers, forming a V.

"Make it two."

Fucking greedy bastard. Without thinking twice, I tore out another hundred-dollar bill from the clip. Before I could hand it to him, the son of a bitch snatched it from me and then pocketed the two bills with a triumphant smirk in lieu of a thank you. My heart beating madly, he finally unlocked the entrance door. Brushing past him, I dashed inside, running straight to the doors to the theater. Fingers crossed I wouldn't be thwarted by another asshole guard. To my great relief, a young girl, who looked to be an usher, stood outside.

"Can I please see your ticket, sir?"

My heart still racing, I waved the ticket in her face. She snatched it and then scanned it.

"Excellent. You're in Row A, Seat 3 on the left side of the theater."

She handed me a program. Without waiting for her to open a door, I thanked her and let myself in. To loud cheers and applause, my mother was taking the stage. She looked stunning as always in a long black sequined sheath and her glittering diamonds. Breathlessly, I flew down the aisle to the very front row as she thanked the audience for supporting The Royal Latvia Ballet. More cheers and applause.

I swear the aisle felt like a fucking mile…maybe because I was still so wound up from my trip uptown. I finally got to the front row, where my father in his wheelchair was sitting in the aisle. There were two empty seats next to him…I assumed one for my mother and the other for me. My mother always saved me a seat even though I rarely attended her events. My father, looking debonair in his tux, gave me a puzzled look as it had been ages since I attended one of my mother's black tie affairs. Breathing out a "hi," I shrugged off my coat, and took my seat as my mother continued.

"I am very proud to present tonight's benefit per-formance of Stravinsky's *Firebird,* newly choreographed by the company's creative director, the one and only Gustave Fontaine. However, due to an injury earlier today, the part of The Firebird will be danced by Miss Willow Rose."

At the sound of her beautiful name, my chest tight-ened and my already fast pulse quickened.

"Now, sit back and enjoy tonight's performance and I'll see everyone afterward in the Promenade for more champagne and dinner."

Applause. Applause. Smiling, my mother sauntered off the stage as the lights dimmed and returned to her seat, sandwiched between my father and me.

"Why darling, what a wonderful surprise," she blurted as the curtain rose, revealing a whimsical forest-like backdrop.

"Hi, Mother," I mumbled, my eyes glued to the stage.

The music started up and then my eyes popped when a familiar but unexpected figure dashed onto the stage, launching into a series of dazzling sky-high jumps. The audience applauded madly. It was fucking Gustave. What the hell was he doing on the stage? I thought he was just the choreographer, not one of the leads. I quickly glanced down at my program and saw that the prick was playing the male lead, Prince Ivan. What the fuck? He was dancing with Willow!

THIRTY-FOUR

Willow

An announcement: "Due to an injury earlier today, the role of The Firebird will be danced by Miss Willow Rose."

At the mention of my name, every nerve in my body sparked. I almost had to pinch myself to make sure this wasn't a dream. But then, as the electrifying music started up and the curtain rose, I knew this was for real. I, Willow Rosenthal, was about to dance on stage at Lincoln Center in one of the most coveted roles ever created for a ballerina!

Stravinsky's *Firebird.* I knew it all too well. Standing all alone in the left wing, I watched as Gustave dashed onto the stage in the role of Prince Ivan. Holding a bow, he was lost in an enchanted forest as he hunted for a princess. Effortlessly, he spun and leaped to great bounds. His dancing was big and bold, unleashed by the freedom of having the stage to himself. My heart pitter-pattered. In a few minutes, it would be my turn to join him and take center stage.

And then my cue! My heart leapt to my throat as if

it was doing a sauté. With a steeling breath, I leaped onto the stage performing a series of grand battements while Gustave flew off it. I heard the audience's thunderous applause, but it was merely an accompaniment to the orchestral music that played in my ears. With each leap, my nervousness dissipated and within moments, I was the mythical bird flying high. The feeling was sublime! Otherworldly.

I continued with pirouettes, my arms fluttering like a bird's wings. *Shimmer!* I heard my master call out to me in my head. Then, a few minutes later, Gustave rejoined me on stage, chasing after me. Playing a game of cat and mouse, he finally caught me.

The firm touch of his hands splayed on my hips sent a shiver through me as his warm breath heated me. Not before long, we were doing a sensual pas de deux, Gustave, holding me by my waist, as I did arabesques and back bends, my arms still fluttering and all the while feeling his intense gaze on me. I began to relax, trusting him to make me shine. Then, he lifted me over his head as if I weighed nothing at all, and spun me. Rather than getting dizzy, I was getting high like I was on some kind of drug. And I knew it right then. Ballet was my drug. I needed to dance as much as I needed to breathe.

THIRTY-FIVE
Ryan

My eyes stayed glued on Gustave. Beneath his sparkling tunic, he was wearing tights that showcased every muscle of his powerful legs as well as muscles in his ass that I never knew existed. But what astonished me the most, making my eyes bug out, was the enormous bulge between his legs. Holy shit! I was endowed, but this bastard was packing a football inside his tights. And nuts the size of baseballs. And that was without an erection.

I swear to God I'd never been envious of other men's packages, but this fucker's was like none other I'd ever seen. He was hung like a horse. I could feel jealousy rearing its ugly head. I swear there was no fig leaf in the world that could cover it.

Then, dressed in a breathtaking red and gold costume, made of feathery layers of tulle, and a glittering headpiece with assorted plumes, Willow flew onto the stage, joining Gustave. I almost didn't recognize her. She was wearing a ton of makeup, her lips painted bright red, her long-lashed eyes thick with mascara, the lids coated in gold glitter that caught the bright lights, and her wild red hair pulled into a tight chignon that accentuated her high cheekbones and swan-like neck. She looked in a word: Exquisite. Fucking exquisite. Mesmerized, my eyes stayed on her as she began to dance circles around Gustave with a series of dazzling leaps and spins, fluttering her toned arms in a way that made them seem like the wings of a bird. With her grace, beauty, and agility, she was a sight to behold. The audience again broke into raucous applause and cheers as I battled with my heart to not leap onto the stage and steal her from the bastard.

The connection between Gustave and Willow was intense. Sitting in the front row, I could feel their heat radiating off one and other. Their sparks flying. I don't know if she saw me because her eyes were focused only on Gustave. Following his every move. In perfect sync. Entwining her body with his. Letting him lift her in the air and hold her as she extended her leg high, so high I didn't think it was humanly possible. Red-hot jealousy heated my bones. I felt myself turning the color of her feathers.

Before leaping off the stage, Willow plucked a feather from her ensemble and handed it to Gustave. A thank you for sparing her life. I impatiently watched the next part of the ballet where Prince Ivan encountered a bevy of princesses, under the spell of an evil sorcerer, and fell in love with one of them. I only wanted to watch *my* princess dance. When would she return to the

stage? My interest picked up when a horde of dancers
dressed up as fantastical fairytale-like monsters flew
onto the stage and attacked Prince Ivan. In my heart, I
wished they'd really destroyed the bastard, torn him to
shreds, but using his magical red feather, he summoned
The Firebird. And then, Willow leaped back on stage
and used her magical powers to put the monsters and
the evil sorcerer to sleep. What followed was an
incredible solo from Willow. I was in awe as she
danced center stage on her toe shoes to the compelling
music. Enraptured. So turned on by her shimmering
beauty and grace, my erection strained against my
pants. The audience so quiet you could hear a pin drop,
I squirmed in my seat to relieve my throbbing cock.
Again, I had to fight the urge to jump onto the stage and
claim her as mine.

Then, jealousy reclaimed me as Gustave returned to
the stage and they did their final pas de deux. The
chemistry between them palpable. The fire, all-
consuming. There was no doubt in my mind that they
were lovers. As the forty-five minute, one-act ballet
concluded with the audience rising to their feet with a
loud standing ovation, my blood curdled. Every muscle
in my body tensing, I forced myself to stand up and
clap my hands.

As the standing audience applauded and shouted
bravo over and over, the dancers took their bows. Next
to last was Gustave for whom the cheers grew louder—
I swear I wanted to throw something at him—and

finally my Willow, stepping forward with a sweeping curtsey that had the audience going wild. Ushers stepped on the stage to bestow her with extravagant bouquets of red roses. One after another. Fuck. I wish I had one to give her. Gustave took Willow's hand, and as they bowed together again, my heart sunk to the pit of my stomach. My cock sank, too, and ached as much as my heart.

I had just lost Willow Rosenthal to her first love. The ballet world owned her. She belonged to another. Gustave Fontaine.

THIRTY-SIX

Ryan

The dinner reception was taking place in the Promenade, the sprawling five-story mezzanine area of the theater overlooking the plaza's lit up fountains. The space looked spectacular. With her impeccable taste, my mother had transformed it into an homage to Stravinsky's ballet with candlelit tables draped in crimson velvet and adorned by centerpieces of tall vases holding exotic arrangements of long-stemmed red roses and gilded feathers. Classical music was piping into the hall.

My mother's elegantly dressed guests, who all seemed to know each other, were buzzing about the ballet as they made their way to their assigned tables.

"Wasn't she magnificent as The Firebird?" I overheard one matron gush.

"Absolutely divine," replied her friend.

"And what about him? Wasn't the chemistry between them so beyond?"

My blood was still simmering as I aimlessly wandered through the crowd. I had no idea where I was sitting or if I even had a seat.

Many of the ballet dancers, now out of their costumes, began to infiltrate the crowd. In the distance, I saw my mother, already holding a glass of champagne, mingling with both patrons and dancers. She was in her element. From the corner of my eye, I spotted my father already seated all by himself at their table in his wheelchair. He was nursing his favorite drink—an expensive Scotch—and he looked lonely. I actually felt sorry for him.

I wondered if there would be a seat for me at their table since I'd never RSVP'd to the event. And I wondered if that's where Gustave Fontaine would be sitting. With his prima ballerina…Willow. My chest tightened as my eyes darted from corner to corner in search of them. A torrent of emotions whirled around inside me. The truth is I was unsure how I would react when I encountered them. Accolades might get buried in a burst of rage.

A vaguely familiar voice broke into my mental turmoil.

"Well, well, well. We meet again."

I spun around. It was Mira, on crutches. My eyes traveled down her seductively clad lithe body, landing on her bandaged ankle.

"Hi," I stammered. "Sorry about your foot." Man, was I. If Mira hadn't sprained her ankle, Willow would have never danced the role of The Firebird. And I wouldn't be here feeling as fucked up as I did.

She scoffed at me. "It'll heal, and when it does, your little girlfriend can say goodbye to her dreams. She's not Gustave's type. And never has been. She's too short and fat. The talentless little shrew doesn't have what it takes. She's a fucking pigeon, not a firebird."

Her scathing insults went in one ear and out the other as I spotted the twosome making their way into the crowd. A photographer was following them, snapping his camera. They were arm in arm, and Willow, now wearing a sexy, strapless red cocktail dress and spiky red heels, was beaming. It was like the chandelier above was shining only on her. On them. A hoard of guests mobbed them, but I was in no mood to fight my way through the crowd to congratulate her. And truthfully, congratulating her was the last thing I wanted to do. Gustave, in his black tie attire and holding his cane, looked smug as Willow dangled on his other arm like a dazzling jewel. While she lit up the room, he dominated it. The connective tissue in my body sparked like a broken power wire. I was burning up. Glowing green in this sea of red. I heard Mira snort as she hobbled away.

More aimless wandering. I wanted nothing more than to get the fuck out of here. Then another familiar voice, this time welcomed, sang in my ear.

"Yo, dude."

I spun around. Duffy!

As he gave me a man pat on my back, relief flooded

me. "Hey, man, what the hell are you doing here? I thought you were still on your honeymoon."

"Came back last night. Covering the event for A&S. Danielle Sanders, our regular dance editor, came down with a bug."

"Is Sam with you?"

"No. She's home. She wasn't feeling well."

"Sorry about that."

"I think it's just jet lag. Maybe a touch of pregnancy fatigue."

We chatted a bit about their honeymoon in Tahiti and then I changed the subject. "What did you think of the ballet?"

"Honestly? I don't know shit about ballet, but I thought it was fan-fucking-tastic. Your girl was amazing."

My heart stuttered. "I don't think Willow's my girl anymore."

Duffy cocked his brow. "What are you talking about?"

"I think I've lost her to that asshole with a brick for a dick."

Duffy followed my gaze over to Gustave and Willow, both still the center of attention.

"That pompous, arrogant pansy?"

"You know him?"

"I wanted to interview him for the magazine, but he wouldn't give me the time of day. Said he would only talk to the *New York Times* or the *New Yorker*."

Gustave was all about control. Control gave him power. I could see it here in this space. I could see it on the stage. I could see it at my parents' cocktail party. And there was no doubt in my mind he exerted control in the bedroom. The thought of him banging Willow and making her his submissive sent a rush of nausea to my chest.

"They look good together," I mumbled.

"Anyone would look good with Willow. She's a fucking knockout."

"She's not even looking for me."

"Maybe she doesn't know you're here. Did you tell her you would be?"

Duffy made a good point. I'd never called or texted her to let her know I was attending the gala. Though it surprised me that she didn't see me sitting in the front row, maybe, blinded by the lights, she couldn't. Or…maybe she only had eyes for him.

And then as I glared at them, my eyes widened and my spine stiffened. "Fuck. He put his arm around her."

Duffster gave me a jab. "What the fuck are you doing standing here talking to me?"

"What should I do?"

"It's simple. Claim her."

It never ceased to amaze me how Duffy had become a regular dispenser of love advice to the forlorn.

"Go, pal, and while you're at it, give me something to write about."

Without thinking twice, I hurried off in Gustave and

Willow's direction, taking giant steps and elbowing my way through the crowd.

Along the way, I bumped into my mother.

"Ryan, darling," she said after draining her champagne, "I've been looking all over for you. We may have found a seat for you at Table 8."

"No need, Mother. I won't be staying."

Confused, she stared at me with her glazed eyes. God knows how many glasses of champagne she'd consumed. Without saying another word, I continued on my warpath. The closer I got to Willow and Gustave, and the closer they got to each other, the more my rage and jealousy fueled me.

The crowd thickened with women trying to get a photo taken with the two stars or their programs signed. Occasionally, I muttered, "excuse me."

Finally, when I was a few feet away from them, my eyes made contact with Willow's. She gasped.

"Oh my God, Ryan, what are you doing here?"

With force, I grabbed her elbow and wrenched her away from Gustave. "Let's get the fuck out of here. We need to talk."

Gustave's face contorted with rage. "Who the hell do you think you are? She's with me."

"Not any more, ballerina boy." Then, on my next heated breath, I fisted my right hand and sent it straight to his nose. He groaned. Staggering on his feet, he cursed under his breath as he wiped away the blood that poured from his nostrils.

Without another word or looking back, I marched Willow out of the theater. I didn't give a flying fuck if people were looking at us. Maybe I'd given Duffy something to write about.

THIRTY-SEVEN

Ryan

"Jesus, Ryan. What in God's name did you do in there?" panted Willow as I hauled her out of the theater. A chill slapped me in the face as we stepped outside.

"Just what it looked like," I growled, not slowing my pace.

"How could you do that?"

"He had it coming."

"I need to go back."

"You're not going anywhere except with me." I quickened my already frantic pace.

"I'm cold."

"Put on my coat." Shrugging it off, I handed it to her and paused for a second as she slipped it on. Then, clasping her hand, we were back on the move.

"Ryan, slow down! I can't walk this fast. My feet hurt. Where are we going?"

"Home," I barked. With my new bed, my place was her place. Or it was supposed to be. I didn't stop.

"Why are you doing this to me?"

"*Why?* Give me a fucking break." I was tinkering between sanity and madness, the latter winning.

"I can't keep up. Please. I'm going to trip." Stumbling, she missed a step.

I'd be lying if I didn't say there was a part of me that wanted her to break a leg. And never dance again. But I cared too much about her.

She stumbled again and I had no choice but to stop and throw her over my shoulder. My rage got in the way of enjoying her in this position. My blood bubbling, I was on a mission.

"Jesus, Ryan. What the hell are you doing? Put me down!" She began to pound me with her fists. And kick.

Still raging, I gave her tight ass a firm whack. As she yelped, I squeezed the area below her seat tighter and marched her to my bike. I'd gotten a ticket for an expired meter, but I didn't give a shit. I set her down, tempted like sin to bend her over the bike and fuck her hard from behind. But there were too many pedestrians passing by, and with my luck, some cop would be among them and throw me in the slammer. So, calling on all my willpower, I ordered her to mount it.

"Get on."

She gave me a what-the-fuck look. I gave her a look back that shouted: don't fuck with me.

"NOW!"

I watched as she silently spread her long, supple legs and straddled the back seat of the bike. It was a lucky thing the skirt of her cocktail dress was full, allowing her to part her legs. Little did she know she'd be parting them a lot wider shortly. Adrenaline pumping through my veins, I hopped onto the bike.

"Hold on," I shouted as I revved it up. The bike rumbled and we zoomed off, her arms wrapped tightly around my waist. Weaving in and out of the Saturday night traffic, I recklessly headed downtown, dodging cabs and running red lights.

"Jesus, Ryan, you're going to get us killed," she shrieked.

I didn't respond. Truthfully, I almost didn't give a damn if we crashed and burned. That's how mad I was.

Twenty death-defying minutes later we reached my loft where I rode the bike straight into the elevator. I hopped off and lifted Willow off the bike. Making a fist, I yanked at her bun, now a mess from the wind, until her wild mane of hair fell loose. She winced.

"You like pain, Willow?" I swear I didn't recognize my own voice as I shoved her against the back wall and yanked off the coat. Gripping her shoulders, I bit down near her neck, marking her flesh, as she winced again. I then pinched her nipples as hard as I could, twirling them as they hardened and elongated.

"Oh, God," she groaned, her bottom lip quivering.

"Tell me, do you like it hard?" With a quick, sharp movement, I hiked up her dress and slipped my hand through the leg opening of her G-string, then plunged my middle finger up her pussy. She let out a gasp.

Sweet Jesus. She was as wet as fuck. Dripping for me. I gave it another forceful thrust, hitting her soft womb, and then slid it out, her slickness coating my digit. My dick stood at attention, stiffening against the fabric of my tux pants. Our erotic ballet had just begun. *Our* pas de deux.

"Extend your leg," I commanded.

Wordlessly, she lifted her bare limber leg so high and straight I was able to grab her slender ankle, and hook her foot over my shoulder. With her six-inch heels on, it was within easy reach. Her skimpy black lace G-string with its soaked cotton crotch exposed, it was the most erotic sight I'd ever seen. Breathing hard with my arousal, I snapped the G-strings, one after the other, then tore off her panties. I scrunched the damp lace scrap in my hand before tossing it to the floor. Then, I grabbed her glistening pink pussy and squeezed it hard. *Mine.*

She groaned again, her breathing ragged with her arousal. Holding her pinned against the wall with one hand, I yanked down my fly, freeing my enormous throbbing cock.

"You like it big? I'll show you big. You like it hard? I'll give it to you hard."

On my next fierce heartbeat, I curled my free hand around the wide base and put the crown to her entrance. With a grunt, I rammed my cock inside her, taking her to the hilt. She shrieked again.

"It's my turn to dance with you, Firebird," I grumbled. Clutching her cinched waist to balance her, I began to pummel her. Fuck her without mercy. Bang her against the wall, each thrust faster and more forceful. The depth of penetration in this erotic position was like nothing I'd ever known before. So fucking deep. So fucking amazing.

"Is this hard enough for you, Willow?" I ground out.

"Oh. My. God." She whimpered, her neck arched back, her face exquisitely contorted.

"Is this how *he* fucks you?"

"No," she cried out.

Every muscle in my body tensed. Fury flooded my veins. Pulling her away from the wall, I slipped my hand under her dress and cupped her bare ass with my hands, allowing me to go deeper, as she balanced on one leg. She glommed on to my shoulders, the two of us face to face, our mouths almost touching, our breath almost one. Madly, I continued to fuck her. We were on fire, the fire spreading from the inside out. The incendiary heat consuming every cell, every molecule of my body. Melting me. Melting her.

"My little Firebird," I breathed out, not slowing down, "I'm going to ruffle your feathers. Make you fall apart."

We made our own music—a symphonic blend of pants, moans, and groans—and built to a crescendo. Her groans became whimpers; her whimpers became sobs; her sobs became shrieks.

"Oh my God, Ryan, I'm so close to coming."

For a nano-second, I thought about pulling out of her, of making her beg, but the truth was I was so close to the edge I couldn't. On my next powerful thrust, I sent her flying with a scream of my name as my own epic orgasm soared and chased hers.

Her body limp, I held my Firebird like she'd been shot down from the sky.

I wasn't done. Our dirty dance had just begun.

"Turn around," I ordered.

Submissively, she did as I asked.

"Bend over the bike." Act 2. I was about to choreograph my fantasy.

THIRTY-EIGHT
Ryan

A ct 2. Over. She hung over the seat of my bike like a limp ragdoll as I pulled out of her. Her red chiffon dress draped over her back while her mass of red hair hung loose everywhere.

Breathless from my epic orgasm, I stared at her gorgeous ass, all rosy pink from slapping it a few times and squeezing it. I'd never fucked a woman in the ass before, and I more than liked it. Spreading those exquisite round cheeks, lubricating her with my seed, and then hammering her. Fast and furious as she sobbed. She didn't beg me to stop, so I kept at it, at once fingering her swollen clit—a hot wet reminder of our previous climax just minutes ago. It so fucking turned me on, bringing us each to another stratospheric orgasm.

But, now as we recovered and sanity returned to me, I felt like shit.

I'd fucked her hard without mercy. I couldn't help myself. A mixture of possessiveness and rage had consumed me. Breathing hard, she could barely stand up as the elevator opened to my loft.

"Why are you limping?" I asked as she stepped out, thinking it was all my fault.

She winced. Quietly, but loud enough for me to hear her.

"It's my feet." I was surprised by her answer, thinking it must be on account of her ravished pussy or ass.

"What do you mean?"

"They're sore from dancing."

Relieved, I lifted her into my arms and carried her into the living room where I set her down on one of the leather couches. Her beautiful face contorted in pain.

"Would you mind taking off my shoes?"

I did as she asked, slipping the red stilettos off her slender feet. My eyes grew wide. Her blistered toes were a bloody mess.

"Jesus!"

She grimaced, her brows knitting together. "The life of a dancer."

"Sheesh. I need to bandage your toes."

A small grateful smile curled on her lips.

Five minutes later, her toes were covered with Band-Aids.

"How do your feet feel?" I asked, observing my handiwork and thinking how much I loved taking care of my frail but feisty ballerina.

She wiggled her feet and grimaced again.

"They're still sore?"

She twitched a pained smile. "Yeah. They're

cramped. It's been a while since I performed."

"Sit back. Let me massage them."

"Really?" She gazed up at me with eyes that reminded me of a puppy's begging to be pet. Leaning back against the armrest, she stretched her long, limber legs across the couch. I sat cross-legged facing her, still in my tux.

"Put your feet on my lap."

She did as I asked, my dangerously close cock flexing as her heels touched down. Gently, I took her right foot in my hands.

"Close your eyes, baby. This is going to feel good."

Her glittery lids lowered as she surrendered to my touch. Expertly, I kneaded her arched sole with my thumbs, going deeper and deeper, hitting all her trigger spots. Despite the calluses on her heels, her feet were as soft and smooth as her satin ballet slippers.

My eyes glimpsed the expression on her face as she arched back her head. It was one of pure ecstasy. She moaned.

"Oh my God, Ryan. That feels so good. How did you learn to do this?"

Allee. For a split-second, the memory of Allee teaching me how to do foot massage flashed in my mind. "It's like making love to your feet," she'd told me.

Forcing myself back in the moment, I simply told Willow I had a good teacher as I pressed harder into her soles. She moaned again, louder.

Yes, I was making love to Willow's tender foot, her soft moans arousing me. My cock throbbed, and I longed to spread her legs, knowing she was bared to me beneath her dress. My eyes closed as I imagined massaging her beautiful clit and ravaging her all over again. As if she knew what I was thinking, she slid her left foot on top of my rigid cock and began to rub it.

I hissed, positive my cock was going to burst through my fly, and managed a few words. "Are you still sore?"

"Please, Ryan, more," she breathed out.

The throbbing so great, I could no longer hold back. With my free hand, I unfastened my trousers and pulled down my fly with a whoosh. Willow's moans drowned out the sound, her eyes still closed as my huge erection sprang out. On my next heated breath, I curled my hands around her slender ankles and slid her down the couch. As she let out a gasp, her eyes snapped open. At the sight of my erection, they smoldered.

"Baby, I want to fuck you again. Sit on me."

The lustful expression on her face was all I needed. She lifted the skirt of her dress and mounted me, squatting over my folded legs, a position that only a lissome dancer could manage. So fucking sexy. So hot and erotic. Her supple legs spread far apart and her hands clutching my shoulders, she lowered herself onto my cock, taking me in inch by raging inch.

She felt so fucking good. My fingers caressed her pussy as she went down on me.

"Jesus, you're so fucking hot and wet for me."

"The massage," she murmured.

The heat of her pussy intensified as I penetrated her. Pushing deep inside her, I splayed my fingers on her haunches to support her.

"Ride me, baby. Ride me hard. Fucking take me to the moon."

As I began to pump her fast and furiously, her hips bucked up and down, meeting my every deep thrust. Our ragged breaths filled the room as she rode me to ecstasy. An orgasm of epic proportions was building quickly and I hoped she was as close to coming as I was.

"Oh my God, oh my God," she repeated, her voice between a cry and a whisper.

Then, everything broke loose as she sobbed out her orgasm, her pussy pulsing all around my combusting cock. I cursed under my breath as I emptied into her while her head fell forward onto mine.

I kissed her lips as I rode my orgasm out. Tonight, *my* Firebird had taught me how to fly.

A few minutes later, we were soaking in my deluxe Jacuzzi tub…yeah, the one fucking Charlotte had insisted I install in my loft. I'd never used it with the psycho bitch… only with Allee, and now, for the first time in five years, with Willow. I'd forgotten how amazing it was.

Willow's beautiful lithe body was in my arms, between my legs, her back to me. The powerful jets caressed us.

"Are you okay?" I breathed into my beauty's ear.

"Yeah," she hummed back. "This feels amazing."

"Is the water too hot?"

"It's perfect."

"Are your feet okay?"

She let out a soft moan that could barely be heard above the sound of the gurgling water. "They feel great. In fact, every part of my body feels great."

I couldn't agree more as I ran a large sponge around her pert breasts. Her body was perfect. Perfect for me. And I didn't want anyone to touch it. Especially that bastard, Gustave. I wanted to banish him to the back of my mind, but his ugly presence lingered. And despite my oneness with Willow at this moment, burning questions whirled around in my head.

"Butterfly, that was a one time thing, right?"

"What are you talking about?"

"You know…dancing. Performing."

I could feel her body tense up. "I-I don't know."

I parted her curtain of hair. "What do you mean you don't know?" Anger crept into my voice.

"Simply, I don't know. I'm tired. It's been a long, emotional day. I don't want to talk about it. Or him."

Him? My blood curdled. "Fine," I snapped back, wishing I'd taken the bastard out or at least kicked him in the balls so hard he could never walk, dance, or fuck again.

Willow spent the night, spooned naked in my arms in my new bed. Exhausted, she fell asleep quickly while I stayed up for hours worrying about our future. I loved Willow Rosenthal with all my heart and soul, and I didn't want to lose her.

After a few hours of shuteye, I woke up early at seven while Willow remained fast asleep. Slipping out of bed, I admired her as she rolled over onto her back, her flaming red hair fanned out on the white bedding, her chest rising and falling. My sleeping beauty, in her naked glory except for my necklace around her neck, the diamonds of the ballet slipper charm capturing the morning sun. Quietly, I threw on my robe and went downstairs to make a pot of coffee before heading outside to retrieve my *Sunday New York Times*. My Sunday morning ritual. When Allee was alive, we always purchased the paper at a nearby newsstand on a Saturday night, but after her passing, I had it delivered. It was too hard to visit that newsstand.

The paper tucked under one arm, I marched back upstairs with two mugs of steaming hot coffee. To my surprise, Willow was awake sitting up in the bed, my comforter pulled up over her chest. Propped against the pink tufted headboard, she looked like a pre-Raphaelite beauty.

"Hi, baby," I said brightly. "You sleep well?"

She twitched a small smile. "Yeah, I did."

Not telling her about my tormented night, I handed her one of the mugs and rejoined her in bed.

She lifted the mug and inhaled. "Mmm, the coffee smells so good." She took a sip as I set the thick Sunday paper down on the bed. It didn't get better than this on a Sunday morning—fresh coffee, the *Times*, and the girl you loved. The tumultuous events of last night drifted to the back of my mind.

Sipping my coffee, I flipped through the paper until I found my favorite section. The section I always began my Sundays with. *The New York Times Book Review*. I immediately turned to the bestseller lists. My book, *Undying Love*, was back on the mass-market chart. Number One. My appearance on *Good Morning America* and the recent announcement that Ryan Reynolds had been chosen to play opposite Emma Stone had re-kindled interest in the book. I smiled while Willow pulled out the *Arts and Leisure* section.

"Oh my God!" she cried out, startling me.

"What's the matter?"

"There's a review of the ballet on the front page!"

My pulse quickened. I was more anxious than thrilled.

"What does it say?"

She began to read it out loud, beginning with the headline, and with every word, I could feel my blood pressure rising.

Headline: *A Firebird on Fire*

The Royal Latvia Ballet may have shined last night during a benefit of performance of Stravinsky's masterpiece, choreographed by Gustave Fontaine at Lincoln Center's Howard Koch Theater, but principal dancer, Willow Rose, who played the title role of the Firebird, literally shimmered, her feathers glowing and in perfect form. Her speed, precision, and artistic expression made sparks fly, bringing the audience to their feet. Known mostly in Europe, this a dancer to watch. She is bound to set the dance world on fire.

My chest tightened as Willow's voice trailed off with the glowing review of her coupling with Gustave. *Stunning…dazzling… explosive chemistry…a match made in heaven.* I wanted to puke.

Lowering the paper, my companion clasped her mouth.

"Oh my God! I need to go."

My nerves buzzing, I shot her a puzzled expression.

"I need to get over to my dad's deli. Before he reads this or some customer tells him about it."

"He doesn't know you danced last night at Lincoln Center?" I asked, now wondering why her father wasn't there.

Setting her mug of coffee on the nightstand, she jumped out of the bed. All naked. All panicked. In a frenzy, she slipped on her red cocktail dress, which I'd folded over my desk chair, and then retrieved her stilettos. She cursed under her breath as her bandaged toes squeezed into the spiky shoes.

"Ryan, do you have something I can borrow? I mean, something I can wear over my dress?"

Five minutes later, wearing my way too big over-coat, she dashed out of my loft.

Leaving me alone with a cold cup of coffee and my *New York Times*.

I tore up the *Arts and Leisure* section and then went for a run.

THIRTY-NINE
Willow

Breathlessly, my feet killing me, I hobbled into my dad's deli. Not even eight a.m., the place was packed with regulars, who were either working their cell phones, reading a Sunday paper, or attending to their families. Sunday morning was one of our busiest days, with New Yorkers from all parts of town flocking to Mel's for the best breakfast in the city. My eyes bounced around the busy restaurant in search of my father. Embarrassment creeping through me as I did my walk of shame, I asked one of the counter guys if my dad was around.

"He stepped into the kitchen," he replied. "He should be back any minute."

My chest tightened; my feet throbbed. Maybe I should run upstairs and deal with things later. With this thought and no longer able to bear the pain, I tugged my stilettos off my feet, one after the other. Closing my eyes for a brief second, I sighed with relief. When I blinked them open, there he was. My father.

He met my gaze as I nervously hugged Ryan's big

coat, acutely aware I was not wearing underwear. My father's eyes roamed down my body, landing on my bandaged toes. His expression stern, he ambled toward me. My heartbeat quickened, my muscles clenched. Shit. What was I going to tell him? After my physical and emotional breakdown eight months ago, the last thing my father wanted was for me to dance professionally again.

He stood before me and I suddenly felt like I was three feet tall in front of this burly bear of a man. As I cringed, his lips pressed thin.

"Why didn't you tell me?"

My cheeks heated. He knew.

"I read the review."

My mouth twitched.

"I would have liked to have been there."

"I-I'm sorry, Pop. I should have told you, but I was afraid you'd get upset. It was a last minute thing… And with your heart condition—"

He cut me off. "Does this mean you're resuming your dance career?"

"Pop, I don't know." I deliberately kept things vague, but there was no denying that dancing on stage had made me feel more alive than I'd felt in months. I didn't know until last night how much I missed it. Ballet was in my blood. It was my oxygen.

My father's dark eyes wavered from me. "You have a visitor."

His face pinched as a familiar, accented voice

sounded in my ears.

"My *petite oiseau…*"

I whirled around. Swaggering toward me was Gustave, carrying my pink ballet bag in one hand, his cane in the other. He was clad all in black except for a white cashmere scarf that draped over his fitted velvet jacket.

My heart stammered. "P-pop, this is—"

"I know who he is." My father cut me off, his voice as cold as ice.

"*Enchanté.*" Gustave smirked as he gave my apron-clad, still meaty father the once over. "Obviously, your beautiful and talented daughter inherited her genes from her mother."

My blood ran cold. Gustave could be so charming in one breath, so cruel and cutting on the next. His onyx eyes zoomed in on me.

"We need to talk, *oiseau.*" He tapped his cane as he shot my father a dismissive look. "Privately."

My eyes flitted to my father. I could tell from the reddening of his face that anger was bubbling in his blood. "Pop, would you excuse us for a few minutes?"

My father scowled. "Fine, but don't make it too long. I could use your help. I'm down a waitress." Without another word, my father stalked off.

"Can we sit down somewhere?" asked Gustave as soon my father disappeared. "Perhaps over there?" he added, pointing to an empty table in the corner with his cane.

A few moments later we were seated at the table facing each other. His nose was still swollen from Ryan's assault.

"I'm sorry if my friend hurt you last night," I murmured, not knowing where to start.

"That is not why I'm here. I have no time to waste on that despicable lowlife." He adjusted his scarf. "I shall simply get to the point. I need you."

"What do you mean?"

"I want you to return to the troupe. I shall make you principal dancer. A star."

"I don't know if that's what I want." My voice was shaky.

He huffed a haughty breath as a waitress, lugging a loaded tray, scurried by us. "Puh-lease. Is this the pathetic life you want? Wearing a dirty apron and serving peons?"

"I respect waitresses." I really did. They were honest, hard-working human beings.

He laughed. "You're only fooling yourself, Willow. You were born to dance and you know that. Did you see any of the reviews?"

"I saw the one in the *New York Times*," I said hesitantly.

"They're all like that. You're all over the Internet and the Twitter world can't stop buzzing about you."

Shock coursed through me. I had no idea.

"I need you to return to the company. With Mira's injury, I have no one who can dance the White Swan."

I registered his words. The White Swan in Tchai-kovsky's *Swan Lake*? He wanted me to perform that role? The coveted role every ballerina in the world dreamed of dancing.

"We shall be touring the world, starting in France at L'Opéra de Paris."

His words whirled around in my head while my heart pounded in my chest. I'd always dreamt of dancing in Paris at the grand L'Opéra. Oh my God. And to dance the role of the White Swan there?

"My *oiseau*, you will become an international star of mega-proportions. This is the opportunity of a lifetime."

Words were trapped in my throat. I was speechless.

"Do you want to spend your life here in this egg-shell or do you want to set the world on fire with your dancing? Think about it, my little bird, and let me know in twenty-four hours. We depart tomorrow afternoon."

And with that, he grabbed his cane and walked out of the restaurant, leaving my emotions in a tempest.

FORTY

Ryan

From the minute Willow fled my loft, I felt like my life had become a ticking time bomb. Over dinner at her father's deli, she told me her plans. She was going to rejoin Gustave's ballet troupe and resume her dance career. Upon hearing this news, rage pummeled through me. A huge fight erupted.

"No fucking way!" I yelled at her.

"Please, Ryan, try to understand."

"I get it. You've chosen him over me."

"No, Ry-man, it has nothing to do with him. It has everything to do with me."

"Bullshit. You're fucking obsessed with him."

This is how the conversation bounced back and forth. My rage rising with each harsh breath. Before we ended our relationship right then and there—and I combusted—we reluctantly agreed on a next step. Something I'd resisted. Couples therapy.

"So, what brings the two of you here?" asked Dr. Goodman, adjusting his glasses on his nose. He was sitting in a leather armchair facing Willow and me, the two of us seated on the couch. Though we were sitting side by side, it felt like miles separated us. The tension between us was so thick a knife couldn't cut through it.

"We have a major problem." We blurted out the words together.

Dr. Goodman's brows lifted. "And that might be…"

Willow and I exchanged a glance. Who should answer?

I jumped in. "Willow wants to go to Paris and pursue her career as a ballet dancer."

Dr. Goodman's impassive reaction to the news floored me. He simply folded his hands in his lap. My body tensed as Willow spoke up.

"I've asked him to come with me."

Our shrink's gaze stayed on us as he asked calmly: "Ryan, why is that a problem?"

Jesus fucking Christ. After all these years in therapy, did he not have a clue? Time to inform him.

"Seriously, Doc?" My voice rose with anger as I grasped at the roots of my hair in frustration. "It's where Allee spent her last days on earth and turned to dust. I can *never* go back there."

"It's the City of Love…the City of Lights," he responded, his voice even-keeled.

"Are you kidding? For me it's the City of Death. The City of Gloom."

The doctor stroked his beard. "I see."

I see. Is that all he could say? What part of this fucked-up situation wasn't he getting? I searched my mind and then spit out, "I don't understand why Willow has to do this."

Dr. Goodman looked at Willow. "Willow, can you explain your reason."

She gave him the same reasons she'd given me. That ballet was in her blood; dance was calling her. It was the opportunity of a lifetime.

"But, there are other companies you can join," I protested. "What about the New York City Ballet?"

"The NYCB rejected me. I wasn't good enough for them."

"Audition for them again!"

"It doesn't work that way. I'm too old to do that."

Desperation rose in my chest and I took another tactic. "Doc, how can you let her go back to that monster—"

He cut me off. "Are you referring to Gustave?"

Obviously, he knew whom I was talking about. "Yes, that psychopath. The man is violent and abusive. I read he even raped a dancer. For all I know, he sexually abused Willow!" With a jerk of my head, I turned to face Willow. "Tell me, did he?"

Silence was my answer. My companion fidgeted with her ballet-slipper necklace as my mind flashed back to one of our earliest conversations. The lunch following her father's heart attack.

"I was in an abusive relationship."

"You let some guy hurt you?"

"It's complicated. Let's not go there yet."

"A boyfriend?"

"Please, Ryan. Drop it."

This time I wasn't going to drop it. The pieces of Willow's shattered past were coming together like the pieces of a jigsaw puzzle.

"Now, I get it. That's why you took a sabbatical. That fucking asshole abused you. Shredded you to pieces!"

"It wasn't like that!" Willow cried out. "I was weak. Needy. Obsessed. I let him…"

"Sexually assault you?"

Tearfully, Willow shook her head. "No, it was always consensual."

I looked at Dr. Goodman. "Is that true?"

"Ryan, I can't divulge that. Doctor-patient privilege. You will have to take Willow's words at face value."

Frustration was surging along with my anger. I wanted to shake someone. Knock some sense into them. "Jesus, Willow, how can you go back to him?"

"He's changed. I've changed." Her voice quivered.

"Bullshit!" I cried out.

Dr. Goodman lifted his glasses and pinched the bridge of his nose. "Willow, Ryan's right. It may not be wise—"

"Not wise!?" My voice rose several decibels with

anger. "Are you kidding me? It's insane! Stop her!"

Dr. Goodman lowered his glasses. "I can advise against it, but I can't stop her, Ryan. She's an adult woman, who is perfectly capable of making her own decisions."

Panic set in. "You've got to! Tell her not to go!"

"Ryan, that's your job, not mine."

I turned again toward Willow. Cupping her shoulders so she was facing me, I looked deep into her watering eyes. "Willow, please don't fucking go."

Unable to hold my gaze, she looked down and chewed her trembling lip.

Then to my surprise, Dr. Goodman threw her a curve ball. "Willow, why do you feel you're ready to go back?"

Willow fidgeted again with her necklace, batting back tears. "I've grown a lot stronger over the last year. I have control over my emotions and my body. I no longer need to be hurt to feel alive."

"Oh, the tables have turned," I snapped. "So, now you like to dish it. Hurt others."

Tears began to fall. "Please, Ryan, I'm not doing it to hurt you."

My cheeks flared. "Oh, you could have fooled me."

"Please, Ryan, don't do this to me." Her voice cracked with desperation. "Don't make it harder than it already is. We'll figure things out...we'll write...we'll talk. I'll be back. Remember, with love, there are no goodbyes."

I thought I was going to implode. Allee's words to live by. Or die by.

"Screw you, Willow."

With that, I stood up and walked out the door. And out of Willow Rosenthal's life.

FORTY-ONE

Ryan

What the hell was I thinking? During a long, grueling run the next morning, I came to my senses. I needed to see Willow. Make things right. I couldn't end things with a fight like that. In fact, I didn't want to end things at all. I wanted her in my life and somehow, I needed to figure out how. With sweat clustering on my chest and my heart rate elevated, I turned around about five miles in and ran straight down Broadway until I got to Mel's Deli. Not bothering to stretch, I hurried inside, breathing heavily.

It was noon, and the place was already packed for lunch. My eyes searched for Willow, but she was nowhere in sight—neither helping behind the counter nor seating the long line of diners. Then I saw Mel trudging down the stairs. I dashed up to him.

"Mel, is Willow around?" My voice was frantic.

He heaved a breath. He didn't seem his normal jovial self. A cloud of sadness shrouded him.

"She's gone."

My heart skipped a beat as his words twisted in my

head. The line in my book announcing Allee's death—
And in the morning, she was gone— stabbed my brain.
No, it can't be!

"Sh she   " I could barely form words. I could barely breathe.

Mel cut me short. "…flew to Paris this morning
with The Royal Latvia Ballet. A chartered flight." He
pressed his lips thin in a tight, grim line. "I couldn't
stop her."

While I should have been relieved that Willow was
all right, I couldn't fight the despair that was swallowing me.

"Mel, did she say anything about me?"

Forlornly, he shook his head. "It all happened very
quickly. Gustave Fontaine came by in a limo to pick her
up."

Fucking Gustave. I'd like to hang him by his balls.
"Is it too late to call her?"

Mel glanced down at the worn leather-band watch
on his wrist. "The plane took off a half-hour ago."

Fuck. Shit. Fuck. That meant I would have to wait
close to eight hours to call her. Dammit. Why didn't I
try harder to stop her? I'd managed to stop Allee from
going to Paris. From pursuing her dream of living in
The City of Lights. All I had to do was ask her to marry
me. Then, it dawned on me. More like hit me like a bolt
of lightning. That right there was the problem; I'd made
no commitment to Willow and she'd called me on it.
And I knew in my heart why. I was afraid of commit-

ment. Afraid of getting attached to someone and then having her ripped away from me. Of losing a great love again. It just hurt too much.

With a ring or without one, I'd lost Willow. With the way I had walked out on her, the chances of her coming back to me were slim. As reality stabbed at me, my aching heart sank deeper and deeper into the pit of my stomach.

"Ryan, can I get you a bite to eat? A sandwich to go?" asked Mel, sensing my despair.

"Thanks, but no. I've got to go."

"I know how you feel." I suddenly realized he had lost Willow too. His precious daughter to that fucking bastard. Then, he slapped his forehead.

"Sheesh. I almost forgot." My eyes stayed on him as he hurried behind the cash register, squatted down, and then returned holding a takeout bag.

"Honestly, sir, thanks but no thanks. I'm not hungry."

"No, it's from Willow," he said, handing me the bag. "She wanted me to give this to you."

Curious, I reached into the bag and instantly knew what was inside. Slowly, I pulled out the contents and glared at the worn little monkey, his sad, scratched glass eyes staring back at me. Baboo.

Around his withered neck was a frayed pale pink ribbon tied into a bow. I was positive it was one of the ribbons from the childhood toe shoes that hung from Willow's bed. I tried to make sense of Willow's rendering. Baboo was a part of her; she'd had him since she was a baby. Lifting him closer to my face, I could even smell her essence. After a whiff, I studied the satin strand. The Harvard literature major that I was, I wondered—what did it symbolize? Was it the string that tied us together? Or did it mean Willow was cutting me out of her life? Was it our lifeline or the end of the rope?

A shudder, like an unraveling ribbon, spooled through me.

Clutching Willow's childhood treasure, I told Mel I had to leave. With the tiniest glimmer of hope in his eyes, he gave me a bear hug. "Hang in there, Ryan. If I hear from her, I'll let you know."

The next few days were living hell. Pure torture. Though Mel called to let me know that Willow had landed safely in Paris, I couldn't reach her. Every time I called her cell it went straight to voicemail, and the numerous, desperate texts I sent her all went unanswered. It was like she was completely avoiding me. Shutting me out of her life. Moving on.

I numbed my pain by pounding the pavement, running miles, or escaping the city on my Harley, speeding down the Jersey Turnpike and letting the roar of the engine dull my senses. The nights were even more painful than the days. I drank myself to sleep and conked out on the couch. I couldn't bear sleeping in the new bed that Willow and I had briefly shared. And might never share again. Much like the way I felt after Allee's death, I thought my life was over.

My only comfort was Baboo, who never left my side. I was convinced the little monkey missed Willow as much as I did. When his bow became undone, instead of re-tying it around his neck, I tied it around my wrist and wore Willow's pink ribbon like a love bracelet, never taking it off. Admittedly, sometimes I thought it was more like a mourning band, and other times, I wished it was long enough to tie around my neck like a noose. A few times, I thought about calling my sister, but zombie me was in no condition for a confrontation; she'd probably chew my ear off, telling me that I should have never gotten involved with someone I hardly knew. Making matters worse, Dr. Goodman was away for a few weeks at some shrink conference and wasn't taking calls. There was no news from Willow, not even from her father, who hadn't heard from her since her initial call.

Duffy, the other person I could confide in, was also out of town on business. However, the day he got back, he texted me and told me to meet him for drinks. Despite my sorry state, I agreed.

I met Duffy at our regular hangout, the neighborhood pub. As usual, he was there first and had a Guinness waiting for me. At the sight of me, he furrowed his brows.

"Hey, man. You okay? You look like shit."

He was right. My eyes were glazed from lack of

sleep, I needed a haircut, and my beard was unkempt from not taking care of it. A mixture of sadness and stress was written all over my face. I was fucking depressed. A total train wreck.

I took a long sip of my cold, frothy beer. Except for quenching my thirst, it did little to help my state of being.

"I *feel* like shit," I mumbled.

"You sick?"

Yeah, I was sick. But not that kind of sick. I was suffering from another kind of disease I knew too well. Heartache. Duffy continued.

"There's a nasty bug going around. Half the office has it."

I took another chug of my beer as Duffy rambled on.

"Hey, I meant to tell you that my glowing review of *The Firebird* got over a million hits. Willow is something."

Was something is more like it. Setting down my mug, I just blurted it out. Got it off my aching chest. "She left me."

Duffy's eyes widened like saucers. "What!?"

"She went to Paris with Gustave."

"That prick with the brick dick? She's fucking him?"

"No, but they did. And she still has an obsession with him. Dancing *The Firebird* last week awoke her need to dance. He's making her a principal dancer and asked her to come with him and his company to Paris.

Then, they're going on a world tour."

"Man, why didn't you go with her? There's nothing holding you back here."

"I couldn't. I didn't think I could handle it. You know, with Allee dying there and everything."

Pressing his lips thin, Duffy nodded. "I get it. How did you leave things?"

One word: "Badly."

My buddy's eyes stayed on me, squeezing me for more information.

Hedging, I ran my fingers through my unruly hair. "We had a big fight. I walked out on her."

"And…"

"The next day, I went over to her dad's deli to talk to her and try to work things out, but she'd already split for Paris."

"Did you try to call her? Text her?"

"Yeah. I've been trying. But my messages go straight to her voicemail and she hasn't responded to my texts. She probably never wants to hear from me or see me again."

"Bullshit. Don't jump to spurious conclusions."

"Duff, I don't know what to do." My voice lowered. "I love her."

"Then, tell her that."

"I don't know how to. She's unreachable. Even her father doesn't know how to get hold of her."

"Bro, do what you do best."

My brows jumped up. I was all ears as "Dear Duffy," my relationship guru, went on.

"Write. Write her a letter."

"But I don't know where she's staying. Nor does her father."

"Send her an email. She's bound to get it some-time."

What would I do without Duffy? Paying for the beers, I sprinted home. My fingers were as twitchy as my dick. The words in my head were already flowing.

As soon as I got home, I raced up the stairs to my bedroom and made a beeline for my desk. On top of it sat my computer...the very laptop with which I'd written every word of *Undying Love*. I was due for a new one, but somehow I couldn't part with this Mac. Memories trumped technology. Sitting down, I flipped open the case and went straight to my Gmail. I hit "Compose," and then in the subject line typed two letters: U-S. Us. As my heart beat with hope and determination, my fingers danced across the keyboard.

My beautiful butterfly~

The next morning after our session with Dr. Goodman, I went to your dad's deli to see you before you left, but you were already gone.

It's only been a few days, but my life has no meaning without you. With every step I take, I wish you were here with me. My loft is empty without you. It's you I dream of and wish were in my bed at night. I miss your lightness of being; every day is dark, my heart heavy.

Allee is still in my heart, not just a memory, but a treasure I will always cherish. You are a treasure too. A brilliant, shimmering jewel that can light up a room as well as a stage. Most of all, you, only you, lit up my heart and showed me that I could love again. Allee always wanted me to meet someone new after her death, and you are that special person.

Perhaps it was fate that you were already on your way to Paris when I came by. Allee taught me a universal human truth. In love, there are no goodbyes. So, hello, my beautiful butterfly, and I hope all is well.

When you come back and I pray you will soon, there's something I want to ask you and we'll figure out a way to make things work. I understand your need to dance. It is not much different than my need to write. Your *stage is my page. It is who we are...what defines us.*

Allee wanted me to have Plan B as in B-E, to go on and live my life to the fullest. I know now, my beauty, I want to live my life with you and be wherever you are.

I'm not giving up on us.

With all my love—
Ry-Man

I re-read my letter, and as I did, a warm breath of air dusted the back of my neck as if someone were standing behind me. I looked over my shoulder and for a flash instant I saw Allee. An approving smile graced her angelic face. She'd read what I'd written. The near final words of her farewell letter whirled in my head. *Madewell, I'll be reading every word from wherever I am.* In the blink of an eye, she disappeared. My pulse in overdrive, I turned around and hit send. I blew out a deep breath. Now, I had to play the waiting game.

FORTY-TWO

Willow

This was so not Paris. Not the Paris I envisioned with bustling streets, cafés on every corner, and a view of the Eiffel Tower everywhere one walked.

To my surprise, Gustave sequestered us in a remote chateau owned by one of his benefactors in the countryside. I had no idea exactly where we were or how far we were from civilization. Upon our arrival, he made us relinquish all our devices, including laptops, cell phones, tablets, and iPods. He didn't want us to have any distractions and besides, there was no Internet service where we were staying. Our focus was to be on dance 24/7. He wanted us to live it and breathe it.

Re-entering the world of ballet—Gustave's world— was a rude awakening I wasn't prepared for. Maybe I'd shined as The Firebird on stage, but I knew now that my performance had been fueled by pure adrenaline. I'd been away from the reality of what it took to be one of "Gustave's girls" for almost a year. Along with the others, I was immediately put on a diet of music to nurture us. Meals were sparse, a bit of protein and some vegetables; nothing over a few hundred calories. While Gustave taunted us with the fine wine he drank at dinner every night, we were allowed none. I missed my dad's delicious sandwiches, blintzes, and matzo ball soup. Within a week, I was definitely "elongating" to use Gustave's pet word to mean I was getting skinny. My collarbone was protruding as were my ribs. I found myself chilled to the bone, having to layer myself with heavy sweaters, scarves, and leg warmers every minute of the day, including practice. It didn't help that the massive chateau had poor heating, which Gustave felt kept us sharp and on our toes, no pun intended.

The days were grueling—all work and no play. Breakfast was served at seven o'clock in the dining room, and by eight, we were in class, doing barre exercises and Pilates as well as practicing moves. Lunch was served at noon, and soon afterward, rehearsals began and continued until six or later if there weren't any emergencies. And there was always something… a dancer coming down sick, straining a muscle, or having a catfight with a fellow ballerina.

The only way I kept track of time was that we were constantly reminded of how many days away we were from the Paris performance. With each passing day, our warm ups and rehearsals became more grueling. On his ruthless quest for perfection, Gustave became more temperamental, more demanding, more intolerant.

And with each passing day, I grew weaker, more depressed. More imperfect. My dancing wasn't as good as it should be. Constantly, Gustave yelled at me and belittled me, criticizing every move while Mira, who had recovered from her foot injury and was playing my nemesis, the evil Black Swan, looked on with a smirk. My leaps weren't high enough, my footwork not fast enough, my armwork not fluid enough. I became a body in motion without any meaning because I was losing belief in myself.

As Gustave broke down my spirit, my body broke down in tandem. I felt dreadfully thin, my hipbones now jutting and my tummy concave. Every muscle hurt, and my feet were so sore there were days I almost couldn't take another step. Not even the ointments, aspirin, or bandages at night could relieve the pain as Gustave worked me harder and harder to the point of exhaustion. My reflection frightened me. Gone was the spirited, determined, healthy girl who had arrived here. In her place, stood a gaunt skeleton of a woman with sunken cheeks, dark circles under her eyes, and veins popping along her emaciated neck.

And I looked sad. Terribly sad. Something more was eating at me. Bringing me down. Destroying all of me. After so many years in this insulated world of dance, I had been seduced by real life. And by one special man, who I couldn't get out of my mind or my heart. Ryan Madewell. My love for him was far greater than my love for dance. Deeper, more encompassing. I missed him so much and it frustrated me to no end that I couldn't communicate with him. The way I'd left him with no closure or hope gnawed at me. Oh, God! What had I done? Regret filled every cell, every muscle, every bone of my body as my aching heart sank deeper and deeper, taking with it my joie de vivre, my joie de dance. I had made a terrible, terrible mistake leaving Ryan, the man I loved with all my heart and soul. The man who loved me as much as I loved him. Maybe more, if more was possible. Only the wise and compassionate Madame Kapinski sensed my emotional and physical turmoil, which was compounded by worry for my father, but there was nothing she could do. *"Ma chérie,"* she told me after one particularly hard rehearsal, "your dance career *eez* fleeting, but true love never ends." She was right; it would likely be over by the time I was thirty, maybe sooner. Then what? Would my greatest love be my greatest loss?

Hopelessness consumed me. I felt trapped in this castle, trapped in my own body. Rather than dreaming of curtains rising and standing ovations, I found myself crying myself to sleep every night, and shortly after darkness claimed me, the nightmare that had plagued me throughout my dance career returned to haunt me. It took place in a cemetery, the one my mother was buried in. Except instead of one tombstone, there were two. Hers and mine side by side. Stacked against hers, a bouquet of fragrant Asian lilies; against mine, a bunch of blackened, dead roses. And there I was—dancing on my grave—unable to stop, no matter how exhausted I was. As if I was cursed to dance until I dropped. Night after night, the dream recurred until the sound of my own desperate screams awoke me. Shaking to the bone and drenched in cold sweat, how I wished Ryan was next to me, to hold me, to comfort me, to love me.

Unable to fall back to sleep in a bed that was as empty as my aching heart, my insomnia and depression took a toll on me in practices and rehearsals. I was on the edge of hysteria, the verge of collapsing. And then it happened, two days before we were scheduled to go to Paris, the first stop of our European tour, I did a pirouette in practice and lost my balance. There was no way I could stop myself from falling to the hardwood floor. Crumpled in a pile of tulle, I burst out in tears. Sobs wracked my body.

While a number of my peers hurried over to see if I was okay, I heard Mira cackle.

"Hahaha! You are so pathetic!"

My tears fell harder, faster. Then, another harsh voice, thundered in my ears. Gustave.

"Rehearsal over. Everyone dismissed." He slammed his cane on the floor, the sound reverberating in my ears. "Get of here. *Allez, allez!* Now!"

The air filled with the pitter-patter of feet scuttling out the room like frightened mice as I remained huddled on the floor, still sobbing. Then, another sharp bang of Gustave's cane ripped through my ears.

"Get. Up."

The two little words swirled around in my head as if they were foreign and I was trying to comprehend them.

"Did you hear me?" Gustave's voice grew harsher, louder. "GET UP!"

Curling into a fetal position, I hugged my knees and let my sobs rock my body. As tears poured from my eyes, I could feel him looming over me.

"There's only one letter that separates a mouse from a muse. Which one are you, Willow?"

I couldn't get my mouth to form words. Not even one syllable ones. As I hugged myself tighter into a ball, he slipped the tip of his cane under a spaghetti strap of my leotard and tugged at it.

"Well, which one?"

I felt like neither. I felt like nothing.

"Answer me!" His voice thundered with a mixture of impatience and anger. Then, with his cane, he snapped the strap, detaching it from the stretchy garment. The fragment crawled along my chest like vermin.

"ANSWER ME!"

My sobs only grew louder in heaving waves as red-hot tears burned my cheeks. And then—*WHACK!*—I shrieked. Oh the pain! Gustave had hit me with his cane! Rubbing my throbbing thigh with my right hand, I managed to lift myself halfway up onto my other elbow. My watering eyes met his. Madness flickered in his charcoal orbs, and without warning, he struck me again. This time harder. The excruciating pain radiating throughout my body, I cried out again.

"Gustave, why are you doing this?"

His eyes smoldered as a wicked smirk curled his lips. "Don't you know? You need discipline. Or should I say need to be disciplined."

"W-what do you mean?"

"You need to ask that?" His face darkened with fury. "I put so much into you, gave you a second chance...the opportunity of a lifetime... but you've lost your passion for dance."

My eyes stayed on him, my heart pounding, as he played with his cane, shifting it from hand to hand. Trembling, I scooted away from him, fearful he would whack me again.

"Where do you think you're going, my *oiseau?*"

As I scooted back further, he followed me, taking long undeterred steps, his cane stamping the floor with each one. *Tap. Tap. Tap. Tap*. My heart beat double time with each ragged breath, my sobs punching through my pained muscles, bones, and flesh.

"P-please," I begged tearfully. It was the only word I could manage.

My eyes stayed on him as terror filled every cell of my being. His nostrils flared, his eyes narrowed, his lips snarled. He breathed in and out of his nose as his face heated with a mixture of madness and lust. I'd seen this expression before and a new fear seeped into my veins.

Then, a few feet away from me, he paused and turned his cane upside down. Relieved, I didn't see it coming. In one swift move, he hooked my neck with the handle and hauled me toward him. I gasped in pain and in need of air.

"You're hurting me," I choked out as he applied more force.

Leering at me, he laughed. "You should be used to pain, my *oiseau*. It's what a dancer's life is all about. No pain, no beauty."

To my horror, he kicked me hard again, and as I winced, he dug the toe of his ballet slipper into my cheek, crushing it as if he was putting out a cigarette. As if I was to be disposed. Trembling with fear, I put my hands to my face to shield it.

"Don't worry, *ma chérie*. I would never harm that pretty face of yours. I need you to look flawless in Paris...unless you want me to replace you with Mira. My other sweet little muse would kill to play the part of the White Swan."

Quivering, I processed his words. There was no doubt in my mind he was still fucking Mira. And would bash my face if I didn't acquiesce.

"I-I want to dance in Paris, Gustave. I-I do."

His cane still hooked around my neck, he kneeled down beside me. He was wearing tights and a T-shirt that revealed every rugged muscle of his chiseled body. Between his powerful thighs, an enormous erection bulged. I looked away only to have him jerk my head forward with his cane.

"Look at me, Willow. I have so much to offer you. Or have you forgotten?" Snatching one of my hands, he forced it onto his colossal cock and smiled wickedly.

Bile rose in my chest and I swallowed hard to keep myself from vomiting.

"Do you know what your problem is, my little bird?" he asked as he moved my hand up and down the curve of his thick, pulsing shaft.

Biting down on my lip, I shook my head.

"I think you're distracted." He groped a breast. "By that pathetic boy toy in New York." He squeezed harder, eliciting a whimper.

"N-no. He's nothing to me." *He's my everything.*

To my relief, he released my neck, setting his cane down beside him. My relief was short-lived. On my next breath, he gripped my shoulders and shoved me down onto the floor. My head hit the hard wood with a thunk as he threw my legs over his shoulders. Kneeling between them, he stretched the crotch of my leotard with his hands and sunk his teeth into the spandex.

"Gustave, what are you doing?" I croaked as he moved his thick fingers to the small hole he'd made. S*WOOSH!* My legs shook as he ripped apart the fabric and then yanked down my tights to my ankles.

"You need to be fucked. By a *real* man who knows how."

Oh, God. NO! Gustave Fontaine was going to fuck me.

"P-please don't do this to me."

"Shut up and spread your legs," he growled, ignoring my plea.

A mixture of fear and dread filling every cell of my

body, I did as he asked. With my tights still on, my movement was limited.

His lascivious eyes zeroed in on my folds. They lit up like spotlights.

"My little bird, such a sublime ballerina-pink pussy." He rubbed it and I froze, feeling nothing but numbness. "Still one of the finest and so beautifully preened."

Gustave's ballerinas had to be hairless. No leg or arm hair, no armpit hair, no pubic hair. There was an on-staff Russian woman who waxed us regularly.

His eyes narrowed as he stared at my mound.

"Whoops! What is this?" Disgust colored his voice as he pinched a stray pubic hair that must have eluded the waxer. I held back a wince.

Leaning into me, he bit off the stray. I couldn't help a yelp as he spit it out with a *pfftt*. I felt so utterly vulnerable and vilified as he stroked the flawless surface.

"Much better now. Perfection. You're as smooth as satin." A wicked smile lifted his lips. "Do you remember Mr. F?"

Mr. F. I shuddered at the two words. It's what he called his repulsive penis. Short for Mr. Fuck, as some of the other ballerina's he'd seduced referred to it. My pulse in my throat, I didn't respond.

"Well, then, my *oiseau,* it is time you get reacquainted."

My eyes, wide with terror, stayed on him as he slid

his tights down to his knees.

His huge, veined, uncircumcised penis jutted at me. It had to be close to a foot long, much bigger and darker than I remembered it to be. Maybe he had it enlarged.

"Say hello again to Mr. F." To my horror, he put my hand to the hooded crown and forced me to rub the foreskin up and down. Both the touch and the pungent scent of it repulsed me. Nausea rose in my chest as he hissed.

"And now, *ma chérie*, let's dance." Putting the searing tip to my entrance, he growled again.

My heart galloped in my chest; my stomach twisted. My master was a monster. He was about to ravage me. Choreograph a rape. Panic gripped me. Oh, God! *Think, Willow, think!* Then, I eyed his cane to the left of me. His other big hard stick. My mind raced. I needed to distract him.

"Kiss me, Gustave, and then come inside me."

"Oh, *ma chérie*," he groaned, so aroused.

Lowering his eyelids, he leaned into me, and as he crushed his vulgar lips on mine, I grabbed his cane.

Not wasting a second—WHACK!—I smacked it across his hideous organ. The sound echoed in my ears like the climax of a symphony.

Jolting, he roared out in pain. "You fucking cunt!"

"You fucking monster!" I barked back. As he rubbed his swollen, beet-red cock and moaned, I whacked him again harder, bashing his balls. This time, he crumpled onto his side, writhing and cursing between agonized groans. With a victorious smirk, I leaped to my feet, pulled up my tights, and dashed out of the studio. Battling the pain in my thigh, I raced down a long corridor in my pointe shoes, making my way to the entrance of the chateau. Fortunately, it was dinnertime and everyone was in the dining hall. No one saw me or stopped me. When I got to the massive front door, I let out a sigh of relief that no security guards were standing by. They, too, must be eating dinner. Praying there were none outside, I swung open the heavy wooden door…Yes! Not one!—and darted outside.

The blast of the mid-December air was a shock against my skin. The temperature must have been near freezing, and a thick fog blanketed the night sky. Shivering, almost bared, I refrained from hugging myself as I sprinted down the long winding, unlit road that led to the chateau. My teeth chattering, my thigh throbbing, I kept running and running. I had to escape this prison! That monster! I had to! I had to! I had to get home! I wanted to be back with my father! And above all, back with Ryan! My love!

Charging out of the ungated property, I found myself on another long dark, desolate road. I had no idea where it led to or where I was going. All I knew was that I had to get as far and fast away from Gustave as I could. Every limb burning, my lungs on fire, I willed myself to keep running. Maybe with luck, a kind driver would pass by and give me a lift into Paris; it couldn't be that that far. I had no money with me—nor my clothes or passport. But maybe, someone at the U.S. Embassy would take pity on me, get in contact with my father or Ryan, and help me get home.

About a mile in, my wishful thinking came to fruition. I saw headlights coming toward me. Without thinking, I ran into middle of the road and waved my hands at the vehicle. Snowflakes, the size of silver dollars, began to fall.

"Help," I cried out, jumping up and down.

The speeding vehicle, with its bright lights, got closer. My heart pounded with anticipation. Hope. As I stood in the middle of the road, still brandishing my arms and screaming for help on the top of my lungs, it began to blizzard. The falling snow mingled with the fog, creating a dense white veil. The headlights got closer and closer, but why wasn't the car or truck slowing down? Then it hit me... too late. Oh God. In my white leotard and tutu, I blended in with the chalky landscape like a snowflake. The driver didn't see me!

"Stop!" I cried out, the headlights a few feet ahead of me on the slippery road. A loud horn roared like a siren as the vehicle's brakes screeched in my ears. Like a deer in the headlights, my unblinking eyes grew wide and I couldn't move. My mind shut down and then— SMACK!—I was thrown a hundred feet, twisted in the worst pain I'd ever felt in my life. A mangled heap of muscles and bones. The excruciating pain radiating from my head to my toes.

"*Oh, mon dieu!*" I heard a husky masculine voice cry out as the vehicle door swung open. Heavy, rapid footsteps, crunching through piles of dead, snow-laced leaves, thudded in my ears.

As I lay there on the icy road paralyzed in agony, the man rushed up to me and covered me with his jacket, mumbling something in French I didn't understand. A Hail Mary? With the little that tethered me to this earth, I met his forlorn eyes.

My consciousness waning, I watched him pull out his cell phone and, after punching a few numbers, talk rapidly into it. It was all mumbo jumbo to me as life ebbed out of me. I'd read once that you never know who'll be the last person you see as death takes hold of you. As my eyelids lowered, I managed to reach for the necklace I never took off and rubbed the ballet slipper charm between my feeble fingers. My eyes closed. I was in Ryan's arms dancing with him on a moonlit beach. I mumbled his name as the haunting Kol Nidre played in my head. And then the pain subsided. Blackness claimed me.

I was no longer dancing on my grave.

FORTY-THREE

Ryan

I lost track of time. If it weren't for the Christmas decorations that lit up the streets, I wouldn't have known what month we were in. It was mid-December. Somehow, November had gone by. Despite invitations from my parents, my sister, my bud Duff, and even Mel, I spent Thanksgiving alone. I had nothing to be thankful for. My email to Willow had gone unanswered. I was in a comatose state. A zombie. It was an effort to get out of bed. Or leave my loft. I even stopped seeing Dr. Goodman, which was probably a big mistake.

The only person I communicated with regularly was Mel. He, too, had not heard from Willow since her departure to Paris. He was worried sick. I assured him that she was fine because for sure he would have been notified if something had happened to her. Yet, the burning question remained: Why hadn't she gotten in touch with us? It had been over a month.

On a cold, blustery Friday, I decided to pay him a visit. Close to two o'clock in the afternoon, my rumbling stomach told me I had to eat something. In my sorry state, the only thing that would do was some chicken soup for the soul. And Mel made the best in the city.

Bundled up in a puffer jacket, scarf, and beanie, I trudged down the street to his deli. Despite my layers, the chill in the air ripped through me. I'd better get used to it. It was going to be a long, cold winter.

Mel's Famous, as usual, was busy. There was joy in the air, many diners carrying colorful shopping bags filled with Christmas and Chanukah presents. Fuck. I hadn't even started my holiday shopping. And I had a shitload to do, from finding the perfect gifts for my parents to sending one to my adorable niece, Violet. I just wasn't in a joyous, giving mood. Maybe I'd hire a personal shopper and get it done that way. As for me, the only thing I wanted was to be with Willow. I'd even settle for a letter, an email, or a text as long as it ended in "xo."

My eyes darted around the crowded restaurant in search of Mel. I spotted him at the cash register. Our eyes made contact as he waved me over.

"How'ya doing, Ryan?" he asked, ringing up a bill.

"Hanging in there. Any news from Willow?"

He shook his head, the expression on his face turning glum.

My heart sunk. The saying "misery loves company" had no meaning for me. I tried to cheer him up.

"Maybe she'll get in touch once the ballet opens in

Paris." The one thing that I'd done was check the performance schedule of the opera house online. The Royal Latvia Ballet's production of *Swan Lake* was set to premier in a couple of days. "Or we can track her down there," I added, not sharing my fear that Willow had abandoned me for Gustave.

"From your mouth to God's ears." Mel shrugged hopelessly. "What can I get you?"

Before I could place my order, his old-fashioned wall phone rang. He grabbed the receiver on the second ring and put it to his ear.

"Mel's Famous." My gaze stayed on him as he listened in silence. His face blanched and his hand trembled. Jesus. Was he having another heart attack?

"Mel, are you okay?" I asked anxiously as the phone slipped out of his hand.

"It's Willow. She's been in a terrible accident."

My heart skipped a beat. "What happened?"

"A truck hit her."

"Jesus. Is she going to be okay?"

"They don't know. She's about to undergo surgery. I need to get to Paris to be with my baby girl."

Paris. A chill ran through me. The City of Lights was my City of Doom. I couldn't even watch French movies anymore.

Mel looked at me, his eyes watering. "Ryan, she's been crying out your name."

I had no choice. We were going to Paris together.

We were fucked. Every airline I looked up online was booked because of the holidays. The first available direct flight to Paris wasn't until after the first of the year. Again, I had no choice. With dread in my stomach, I speed dialed one number. My father's. His longtime secretary, Hazel, picked up on the first ring and I asked her put me through to him. I told her it was urgent.

Holding my breath, I was relieved when I heard my father's voice.

"Hello, son. What can I do for you?" he drawled though his speech was improving.

"Father, I have an emergency."

"You need money?"

"No, I need to use the company plane if it's available.

"Where do you need to go?"

"Paris."

Silence ensued. The City of Lights held dark memories for my father as well. He had flown there to make amends with me, but it was too late; Allee was gone. Reliving our awkward encounter in the Hemingway Bar, my chest tightened.

Clearing his throat, my father asked, "Something to do with your late wife?"

He never referred to Allee by name, which was fine

by me.

"No."

"Something to do with that new girl. Willa?"

"Willow," I corrected. "She's been in a bad accident."

Another stretch of silence. Every second that went by meant that I might never hold her in my arms again. My pulse thudded in my ears with trepidation.

Then, finally…"Hold on. I'll have Hazel check if the plane is free."

While I shared an anxious glance with Mel, my father put me on hold for a minute and then returned.

"Son, it's available. It's yours."

I breathed out a heavy sigh of relief and gave Mel a thumbs-up. His forlorn face brightened a tad as I wrapped up my call.

"Thank you, Father." Three words I rarely said.

"When will you be back?"

"I don't know. But as soon as possible."

"Good luck, son. And may God be with both of you."

One hour later, Mel and I were on our way to Paris with my father's blessings. Praying that Willow would be all right.

Mel and I arrived in Paris seven hours later. A limo met us at Le Bourget Airport and drove us straight to the hospital. The American Hospital in Neuilly. The very hospital where Allee had passed away. Where we'd spent our last night together.

A little after seven o'clock in the morning, the City of Lights was just waking up. Mel, who had never been to Paris before, kept his face pressed against the tinted glass windows. I suppose silently taking in the sites was a means of coping with his anxiety and fear. In the plane, he had tearfully told me that he couldn't bear to lose Willow. I couldn't bear to lose her either.

My stomach was in knots throughout the entire ride. I hadn't been back to Paris since Allee's death. The range of emotions that ran through me was daunting. And there was an awful, sick sense of déjà-vu. I seriously did not know if I could go through with this. Losing one great love in Paris was enough. Losing two was unimaginable.

The trip took us only twenty minutes. Except for a light layer of snow that dusted the grounds, The American Hospital of Paris was just as I remembered it. The sprawling five-story brick complex venerable and stately. Despite our fatigue, we raced through the entrance and up to the information center. Willow, now out of surgery, was in the intensive care unit on the third floor of Building D. The attendant on duty informed us we were not allowed to see her at this time.

"Monsieur, ce n'est pas possible," said the stern, dismissive woman after a distraught Mel begged for the umpteenth time.

Impossible? Fuck this shit. This is when I used my pull. I told the arrogant French woman that I was Ryan Madewell, the son of Eleanor Madewell, who was now the Chairwoman of the American Hospital of Paris Foundation. To prove it to her, I pulled out my passport. Her eyes grew wide and after mumbling, "Pardon" in French, she instantly picked up a phone and arranged for Mel and me to have access to Willow. Her surgeon was going to meet us outside the ICU.

Dr. Beauchamp was a kind-looking, balding man in his early sixties. He spoke English perfectly.

"Messieurs, I am afraid I have good news and bad news."

Bad news. At the sound of those two words, I thought Mel would have another coronary. This time a major one. I steadied him with my hands.

"The good news *eez* that she *eez* going to be okay. Given the force of impact from the truck, it *eez* a miracle. Though she suffered numerous internal injuries as well a serious head injury, she does not have brain damage. She will be able to resume a full and normal life."

I breathed a loud sigh of relief. Mel almost squeezed the life out of the slight man with a hug. "That's great, Doc. So what's the bad news?"

"I'm afraid she will never be able to dance again. At least on a professional level. Her right leg was severely broken in five places. We had to pin *eet* back together."

The big smile on Mel's face fell off. "Will she be

able to dance at her wedding?"

The doctor nodded with a grin. "*Bien sur.* Not only will she be able to dance at her wedding, but she'll be able to dance at her children's too."

Tears leaked out the corners of Mel's eyes. "Can I see my little girl, Doc?"

"*Oui.* But just for a *petit peu.*" A little bit. "She *eez* very tired."

The doctor's focus shifted to me. "You must be Ryan. *Oui?*"

I nodded. "Yes, sir."

"She was crying out for you when she was wheeled into the hospital. And when she regained consciousness after the surgery, she asked for you again."

My stomach twisting, I digested his words and remained speechless.

The doctor continued. "She will be very happy to see you, *monsieur. Attendez-vous ici, s'il vous plaît.*"

Wait here. Dr. Beauchamp escorted Mel to Willow's room while I took a seat in the waiting area. Jumbled thoughts swirled around in my head. How would I feel when I saw her? What would I say to her? And why had she called out my name?

Fifteen minutes later, Mel slumped into the waiting area. His eyes were bloodshot; he'd been crying. I leaped to my feet.

"How is she?" I asked anxiously.

A faint smile flickered on his face. "She's eager to see you, Ryan. She's in room 312."

Allee had been two floors above in room 512. The memory of our last night together jumped to the front of my mind. Frail, wan Allee lying there in bed with me, facing the bitter end. My beloved Allee. I could hear her voice in my head as if she was looking down on me. *Madewell, I want you to be strong for me.* Now, I had to be strong for Willow. I took a deep breath, steeling myself for the worst.

A few minutes later, I stood in the doorway to her room.

"Hi."

The minute my eyes set sight on her, my heart filled with reckless abandon. A small smile lit her face, and when she met my gaze, I rushed to her side, desperately wanting to take her into my arms.

Hooked up to IVs and beeping monitors, she was way thinner than when I'd seen her last. From under a bandage around her head, her long red hair fanned out over her pillow. Her skin was paler than I remembered, but her pallor and weight loss only accentuated her exquisite delicate features. Her leg, in a thigh-high cast, was suspended in traction. I took hold of her frail hand.

"Oh, Ryan, you came!" Her hoarse voice was just above a whisper.

"Shh." I lifted her hand to my lips and kissed the back of it.

"Yeah, I'm here, baby."

"Can you ever forgive me?"

"There's nothing to forgive. We're together. That's

all that counts."

Her heavy-lidded eyes blinked tears as I slid my backpack off my shoulders.

"I brought you something."

"You did?" she murmured, her voice rising just a bit.

Her eyes stayed on me as I unfastened the buckle of the bag and reached inside it.

"Baboo!" she exclaimed as loud as she could as I held him up and waved his little tattered hand.

"I missed you," I said in my best cartoony monkey voice. I certainly was no actor, but my silly impersonation worked.

Despite her fragile state, my Willow giggled. God, I loved that giggle. I smiled, then grew serious, my voice returning to normal.

"But not as much as I missed you."

"I missed you so much too," she said softly as I handed her the plush monkey. She sniffed his worn hand and smiled again.

"He smells like you, now."

I couldn't help but smile back. "Yeah, I slept with him every night. He made me feel connected to you."

"Was he there for you?" She was referring to our conversation that night on Yom Kippur in her bedroom. My fuckedupness.

"Yeah, he gave me hope." I paused, wondering what to say next before blurting out what was on my mind. "Why didn't you write me? Email me? Text me?"

"I couldn't. There was no Internet. Plus, Gustave confiscated all our devices and circumvented all our mail." She fiddled with the ballet slipper charm on the necklace I'd given her. "I thought about you every minute of the day."

"The same." I stroked her hair, relieved that the bastard hadn't taken her necklace. "How did the accident happen?"

A look of terror washed over her. She chewed her bottom lip. "G-gustave assaulted me."

"Jesus! Did he r—"

She cut me off before I could say "rape."

"No, I escaped." She continued with the details, begging me not to tell her father about what had happened.

Rage pulsed through my veins. Fucking, fucking Gustave. I wanted to kill the bastard. He was going to pay. My brave Willow should have chopped off his balls. When I got back to the States, I was going to talk to my sister about pressing charges. I was going to take the motherfucker down no matter what it took.

Stealing me away from my Machiavellian machinations, Willow squirmed in her bed. She shifted her raised leg and grimaced. Every nerve in my body jumped with concern.

"Do you hurt, baby?"

She shook her head. "Not when you're with me."

I caressed her face. "My darling, you're going to be

with me for a long time."

Her eyes widened and her parched but oh so kissable lips parted. "What do you mean?"

Panic set in. I had to do this right, seal the deal, give her a ring. Any ring. Fuck. What ring? Then, as my gaze zeroed in on Baboo snuggled next to the woman I loved with all I had—*Ping!*—a light bulb flashed above my head like they did in comic strips. On my wrist, I was still wearing the pink ribbon that used to be tied around the little monkey's neck. Reaching under the sleeve of my jacket, I undid the ribbon as Willow watched in silence. Holding the ribbon between my fingers, I got down on one knee, then took Willow's left hand in mine.

"Willow, my love, I want to lay my roots next to yours. Make beautiful saplings and watch them grow as we grow old together."

Her eyes shone into mine. "What are you saying, Ryan?"

"I love you with my heart and my soul." My voice loud and clear, I wrapped the frayed pink ribbon around her ring finger, sealing it with a bow. "Will you be my wife?"

"Oh my God, yes," she whispered, gazing at her finger. We were tied together. Bound.

And with that, I leaned into her and pressed my lips against hers. She was too weak to resist me deepening it with my tongue. A moan escaped her throat, one of pure joy, not pain.

I pulled away and traced her moist lips with my finger. Tears were streaming from her eyes. I moved my hand to her cheek and brushed them away.

"My butterfly, why are you crying?"

"Oh, Ry-man, I've loved you from page one."

Undying Love. I swiped my own tears. Here in this hospital where I'd lost Allee Adair, I'd gained Willow Rosenthal. The next Mrs. Madewell.

Willow needed her rest. It was time to leave. A relieved but weary Mel stood by my side waiting for the elevator. Later, after getting some sleep at a nearby hotel, I would tell him that I had proposed to his daughter. A better father-in-law could not be had.

The elevator doors slid open, and the sole passenger's steel-gray eyes clashed with mine. He was holding a large bouquet of black roses in one hand and his cane in the other. He pushed past me. Fucking Gustave!

"Mel, go down to the lobby. I forgot something." I shoved him into the elevator before he could say a word. The doors closed behind me.

Tapping his cane, Gustave swaggered down the long corridor with a slight limp. Ha! He was still aching from Willow's caning. Not wasting a second, I chased after him and caught up to him in no time. Grabbing his elbow, I held him back. He spun around.

"What do you want?" he asked, his voice as cold as dry ice.

I didn't answer him—why waste words on this asshole?—and tightened my grip.

Writhing, he tried to free himself, but it was futile. "Let go of me, you peon."

Ignoring his pathetic plea, I plucked out one of the macabre roses from the bouquet.

"A rose is a rose is a rose." The astute words of one of my favorite writers, Gertrude Stein. Inspired, I rolled the pad of my thumb over one of the thorns. "And a prick is a prick is a prick."

He scowled. "Give me back the rose."

"Fine, but I want to give you *this* first." Before he could blink an eye, I fisted my right hand and plowed it into his face. So hard my knuckles stung. *THWACK!* His groan was like music to my ears.

Blood poured from his mouth. "I'm bleeding," he whined like a pathetic ninny as he swiped at the crimson stream. Rivulets rolled over his twisted lips, some landing on his cashmere turtleneck, others getting caught in his goatee. Lowering his hand, he rolled his tongue over his teeth before contorting his face and cursing in French.

"You knocked my tooth out!" Reaching into his mouth, he retrieved the bloodied front tooth and stared at it in a state of shock while blood still dripped down his chin.

Taking advantage of his stunned condition, I

punched him again harder—this time in his gut. Wincing, he bent over in pain, dropping the rest of the flowers onto the floor. Adrenaline pumping in my veins, I kicked them fifty-feet down the hall and then kicked him in the balls.

"What the fuck?" he moaned, his eyes watering.

"I'm not done with you."

Not wasting a second, I grabbed his cane out of his hand. He cowered, fearing I would hit him with it. And trust me, I was this close to doing it.

"Please," he whimpered, clutching his stomach with one hand and protectively cupping his junk with the other. "Don't hit me again."

I gripped the cane so tightly my knuckles turned white. "You, bastard. If you ever come near my girl again, I'll break you in half like this cane." With my two hands, I snapped the cane in half and tossed the pieces in the direction of the elevator. "Now, get the fuck out of here."

As he gimped down the hallway to the elevator, I shouted out to him. "By the way, don't count on an invitation to the wedding."

FORTY-FOUR

Ryan

Six Months Later

As seated guests waited anxiously for the bride to appear in the vast yard of Willow's grandmother's upstate property, I stood under the bough of the majestic willow tree where Willow Rosenthal and I would soon be exchanging our vows. The very tree under which we'd made love for the first time and on which I'd inscribed an eternal heart with our initials back in the fall. The heart that sat next to the one her father had inscribed three decades earlier.

The early June day couldn't have been more perfect. The temperature was in the mid-seventies and the sun shined brightly in the clear blue sky. The sound of birds chirping accompanied the harpist, who was playing Vivaldi's melodic *Four Seasons*. My heart thudding with anticipation, I watched as my adorable five-year-old niece, Violet, walked down the flower-lined aisle holding a basket from which she tossed purple petals everywhere. Dressed in a poufy ankle-length white tulle dress with a violet sash and a matching band of flowers around her head, the radiant little beauty already walked with the grace of a ballerina.

My ballerina bride would be here soon. The procession started at the lake and it would be a few minutes until she arrived with her father. Standing under the tree with my sister's spouse Beth, a Universal Life Church minister, who was going to marry us, I took in our guests.

We had decided on a small, intimate wedding, but everyone near and dear to us was here. In the front row, my mother was sitting next to my sister and to the right of her was my father in his wheelchair looking the best I'd seen him look since his stroke. Over the last six months we'd grown much closer, and to both my mother's joy and mine, he had made amends with my sister. Thrilled to have a grandpa, little Violet smiled brightly at him as she passed him. My father shot a smile back, their exchange warming my heart on this special day.

Another reconciliation had taken place over the past six months. While Willow was convalescing from her accident at the one-story flat we rented so she didn't have to climb stairs, her grandma had come down to visit her. Willow's near-death encounter miraculously erased the grudge the matriarch held toward Mel. While Willow's mom would never be part of their lives again, both menschy Mel and good-hearted Ida were united by

the near-loss of their beloved Willow. Over a plateful of
Ryan Madewell sandwiches at Mel's deli, memories
were exchanged and a new bond was forged. The
future. Later that night over champagne, I finally gave
Willow her real engagement ring…it was the diamond
ring Mel had given his late wife when he proposed to
her. Mel wanted Willow to have it and though I could
have certainly have afforded something much grander,
this ring with its small square solitaire diamond was
special. The happy tears my Willow had shed as I
slipped it on her finger filled my mind as I eagerly
awaited her, my eyes still flitting among our guests.

Behind my parents and my sister sat my best bud
Duffy and his beautiful wife Sam along with their
adorable three-month-old baby, Zeke—my godson.
Others seated in the white folding chairs included Nurse
Hollis, who was officially Mel's "gal" as he liked to
call her. Mel's loyal employees were also here along
with some longtime customers, including that curmudgeon I'd made a sandwich for the first day I met
my beautiful wife-to-be. His name was Gus, and it
turned out he used to frequent Willow's grandparents'
hotel with his late wife back in the day. He'd always
thought that Willow's grandma was the cat's meow and
now he was sitting next to her, holding her hand. There
was definitely magic in the air.

Some of my former staffers from *Arts & Smarts*
were also here along with my agent, Paula, and our
therapist, Dr. Goodman and his wife. Last but not least,

Marcus was here, seated next to my beloved nannie, Maria. It meant the world to me that my esteemed former driver had flown in from Detroit to share my special day. Just a little over five years ago he had walked my beloved Allee to me in Central Park. The memory of that day flashed into my mind, and for a split-second, sadness pricked me. But as soon as I saw my stunning new bride heading toward me on the arm of her father, the memory faded and happiness filled me.

All eyes were on her as she slowly walked down the aisle with her beaming and now fifty-pounds thinner father. My eyes, too, stayed riveted on her. Meeting my gaze, a smile crossed her lips. She looked absolutely gorgeous…dressed in a long strapless white tulle gown that resembled Violet's and a band of white flowers circling her loose, wild red hair. She had vowed to walk down the aisle with her father, and after months of crutches, physical therapy, and pure determination, here she was. She still had a slight limp, but in time that would go away. Nothing was going to stop our union. *Nothing.*

Several rapid heartbeats later, I took her into my arms and then held her hand as we both faced Beth. My pounding heart leapt into my throat as Beth began the service.

Rather than writing our own vows like I had with Allee, Willow and I decided we wanted Beth to tell our story. To share with our families and friends the story of a second chance romance—one that was filled with heartbreak and hope...of finding true love again where you least expected it. In a deli of all places. Laughter erupted and I squeezed Willow's hand as Beth continued.

As the laughter died down, I inhaled a deep breath. It was vow time.

Except for the chirping birds and a few sniffles among our guests, there was silence.

Beth: "Do you, Willow Rosenthal, promise to love Ryan Madewell in sickness and in health until death do you part?

"I do." Willow's voice was as soft as a prayer.

My turn. My heart was racing and my stomach knotted. Beth repeated the words she'd just said to Willow.

"Do you, Ryan Madewell, promise..."

In sickness and in health...until death do you part. The words whirled around in my head and nausea rose in my chest. My hands grew clammy.

What if Willow died young? All too soon like Allee? I didn't think I could ever recover again. Even live. I'd discussed this morbid fear with Dr. Goodman ad nauseam, both alone and in couples sessions with Willow. Both of them assured me I had nothing to worry about. Willow even said she possessed her Nana's good genes and would likely be dancing when she was a hundred. Or more. But there was still the possibility of a fatal accident...

At this critical moment, this profound fear rammed into me like a freight train. I was paralyzed. I couldn't get my mouth to move and say two little words.

"Well?" The raspy voice trailed off as my eyes grew wide.

Allee! She was here!! Standing right next to Beth, wearing that white gauzy gown I'd seen before.

Her arms folded across her chest, she rolled her espresso-bean eyes at me. "Madewell, whatch'ya waiting for? All you have to do is say, 'I do.'"

My jaw dropped open.

Her expression softened. "Madewell, do it. Do it for me."

The two little words spilled out slowly, one at a time. "I do."

With Allee looking on, Willow and I exchanged rings. Simple platinum bands, each engraved with a heart and our initials much like the carving on the tree trunk. As Beth pronounced us husband and wife, a butterfly flew by us and that dazzling smile, one I would never forget, spread across Allee's full lips.

"Congratulations, Golden Boy." She gave me a thumbs-up and then disappeared as Beth pronounced us husband and wife.

Amidst cheers and applause from our guests, I took my beautiful new wife into my arms and gave her a passionate, all-consuming kiss that I wanted never to end.

Soon, I'd be swaying her in my arms to the song

we'd chosen for our first dance We'd sifted through so many, but none of them made more sense than one. I think *she* chose it for us. It was the song that connected the three of us, made me think of the past, the present, and the future. The song that had given me hope and made me whole again.

"I Won't Give Up."

EPILOGUE
Ryan

Four Years Later

T he first Sunday of November couldn't be more perfect. The temperature is unseasonably mild, in the low-seventies; the sun-kissed sky is picture-postcard perfect, and the still blooming flowers have once again proven they are mightier than the winter snow. Winter will claim them soon, but they will be back in the spring with their friends, the butterflies, all around the small but charming backyard of our townhouse in the West Village. The down payment was a wedding gift from my father. Actually, he wanted to buy it out right, but both Willow and I refused. I, however, appreciated his grand gesture. It was his way of making amends with me. While I will never have the close father-son relationship that many guys have with their dads and can never forget the past, he's welcomed in my life. My way of forgiving him. Allee would be proud of me.

The three-story brick house is perfect for us. There's plenty of space including an office where I write and a dance studio in the basement where Willow teaches ballet to neighborhood children. We have a multitude of bedrooms, one of which permanently belongs to my darling niece, Violet, who visits us often. Almost ten-years-old, she's an amazing young ballerina. And an equally amazing cousin.

Our bedroom is on the top floor. Our regal bed with the pink tufted satin headboard dominates it. There's not one night that goes by that I don't make love in it with my beautiful wife. Sometimes countless times. Wedged between our pillows is Baboo and hanging above the bed is the Degas ballerina painting that belonged to my mother. The one that awed both Allee and Willow. My mother gave it to us as a wedding present. She wanted us to have it. Willow says it belongs to all three of us, but we're thinking of donating it to the museum I visit annually on Allee's birthday that houses my former bed.

Our sun-filled room overlooks the backyard, a rarity for any New Yorker. Our garden, with its array of flowers, herbs, and vegetables, is totally Willow's doing. She planted everything by hand herself. In the middle stands a tiny weeping willow tree. One day it will grow big and strong and provide shade to all those who need it. And there will be a swing hanging from one of its mighty branches.

Scattered throughout the garden is some outdoor furniture that Willow and I collected at local flea markets. Among the pieces is a vintage French bench that reminds me of the one Allee and I once shared in the Jardin de Tuileries in Paris. I sit there often as I am about to do with my *Sunday New York Times.*

As I head toward it with the paper clutched under my arm, a little girl with a large paintbrush in her hand skips by me. This past summer she turned three. Our daughter. The child Willow and I love more than life itself.

"Daddy, I go paint a picture." She frolics over to the small easel in the corner of the yard that Mel and Hollis, her other doting grandparents, bought her. Her espresso bean eyes twinkle, and her long chestnut ponytail flies in the warm autumn breeze.

She brings a big smile to my face and lights up my heart. She's inherited Allee's love for art. And she's her spitting image.

"Hey."

The raspy familiar voice catapults me out of my thoughts. Allee! She's sitting on the bench peeking up from a book. Mine! *Endless Love.* The book I started writing the morning after I made love to Willow for the first time in our bed. It's a true story of heartbreak and hope, rediscovery and recovery, fate and second chances. Willow actually helped me write it. Told in dual point of view, it's not my story. It's our story, but with Willow's blessings, I dedicated it to another…

> *To Allee, my endless love.*
> *You will live in my heart forever.*

My jaw drops. This is the first time Allee's visited me in my new digs. I'm frozen in shock, speechless.

"How'ya doin', 1212?"

1212. My breath hitches. Only Allee ever called me that—my bib number when I ran the New York Marathon exactly ten years ago today and she joined me mid-way.

Thinking back to that fateful day, I manage a few words. "I'm good. Really good."

She smiles. "I'm proud of you, Madewell. And Willow, too. She's my kind of woman. Good for her for taking the asshole down."

Following our honeymoon in Fiji, Willow was determined to expose Gustave for what he was. A despicable prick, and that was being kind. With the help of my sister, she pressed charges against him for sexually assaulting her, and after a headline-making international trial in which several other abused dancers testified on her behalf, he was sentenced to ten years in prison and a $150,000 fine, which cost him his dance company and his career. Willow became a star in a way she could have never imagined. A hero to women all over the world. In addition to teaching and being an incredible mom, my amazing wife is now a crusader for the rights of ballet dancers, relentlessly trying to improve their working conditions, benefits, and pay.

"I'm proud of her too," I respond to Allee, who's staring down at the cover of my book.

"Oh, and by the way, the new book is really good.

Nice of you to include me."

Holy shit. She read it! "Really? You liked it?"

"Yeah. A lot."

A compliment from Allee is like finding a needle in a haystack. I'm both shocked and ecstatic.

"Wow, thanks!"

"Are they making a movie version?"

"Yes." The film was already in production with Ryan Reynolds and Emma Stone reprising their roles. Lilly Beaucoup, a new unknown actress and former ballerina, was playing Willow. I'd never seen the movie version of *Undying Love* even though it was a blockbuster, garnering both Ryan Reynolds and Emma Stone Academy Awards. I wondered if Allee saw it, but I didn't ask. Something else was on my mind.

"Allee, was Endless Love as good as Undying Love?"

"Are you kidding me, Madewell? It was better. It made me happy. You got your happily ever after. You deserve it."

With a smile, I gaze at her. She hasn't aged a bit. Her long hair is gathered in a high ponytail and her espresso bean eyes twinkle against her dewy fresh skin. She's wearing running shorts and a tank top that show off her perfect breasts and those amazing legs. The very outfit she wore when she ran the marathon with me.

"So, tell me about the kid."

"Oh, Allee, she's just like you. Feisty, artsy, and smart." I tell her that when I told Willow about my

frozen embryos, she pleaded to have them implanted in her. She knew how much Allee meant to me. I agreed, knowing from her relationship with Violet what a great mother she would be. One out of the three took and Willow joyously carried the baby to full term. One day when our little girl is older, we will tell her the story of her conception. And I'll tell her all about Allee.

Tears are brimming in Allee's smiling eyes. I'd seen enough of them to last me a lifetime. "What's her name?" *she asks.*

"Belle." I glance over to my precious daughter, who is now creating a masterful abstract painting at her easel. We named her after Willow's mother, Belinda.

Allee gazes reflectively at her too. "That means 'beautiful' in French. Just like she is."

"Yeah, I know."

Allee's misty eyes don't stray from Belle. "And her name has two L's. That's good."

I nod as Allee continues to observe her.

"She's quite the little Picasso."

I smile with pride. "She is."

"Ry-man, who are you talking to?"

I look over my shoulder. It's Willow. Taking advantage of the glorious weather, she sets a tray down on our outdoor table—the delectable lunch I'll share with her and Belle. If only she knew there are four of us. Or should I say five because Willow is pregnant again—with a baby we made—a boy, due in February on

Valentine's Day. We're naming him Harry, after Willow's grandfather, Harold. Willow insisted we make his middle name Ryan, and I only hope Harry Ryan Madewell will turn out to be the best man he can be.

"Do we have a guest?" asks my beautiful wife.

I falter for an excuse. "Um, butterfly, I was just thinking my next book out loud."

Willow smiles at me and arranges the table.

My sweet little Belle catches sight of Willow. "Mama!" she shouts, running over to hug her.

Beaming, Willow lifts our daughter into her arms and smothers her with kisses.

I glance back at the bench. Allee has risen. There's a wide smile on her face. Her voice resounds in my head as she fades away.

"Belle will find her Superman. I hope he's just like you. See ya', Golden Boy."

NOTE FROM NELLE

Dearest Reader~

Thank you from the bottom of my heart for reading *Endless Love* as well as *Undying Love.* If you loved these books, it would mean the world to me if you would write reviews at the retailer where you purchased them. They can be as long or short as you wish. Reviews of any length help others discover my books.

Many of you have waited almost five long years for this sequel. I want to thank you for your love, patience, and support.

Believe me, this is the miracle of books. I will be honest—I didn't want to write it and was regretful I included an excerpt of it at the end of *Undying Love.* In retrospect, some books like *Me Before You* shouldn't have a sequel and the future of the protagonist should just be left in the reader's imagination. But I foolishly included a few early chapters of a sequel because I knew my romance readers required a HEA—a happily ever after ending.

Many readers begged for the sequel; others became

angry with me, some cheered me on while others became disbelievers. I often felt like the protagonist in *Peter and the Wolf,* except I cried sequel instead of wolf. Let me tell you, guilt gnawed at me big time every minute of the day.

Over the years since *Undying Love* was published, I wrote chapters of *Endless Love* here and there, never thinking I'd ever finish writing the book. Then, something I read inspired me. "A Modern Love" column in the *Sunday New York Times.* It was a love letter of sorts written by Amy Krause Rosenthal, a critically acclaimed author in her early fifties, who on her deathbed, urged her beloved husband to find someone new after she was gone. Sounds familiar? And uncannily, this amazing woman, who had everything to live for, shared the same last name as my heroine, Willow. Because I envision you smiling at the end of *Endless Love* and/or crying happy tears, I'm not going to include the link. If you do want to read "You May Want to Marry My Husband," email me at nellelamour@gmail.com and I will send it to you.

When I read this moving tribute, I bawled. It reminded me so much of the letter dying Allee wrote to Ryan. I read it again and again. And I shed tear after tear. Just like Allee, Amy passed away soon after and I cried yet again. Through my tears, I knew I owed it to my readers and myself to finish *Endless Love.* And to Allee as well. The words flowed.

And so, almost five years later, Ryan Madewell finally has his happily every after. Just like his Allee wished. I hope that Joel Rosenthal will get his too. That's what his Amy wanted. In fact, I hope that all of you, who have lost a cherished spouse or partner, will one day get a second chance and find a new endless love to make your life whole. There is a reason I didn't type THE END when I finished writing this book. To repeat Richard Bach's poignant words, "A true love story never ends."

Let another one begin. I hope to bring you many more. Thank you from the bottom of my heart for reading *Endless Love* and believing in me…

With love, appreciation, and heartfelt tears…

MWAH!~Nelle ♥

.

MORE FROM NELLE

If *Undying Love* and *Endless Love* are the first books of mine you've read, just know that I write a diverse range of erotic romances. Except for *Undying Love,* they all have happily ever after endings.

Many of my books are bestselling steamy romantic comedies. They include my hugely popular *THAT MAN* series and *Unforgettable* trilogy (both available as boxed sets) as well as my standalones, *Baby Daddy* and *The Big O.* If you love loveable, cocky alpha males with hearts of gold, these books are for you. Be prepared to laugh, cry, and swoon!

I also write steamy romantic suspense. These include my *USA Today* bestselling *Gloria's Secret* trilogy (available as a boxed set) as well as my *Trainwreck* duet. Be prepared for sexy, page-turner excitement.

To sample some of my books, you can download the following anthology for FREE:

NAUGHTY NELLE:
https://dl.bookfunnel.com/r39m1ug4mx

Under the pen name, E.L. Sarnoff, I write romantic

fantasy. Check out *Dewitched: The Untold Story of the Evil Queen,* a standalone, and its sequel, *Unhitched.* Be prepared to see the Evil Queen from *Snow White* in a whole new light as she goes to rehab for her addiction to evil and gets a chance at happily ever after and true love.

Links to all my books follow. I hope you will enjoy reading them as much as I loved writing them. You can also find them on my website: nellelamour.com/books

Thank you again from the bottom of my heart for reading *Undying Love* and *Endless Love*. And for your love and support. Never hesitate to drop me an email or send me a PM on Facebook to let me know your thoughts. Or just to say hello! I respond personally to each and every message I receive.

MWAH!~ Nelle ♥

ACKNOWLEDGMENTS

WOW! I did it! I wrote this book! It took me five long, challenging years and I have many people to thank who shared this incredible journey with me.

First of foremost, a big shout out to my readers who pushed me to write the sequel to *Undying Love* and never lost faith in me. I'd like to single out a few...my beautiful ninja warrior, Cathy Gaudagnino, persistent Mariana Lee, and lovely Wendy Anderson.

Another round of thanks goes to my bestest beta readers. In alphabetical order, they are: Auden Dar, Shannon Meadows Heyward, Shelley Miles, Kristen Myers, Ilene Rosen, Lynette Schaefer, Karen Silverstein, Jeanette Sinfield, and Joanna Warren. Thank you for your honesty and insights. Truly, *Endless Love* is a better book on account of your input. I'm so blessed to have you all in my life.

I want to give special thanks to a couple betas. First, my dear friend and balletomane, Shelley Miles. While I did a great amount of research and had the good fortune of attending breathtaking performances of both *The Firebird* ballet and *The Red Shoes*, Shelley scrutinized the ballet portions of *Endless Love* to make sure I got things right. I was totally blown away when she said I "did a really great job," but equally loved when she told me toes shoes are called pointe shoes in the ballet world and that those who inhabit this world prefer to be called dancers than ballerinas. Who knew!

Secondly, I want to single out fellow writer, friend, and beta, Auden Dar. Not only were her notes astute, but she was also a great cheerleader. Our daily back and forth emails kept me going and believing in myself. Check out her debut book, *Prelude*, on her website. It's so good! Trust me, Auden is one to watch! Website: www.audendar.com

Though not one of my betas, I also want to thank *mon amie* and fellow writer, Fifi Flowers. She, too, was so supportive. Check out her steamy books! Website: www.fififlowers.com

And now a big applause for my ongoing team:

♥ Gloria Herrera, my trusted assistant, who makes all those beautiful teasers you see on Facebook and sends out all my ARCs one by one. Plus, keeps me on schedule with her virtual whip. *Wink*

♥ Give Me Books and Enticing Journey, the wonderful PR companies that hosted my Release Blitz and Blog Tour, respectively. These lovely ladies work so hard to get our books into the hands of readers and deserve hugs.

♥ All the passionate bloggers who featured *Endless Love* (and *Undying Love*) on their blogs. A special shout out goes to those who painstakingly wrote reviews.

- ♥ My ARC readers. I love you all! Thank you for reading and reviewing *Endless Love* as well as *Undying Love* (if you hadn't done that before). Your beautiful, heartfelt words brought tears to my eyes.

- ♥ Mary Jo Toth and Virginia Tesi Carey, my eagle-eye proofreaders, who never fail to make me realize you can't have enough eyes on your work.

- ♥ Arijana Karcic/Cover It! Designs, my amazing cover designer. I adore you and can't wait to work with you again.

- ♥ Paul Salvette/BB ebooks, my patient and meticulous formatter. He's always such a pleasure to work with, and he puts up with my gazillion revisions.

- ♥ Finally, my family. Thank you, my loves, for letting me write. A big hug (Okay, I know you want and deserve more) goes to my hubby for often being Mr. Mom (though I know you're convinced you're Blake Burns).

I think that does it! No, wait!! Thank you, dear reader, for purchasing and reading *Endless Love*. Your love and support means with the world to me. You are the reason I write.

MWAH!~Nelle ♥

ABOUT THE AUTHOR

Nelle L'Amour is a *New York Times* and *USA Today* bestselling author who lives in Los Angeles with her Prince Charming-ish husband, twin now-in-college princesses, and a bevy of royal pain-in-the-butt pets. A former executive in the entertainment industry with a prestigious Humanitas Prize for promoting human dignity and freedom to her credit, she gave up playing with Barbies a long time ago, but still enjoys playing with toys with her husband. While she writes in her PJs, she loves to get dressed up and pretend she's Hollywood royalty. Her steamy stories feature characters that will make you laugh, cry, and swoon and stay in your heart forever.

To learn about her new releases, sales, and giveaways, please sign up for her newsletter and follow her on social media. Nelle loves to hear from her readers.

Check out her cool website:
www.nellelamour.com

Sign up for her fun newsletter:
nellelamour.com/newsletter

Join her on Facebook:
facebook.com/NelleLamourAuthor

Join her intimate Facebook Reader Group:
facebook.com/groups/1943750875863015

Follow her on Twitter:
twitter.com/nellelamour

Email her at:
nellelamour@gmail.com

Follow her on Amazon:
amazon.com/Nelle-LAmour/e/B00ATHR0LQ

Follow her on BookBub:
bookbub.com/authors/nelle-l-amour

BOOKS BY NELLE L'AMOUR

Unforgettable
Unforgettable Book 1
Unforgettable Book 2
Unforgettable Book 3

Alpha Billionaire Duet
TRAINWRECK 1
TRAINWRECK 2

A Standalone Romantic Comedy
Baby Daddy

An OTT Insta-love Standalone
The Big O

THAT MAN Series
THAT MAN 1
THAT MAN 2
THAT MAN 3
THAT MAN 4
THAT MAN 5

Gloria
Gloria's Secret
Gloria's Revenge
Gloria's Forever

An Erotic Love Story
Undying Love
Endless Love

Writing as E.L. Sarnoff
DEWITCHED: The Untold Story of the Evil Queen
UNHITCHED: The Untold Story of the Evil Queen 2

Boxed Sets
THAT MAN TRILOGY
THAT MAN: THE WEDDING STORY
Unforgettable: The Complete Series
Gloria's Secret: The Trilogy
Seduced by the Park Avenue Billionaire
Naughty Nelle

Printed in Poland
by Amazon Fulfillment
Poland Sp. z o.o., Wrocław